Spirit, LEAD ME

NALANI KING

WestBow
PRESS®
A DIVISION OF THOMAS NELSON
& ZONDERVAN

Scripture quotations are taken from the Holy Bible, New Living Translation, copyright ©1996, 2004, 2007 by Tyndale House Foundation. Used by permission of Tyndale House Publishers, Inc., Carol Stream, Illinois 60188. All rights reserved

WestBow Press books may be ordered through booksellers or by contacting:

WestBow Press
A Division of Thomas Nelson & Zondervan
1663 Liberty Drive
Bloomington, IN 47403
www.westbowpress.com
1 (866) 928-1240

Because of the dynamic nature of the Internet, any web addresses or links contained in this book may have changed since publication and may no longer be valid. The views expressed in this work are solely those of the author and do not necessarily reflect the views of the publisher, and the publisher hereby disclaims any responsibility for them.

Any people depicted in stock imagery provided by Thinkstock are models, and such images are being used for illustrative purposes only. Certain stock imagery © Thinkstock.

ISBN: 978-1-9736-1609-2 (sc)
ISBN: 978-1-9736-1608-5 (hc)
ISBN: 978-1-9736-1610-8 (e)

Library of Congress Control Number: 2018901017

Print information available on the last page.

WestBow Press rev. date: 01/29/2018

CHAPTER 1

Trust in the Lord with all your heart; do not depend
on your own understanding. Seek his will in all you
do, and he will show you which path to take.
—Proverbs 3:5–6

Cayleen Jamison bolts upright in bed, blue eyes open wide, and grasps the pillows around her with both hands. *Breathe.* The night from over a year ago has come back. On the beach in the Bahamas—with her mother and sister nearby at the pool—the bartender who had been serving the fourteen-year-old Cayleen all night had gotten his way. She was too embarrassed to scream. She was embarrassed that she had let herself get in the situation: drunk near the water with a man who was almost ten years older. She was scared speechless when she finally realized his goal. Her naïveté had allowed her to get so far away from the crowd. She was ashamed that she was not able to run away from his grip once the reality of the situation finally clicked in her alcohol-induced mind.

As she turned toward her mother, sister, and the other men who had returned to their hotel after the bar had closed, the bartender grabbed her around the waist and reeled her back in. Suddenly her entire world was shattered. He took her virginity, and he stripped her of any sense of security, trust, and innocence. He could not hold her still for long, and she wiggled her way out of his grasp, buttoning her pants before she reached the others. She was so ashamed that she didn't say anything to anyone. She masked her shame with a smile and joined in the conversation. She felt comforted by the community of people, sure he would not try it again in front them.

The agony she feels from the night so long ago is still with her, and reality starts coming back. The bedroom becomes clear—darkness, curtains, pillows—beckon her back to the present. *It was just a dream.* Little does she know of the unseen spirits in the room. They had been close to her during her sleep, but now with Cayleen awake, they back off, hiding in the shadows of her bedroom.

She takes a deep breath, loosening her grip on the bedding. Though she's able to release the tension she feels, she is still not able to release the shame and embarrassment of the night. As her eyes come into focus, she concentrates on every object in the room in a mediocre effort to regain control of herself and her thoughts: tall dresser in the corner, TV she managed to buy with her own money along with the futon she is lying on. *You're in your room. It's all here. Your brain's not playing any more tricks,* Cayleen thinks, taking a deep breath.

Hands propped behind her, she sits up and crosses her legs. *Well, I'm up for now,* she thinks, not wanting to give credit to the underlying thought of not going back to sleep to face him again. Cayleen grabs a rubber band off the nightstand, tugs her long, blonde hair into a ponytail, and rubs her eyes. Maybe if she can get her hands that close to her brain, she can control her thoughts from going back to that night. Cayleen lets her hands drop to her lap and leans back against the wall.

Tomorrow's Sunday, which means we have to go to church. She controls her thoughts to only be in the present. Cayleen's mother, Jessica, has taken the girls to church for as long as she can remember. Cayleen doesn't think church itself is that bad—it's just that all the other girls her age don't have to go, and it seems like such a waste of an hour. Cayleen has no basis for knowledge or understanding of a Holy Spirit-filled life and has only been shown religion in the form of habit, practiced only on Sundays and only for an hour.

Cayleen thinks back to the time her sister, Cheyanne, had left little white lines of powder on the bathroom counter, waiting for Cayleen when she got out of the shower. Luckily, they didn't make it to church that morning. The drugs had blurred Cayleen's memory, and she can't fully remember why they never made it. Cayleen's thoughts turn to her stint of following Cheyanne along the drug-induced path for several months after the *incident*. She prefers the word *incident*. She does not think of what happened that night as rape. It was just sex that she didn't want to have. After all, Cayleen never screamed. She was too drunk to make the sex not happen. She was sure she said no, but if she really had said no, it wouldn't have happened, right?

> But if the man meets the engaged woman out in the
> country, and he rapes her, then only the man must die. Do
> nothing to the young woman; she has committed no crime
> worth of death. She is as innocent as a murder victim.
> —Deuteronomy 22:25–26

Cayleen buries her face in her hands. *I don't want to think about this anymore. It's behind me now, and the drugs are no longer a temptation with Hunter in my life.* The first spark of hope returns to her clear, blue eyes.

Hunter is the boy she met last year at school, just after the incident. Defying tradition, Cayleen asked him to homecoming, but Hunter's response had been that he didn't like to dance. His refusal had a devastating impact on Cayleen at the time. She stepped into drugs and dove headfirst into boys. She figured that if God had allowed some guy to take her virginity so easily, sex must not be a big deal. Besides, having sex on her terms allowed her some sense of control, which she was so devastatingly denied her first time. Luckily for Cayleen, by spring, Hunter had realized dances weren't just for dancing and had taken Cayleen to the spring dance. Hunter told her he drank, but he didn't do any drugs. Cayleen liked him, so she stopped with the variety of drugs Cheyanne had shown her.

Cayleen didn't think drugs were much fun anyway. They made Cayleen feel silly the next day; she felt like she had done stupid things and couldn't remember everything. Cayleen couldn't remember if she had actually done the stupid things or just thought them. Her pride was too great to ask. The "fun" that her friends who did drugs spoke of was always muted, though emotions ran as high. Cayleen felt fun was supposed to be something colorful, welcoming, and remembered. Drugs didn't do that for Cayleen, but for Cheyanne, drugs were still her choice of fun.

Cheyanne and Cayleen were opposites in that and several other ways. Cheyanne had been active in sports until her back injury in a car accident last year. Cayleen was a straight-A student but not much of an athlete. Cheyanne had many friends in her class, but Cayleen found herself friends with a few girls but thought most of the girls in her class would fit right in with the mean girls she read and watched movies about. Even in appearance, Cheyanne was four inches shorter than Cayleen with darker hair and darker skin, which Cayleen envied. Cheyanne would have tan lines after ten minutes outside, and Cayleen had to lather up in sunscreen to avoid blisters. The only similarity between the girls was in their blue eyes. They were wide and translucent.

Cayleen takes a deep breath, puts her feet on the floor, and lifts herself to standing. *Well, if I'm up, I might as well have a smoke,* she thinks. Cayleen walks into the living room to the fireplace and finds the cigarettes. Her mom, Cheyanne, and Cayleen all smoke there so the cigarette smoke goes up the chimney rather than filling the house. Cayleen decides she wants to be outside and goes out to the lawn chairs on the back deck. As she lights her cigarette, she looks up toward the sky. Intrigued by the lack of clouds, she studies the stars. There are very few city lights coming off of Spring Forks, Colorado, which is not surprising. In the town of less than one hundred thousand, most businesses close for the evening at nine—but not the teenagers.

Cayleen thinks back on her weekend. On Friday night, she had gone out with Hunter. They see each other at school and usually two weekends a month. She likes him a lot and doesn't want to mess things up. She stopped the drugs, and she stopped being sexually assertive. Drugs are not something Cayleen misses. Besides, the interaction she has with Hunter—kissing and hand-holding—is more meaningful than any of the three partners she had taken in the year after her incident.

For her birthday several months before, Hunter gave her a huge teddy bear and roses. He handed them to her all at once, and she didn't have the hands to grab them. Compared to her five-foot-nine frame, the bear went from her head to her hip. She had looked up into Hunter's hazel eyes, beaming with tears of happiness. No boy had ever been so kind. Full of emotion, Cayleen had reached up to give the six-foot-tall Hunter a hug. Between her and the stuffed animal, it ended up an awkward mess. She was grabbing his muscular bicep with one hand and his shirt at the waist with the other. He had steadied her with a strong arm around the waist. The sun was shining down on his dark hair, hitting his collar at the back, and she felt giddy inside.

On Friday night, she had seen a different side of Hunter. Without spiritual eyes being opened, Cayleen couldn't tell this dark side was demonic. They had gone out with a group, and he had been drinking. There was a party at a friend's house—her parents were out of town. Hunter had gotten mad, and Cayleen didn't know what he was mad about. She couldn't understand what the problem was, but she followed Hunter when he stormed out of the house to his truck. She stood nearby, not knowing how to console such behavior. Hunter grabbed the top of the truck and started shaking it. He then grabbed the passenger door and started moving the truck even more. Cayleen was standing there, numbly watching and not knowing how to react. Hunter's friend, Jason, came over and calmed him down. Jason asked Cayleen whether she was ready to go. *Yes, please.* All three loaded into the pickup and drove Cayleen to her house.

Cayleen had needed to process the situation internally and think about it before talking to her mom about it. Cheyanne was high as a kite most of the time or looking for her next high and was not someone Cayleen got advice from.

Cayleen hadn't yet learned to take advice from her mom with a grain of salt—even though the Holy Spirit had already tried to warn her. When Cheyanne found out that Cayleen had been raped by reading Cayleen's diary, Cheyanne told their mom in front of Cayleen.

Jessica had said, "So you were raped, huh?"

Cayleen nodded.

Jessica said, "Well, I was raped at knifepoint! Were you raped at knifepoint?"

Cayleen shook her head, eyes widened at the horror of being raped at knifepoint. Cayleen's empathy for her mother took over, and she listened intently to the rest of the story.

"Remember that cruise we took in Mexico? And the waiter?"

Cayleen and Cheyanne glanced at each other with a confirming look, remembering the waiter and their mother flirting heavily with him. They both nodded.

"I went to his room one night, and he raped me! Knife at my throat, like this!" Jessica put her pointer finger to her throat.

The subject of Cayleen's rape was never brought up again. Cayleen still goes to Jessica with all of her concerns. She sees other girls going to their mothers with their problems and believes it is normal. Cayleen doesn't read or study her Bible regularly. She hasn't had that behavior modeled for her. Cayleen doesn't realize what God has said about cleaving her family; if she did, perhaps she would realize cleaving should be done at an earlier age in her case.

While Cayleen and Jessica are having a cigarette break on the deck, she says, "Hunter scared me last night, Mom."

"What happened?"

"We were at a house party, and there were quite a few people there. I didn't know very many of them and stayed near Jason. Hunter seemed to know everybody and wanted to talk to everyone. I tried to keep up, but he lost me. I found Jason and stuck near him. We were there for a bit, and I ran into Vanessa. You remember Vanessa from my geometry class?" Cayleen waits for the nod of recognition from her mother. "Well, Vanessa and I were talking, and Jason was on the front lawn when Hunter barged out and stomped off toward the truck. He threw the door open so hard the screen door stuck open. He was just so mad! I walked over to the sidewalk to see if I could help. He was pacing in front of the truck. I told him he might get hit walking nearly in the middle of the street like that. He joined me on the sidewalk. I was standing near the cab of the pickup and asked what was wrong. He just grabbed the hood and started shaking it. Then he grabbed the door—through the window 'cause it was open, you know? He started moving the truck even more."

When Jessica doesn't respond, Cayleen says, "I just don't know what to think. I've never seen him drink before. I'm sure that was it, the beer, but we've never been drinking like that together before. I just don't know what to do about it."

Finally, Jessica offers, "What do you think you should do about it?"

Cayleen thinks for a moment and puffs on her cigarette. "Well, is that something that I should have in a relationship? Should I continue with Hunter even though he's like that? Or should I break up with him because he's acted that way? That's what I don't know!"

Cayleen has rarely seen healthy relationships in action. Her parents divorced before she had any memories of them being together. Two years earlier, her dad, Luke, came back into their lives by moving back to town. During that time, Luke started his own construction business and was enticed by a woman. They were expecting their first son. Earlier in the summer, after Luke told the girls their happy news, they invited the girls to Las Vegas for the wedding. It was Luke's third marriage. Cayleen still doesn't know what a healthy relationship looks like.

There is silence between mother and daughter as they both think about the previous night's events. Jessica says, "You know, Cay-K, high school is only four years." Cayleen's middle name is

Katherine, and her mother has used that nickname for as long as she can remember.

Cayleen says, "What's that supposed to mean?"

Jessica says, "Well, when you're my age and look back, these four years of high school will seem like no time at all. Do you want to have a relationship during high school? It's not that long to put up with that type of behavior if a boyfriend is what you want. Besides, then you'll go to college—and there will be more boys to choose from. College has so many options."

Cayleen stares at the night sky, coming back to the present. She looks down at the burnt Marlboro Light filter in her hand, ashes nearly the length of an unlit cigarette. She has been so lost in her thoughts and hasn't smoked much of her cigarette. *Well, there's always more.* Cayleen grabs another one from the pack. Jessica buys the girls cigarettes; she tells the girls if they are going to smoke, she would rather not have them hide it.

Cayleen understands Jessica wants to know what they are doing and usually takes Jessica's opinions of things into consideration before making decisions. Cheyanne, on the other hand, gets a thrill out of not telling Jessica things and taking what she needs from her mother rather than asking. Cayleen turns her thoughts to her sister. *She's probably passed out on the couch at one of her friend's houses.* Cayleen feels sympathy and then a hint of jealousy. *Well, I guess she won't have to go to church with us!*

> You are not to associate with anyone who claims to
> be a believer yet indulges in sexual sin, or is greedy,
> or worships idols, or is abusive, or is a drunkard, or
> cheats people. Don't even eat with such people.
> —1 Corinthians 5:11

CHAPTER 2

Cayleen pulls into her driveway after school, thinking about her next task for the day: getting ready to go to her job at JC Penney. Jessica is out of town with her most recent boyfriend. He owns an antique store, and they go out of town from Thursday through Tuesday twice a month to shop the antique sales around the state. Jessica said they won't be going during the winter, so they need to get as much inventory as possible for his antique store.

Cayleen walks into the house, stomach grumbling. Jessica left Cayleen twenty dollars for food and ordered pizza before she left town, standard protocol. Cayleen allows herself one piece for lunch. If she doesn't eat much, the one pizza can last the entire time Jessica is gone. Of course, she puts the pizza in the freezer after a few days, but if she skips breakfast, eats one piece for lunch, and has two for dinner, she can pocket the money. With all the rest of her life moving forward from her rape, Cayleen doesn't realize there may be lingering emotions still holding on: for instance, the need to be in control.

Cayleen's pants were hurting her stomach a few months ago, which she realized was because her stomach was too big. She's been working on getting the pants to fit without hurting. Last week, she weighed herself and was down to 128. *That is the lowest so far!* She doesn't realize that on her five-foot-nine-inch medium frame, there is such a thing as too thin.

It's a numbers game to her. Jessica has had diet pills in the cupboard and encouraged Cheyanne to take them at twelve years old because she was getting heavy. Cayleen feels she keeps watch well enough that she doesn't need to be told to take the pills. Of her most recent efforts, Cayleen will not allow herself to eat more than five things a day, sodas included.

Cayleen doesn't realize that the reason she has to sleep with her hands cupping her hipbones is because they hurt from the pressure of bone without padding. She doesn't realize the reason she is flabby is her body has eaten all the muscle tissue due to starvation. She eats, so Cayleen justifies she is not anorexic. She doesn't realize that the reason she went through the drug phase—and now the anorexia—is because of the pain she is hiding from the hurt of her rape. First, the drugs and boys were her form of control. Now, her eating is what she can control. If she can be the perfect student, the perfect daughter, and the perfect size, then maybe the pain won't be there. Maybe the fear of being raped again will go away. Rape doesn't happen in a perfect world, right? But Cayleen doesn't realize that yet. All Cayleen recognizes is that, now, the pants fit. Size three.

While savoring every bite of her small, cold piece of pizza, the phone rings.

"Jamison residence. May I help you?" Cayleen answers with the greeting Jessica taught the girls in order to allow them to answer the phone properly while still in elementary school.

"Hey … Cay! It's … Chey." Cheyanne's most recent endeavor was to move out of the house, into a home that Jessica and Cayleen's grandmother had bought, while Cheyanne attends the local college. Cheyanne living on her own is a relief for Cayleen. There isn't that constant worry about where Cheyanne is or when she is coming home or what she is going to take from Jessica next. Cheyanne's habits haven't changed, but Cayleen is less exposed to them—out of sight, out of mind.

"Hey, Chey. What's up?" Cayleen has little tolerance for her older sister when she is high, which she definitely is right now. Cayleen has a little over an hour before work, and she knows Cheyanne can take an hour with one high conversation.

"Cay, can you do us a favor?" Giggling. "We need a pizza." Giggling.

"Well, do you want me to order you one?"

"No! No delivery people!" Cheyanne giggles even more. "We have a pizza. It's in a box … and I have an oven … you know."

You must be kidding me, Cayleen thinks. *What is she on now?* Cayleen knows the kitchen is fully equipped at Cheyanne's house.

Cheyanne says, "I just can't figure out how to turn on the oven. It keeps on looking at me funny. And when I open the door, it's like it's going to eat me."

Cayleen also knows the oven is gas—and the burners are gas. *If Cheyanne touches the wrong button …* "I'll be right over. Don't touch anything! I'll cook you your pizza. Love you, bye."

"Love you, bye." Their closing comes out as one word since it is so commonly used between the two girls and their mother.

Cayleen thinks she will get a speeding ticket from driving so fast, but she doesn't. The thought of having to take care of her older sibling doesn't strike Cayleen as odd. Ever since they were little and Cayleen had to stop a food fight between Cheyanne and Jessica at a restaurant with waiters in aprons and nice white tablecloths, Cayleen has taken on the role of taking care of the other two, most times without realizing it.

Opening the door to Cheyanne's house, she assesses the situation. There are four girls on the floor in the living room area, all sitting in different areas and leaning against the walls. Each girl has her legs tucked close to her, giggling and swaying front to back or side to side, each to her own giggling rhythm.

"Are you here to cook pizza?" one girl askes, swaying slightly but seemingly not opening her eyes. This college student reminds Cayleen of a five-year-old.

"Yes," Cayleen replies without losing a step as she walks toward the kitchen.

"I don't think I've ever been so happy to see someone in my life," the girl says. Her response lacks enthusiasm, and her eyes are droopy.

Cayleen knows this girl is probably feeling extreme happiness right now, but the drugs dull your senses so much there is no expressing it. *Marijuana?*

Cayleen pulls the pizza out of the freezer and starts the oven. Opening the box and unwrapping the pizza, Cayleen calls, "Just one pizza or two?"

A minute later, Cheyanne appears in the doorway. Her movements say she is trying to hurry, but it is obvious the drugs are holding her back.

"One is fine. I don't know if many people will actually eat it. Hi, sister." Cheyanne giggles with a glassy expression and goofy grin. "I'm so glad you're here!" She gives Cayleen a bear hug, and her expression changes to one of extreme excitement. "You can meet our sister!"

After the oven remarks, the expressions, and the crazy actions, it has to be acid, Cayleen thinks.

Cheyanne leads Cayleen into the back bedroom. Two more girls are sitting on the floor. They have the same goofy grins and glazed eyes as Cheyanne. Cheyanne points to the curly-haired blonde.

"This is Summer. She's from Fort Collins. She's adopted. We're the same age. Summer's just a few months younger than me." Cheyanne introduces Cayleen with a wave of her hand and plops to the floor, her back against the wall.

Why aren't they using the furniture? I'm not going to ask. "So how does that make Summer our sister?" Cayleen's question comes out as genuine; she is too sober to see the connection.

Cheyanne says, "Well, Dad started cheating on Mom about that time, and Summer's real mom gave her up for adoption because she didn't want to be a single mom."

Of course, all adopted children were descendants of Dad, Cayleen jokes to herself. *He's fathered so many children.* She decides to go another, less funny route. What Cayleen sees as funny might seem confrontational in their states of mind. "Has Summer ever met her mother?"

"No," Cheyanne replies.

"Then what makes you think that she slept with Dad?" Their dad is known for infidelity—but not exactly statewide.

Cheyanne looks to the ceiling, where the other girls are looking. They are more interested in the galaxies they think are appearing in the room right on top of their heads than the sister conversation. "Summer's adopted mom said so."

Conversation over. The galaxies are more interesting to Cheyanne now than her supposed sister meeting her actual sister.

Cayleen shakes her head slightly with a grin as she walks back to the kitchen, thinking about making decisions. At that moment, Cayleen is happy about her decision to no longer do drugs. Admittedly, she still has an addiction to nicotine, which she is constantly trying to kick, but not the acid and marijuana she sees right now in this house. Her thoughts turn to Hunter and how thankful she is to have him in her life. In her mind, Hunter is the reason she no longer does drugs. Hunter brought her out of that dark place in her life. Hunter is the one deserving of her gratitude. What Cayleen doesn't realize is the power that brought Hunter to her is God—who is ultimately deserving of her praise.

[God will] equip you with all you need for doing his will.
—Hebrews 13:21

CHAPTER 3

Cayleen storms in the door, slamming it behind her. She throws her backpack down in the kitchen and goes for the glasses. As she's filling her glass with water, Jessica walks in. No antique hunting this weekend. "What's wrong, Cay-K?"

"Hunter." One word said through clenched teeth. "It's not as if I'm not willing to!" Cayleen slams her glass down on the counter. The brilliant invention of plastic is the only reason her glass doesn't shatter. Even so, water spills out of the cup with the force. "He just never does anything! He never says anything!" Cayleen pauses her ranting, turns slightly, and throws one hand in the air. "Until now!"

There is another pause. Jessica can see Cayleen is withdrawing back to her thoughts. Softly, Jessica says, "Cay-K, I'd like to help, but I have no idea what you're talking about."

Cayleen stares blankly at the counter.

Jessica can't tell if Cayleen can even see the spilled water her gaze is fixed on.

"He broke up with me. He said that we've been dating for two years and haven't had sex yet—and that's why he broke up with me. All his friends have already had sex. He's turning eighteen in a few months and doesn't want to be a virgin. So, he broke up with me." Since their talk about Cayleen's rape, they've kept Cayleen's sex life off-limits.

"Honey, I'm sorry." Jessica puts a comforting arm around her daughter. "Men are stupid sometimes."

Cayleen looks up at her mother. "Why don't I run to the store and get some bonbons and we can watch movies?" Jessica suggests.

"What are bonbons?" Cayleen asks. "I thought they were just in movies."

Jessica smiles. "You'll see. Any movie requests?"

> Run from sexual sin! No other sin so clearly affects the body as this one does. For sexual immorality is a sin against your own body.
> —1 Corinthians 6:18

The next night, Cayleen is still sulking and not answering the phone. She is on the couch with a blanket and not planning on doing anything. Who cares if it's a Saturday night? Who cares if she hasn't done anything all weekend? She managed to get to work—that counts.

Jessica walks in with the phone. "It's for you." She hands Cayleen the phone.

"Hello?"

"Cay?" It is Hunter.

Cayleen gets nervous, excited, and mad at the same instant.

"I was wondering if you would like to go out with us tonight. We're going to the woods."

Okay, so that is his big apology? Where is the "I'm sorry"? Where are the flowers? Where is the gentlemanly way of meeting face-to-face? Oh, wait, we're talking about Hunter. Cayleen continues in her own thoughts. *It's a good thing I fell in love with him over the past two years.*

"So, I'll see you there in a couple hours," Hunter says without waiting for Cayleen's response.

"Okay. Bye," Cayleen says. Only once had Hunter said "I love you," and only three times had Cayleen said it. She stopped saying "I love you" after not getting a response from him.

"Bye." His ending is clipped and followed immediately with a dead end of the line.

"My people are foolish and do not know me," says the Lord. "They are stupid children who have no understanding. They are clever enough at doing wrong, but they have no idea how to do right."
—Jeremiah 4:22

Cayleen picks up Jasmine, one of her friends, and they slowly make their way to the woods. Cayleen knows where they will be: lighting a small fire and drinking too much beer. She's been here many times before. Her relationship with Hunter has grown in some ways; they spend much more time together, especially since she started driving. She stops by his house after school on days she doesn't have to work, and they hang out on the weekends, watch TV, or go to the woods with friends and beer. Their relationship has not grown in other ways. Hunter is still very short-tempered when drinking. Both have a difficult time talking about things with each other. Hunter hardly talks about anything. *Maybe tonight will change that,* Cayleen thinks as she maneuvers her four-door sedan through the rutted path to the woods. *Tonight, we can talk about what he wants.*

"So, who will be there tonight?" Jasmine asks.

"Jason will be there, Jazi. Unless he's in the hospital with pneumonia, he'll be there. He's always with Hunter."

"Does he like me?" Jasmine asks.

"Honestly, I don't know. Jason and I don't really have any heart-to-hearts." Cayleen thinks, *Jason and I may talk as much or more than Hunter and I do.* "Hunter mentioned last week that he stopped seeing that other girl, Tiffany, who he's been seeing for a while. Okay, Hunter didn't mention it. I pried."

While Jasmine's face lights up the inside of the car, outside the headlights reveal Hunter's decades old Ford pickup. "Well, we're here. Why don't you find out for yourself?" Cayleen poses the question before slowly getting out of the car.

From around the truck, Hunter walks toward them. Even in the dark, with the halo of the firelight, Cayleen can tell it is Hunter. He hasn't grown much in the two years they've been together, but he is over six feet tall. His thin body is just starting to fill out a bit around the shoulders and arms. Cayleen can see the fire and recognizes all the faces. Her relationship with Hunter has also brought her closer to all his friends.

Jason says, "Jazi, why don't you head to the fire. I'll be along in a minute."

Jasmine says a quiet agreement as she moves ahead of Cayleen and passes Hunter.

Cayleen keeps walking toward the fire.

Hunter has to turn and walk with her. "Wait."

Why does it seem he always commands rather than speaks? Obediently, she slows to a stop near the tailgate of the truck. "What?" Cayleen waits, searching his hazel eyes.

The fire reflects in his eyes. He is probably never going to say what he wants her to know, and that means she has to try to figure it out herself.

Hunter shows her one of his hands, which holds an unopened beer. "Do you want a beer?"

Cayleen takes the drink, thinking his form of apology could use a lot of work.

He says, "I didn't mean to hurt you."

"Well, it's not really about you hurting me."

"It's not?"

Cayleen says, "No. You just don't ever talk to me. I'm not against having sex with you, Hunter. It's just that you never made a move. You've never showed me that's what you want. I know you don't talk about things that much, but if you don't talk and you don't show me, I don't know. You could have told me that's what you wanted before you got mad at me for not knowing that's what you wanted and breaking up with me." She drops her hands to her sides and lets out a sigh. "Hunter, what do you want? 'Cause if you just want sex, there are a lot of girls out there who would do that for you. You're right for breaking up with me. You probably wouldn't have to wait for two years to have sex with them!"

"No, but you're the best bet I've got!" Hunter smiles at his own humor. "I want you, Cay." Hunter pulls his head toward hers and prepares to kiss her.

Because he is only seventeen and about as smooth as a cactus, Cayleen knows what is coming. She also knows and accepts that this is Hunter's apology.

> For God bought you with a high price. So
> you must honor God with your body.
> —1 Corinthians 6:20

CHAPTER 4

Cayleen doesn't even notice the other student walk in and hand the teacher a pass. She is working so hard on the problem that she nearly flinches when Mr. Thomas flicks the note in front of her work. "Office needs you. Go."

Mr. Thomas is not known for his pleasantries, but Cayleen sees through the rough exterior to the witty man who yells at each of his math classes and then chuckles under his breath when no one is looking.

Cayleen looks up at him with confusion.

He raises his eyebrows, shakes his head, and mutters, "I don't know what for. Go!"

Cayleen packs her things and leaves the room. On her way out, she thinks she hears Mr. Thomas snickering. "Kids don't think I'm serious anymore."

Once in the office, Cayleen gives the secretary her name. Cayleen stays as far as possible from the principal's office—no matter how nice he is. Cayleen has never actually been in the principal's office, and she hopes it will not stain her record.

The secretary looks at what appears to be logbooks. "Cayleen Jamison? Your mother is waiting out front and has authorized you to leave the building."

What? It's only ten in the morning. Cayleen does well in school. Now in her senior year, she has organized her schedule to have the first and last two hours off of school in releases for the entire year.

It is great for her to work or do fun things after school and not have to be up early in the morning, and she only goes to school for a few hours each day. "Okay. Thank you." Cayleen, though confused, is not going to wait for another answer. During elementary school and part of middle school, Jessica would let her stay home for getting 100 percent on tests. Eventually, Cayleen did so well in school that Jessica had to limit her days off to once a month. As a teacher, Jessica recognizes the value of being in school—most of the time. Cayleen wonders if maybe Jessica opened her ACT scores and saw something.

Jessica is sitting in the passenger seat of her car in the no-parking zone.

Cayleen rushes to the driver's side, gets in, and fastens her seat belt. "What's wrong, Mom?"

"I need you to drive me to the doctor's office." Jessica has one foot on the dash, the other tucked somewhere near the console and seat, and her arms brace her upper body against the dash and the door.

Cayleen throws the car into drive, sees the pain it causes on her mother's face, and tries to be more careful maneuvering out of the parking lot.

Jessica says, "Well, it seems that what the doctors told me about not being able to have another baby when I had you wasn't right."

"You're pregnant?" Cayleen asks.

The doctors had told Jessica that the scar tissue in her uterus after having C-sections for Cheyanne and Cayleen would prevent her from having another baby. It was uncommon for women to have such complications, but Cayleen figures there is even more scarring inside.

"I'm not pregnant anymore," Jessica says with a groan.

"You're sure we don't need to go to the hospital or call an ambulance?" Cayleen asks.

It takes several minutes for Jessica to respond. "I'm just having a miscarriage. The doctor is expecting me."

God's will is for you to be holy, so stay away from all sexual sin.
—1 Thessalonians 4:3

As Cayleen pulls into the parking area and toward the door to make sure Jessica doesn't have to walk far, Jessica explains, "I'll be okay. Jeff is meeting me here. He was just on the other side of town, and you were closer to drive me to the doctor. See." Jessica nods in the direction of Jeff's familiar green pickup. "He's already here." She winces and grabs the top of the open door.

"Call me and let me know what's going on," Cayleen says.

Jessica makes her way to standing. "I'll do that. I will probably stay at Jeff's tonight, Cay-K. I don't want you to have to see this."

Cayleen can't tell if she sees regret or pain on Jessica's face. "Mom, please call. I'll worry."

"Soon," Jessica says, without making eye contact, and makes her way inside.

Please listen and answer me, for
I am overwhelmed by my troubles.
—Psalm 55:2

Ninety minutes later, the phone rings. Cayleen picks up before the first ring is finished. "Jamison residence."

"Cay-K. Thank you for your help today. I really appreciate it," Jessica says.

"Of course, Mom. What is the doctor doing to help you?" There is a pause. "Mom, I'm already involved. It's best to tell me everything."

"Okay. Well, the doctor is going to do a procedure this afternoon … to make things a little quicker. It's called a DNC, and I had one each time I had a C-section, which may be the cause of the scarring due to the incompetent doctors who … I'll be having this procedure this afternoon. I've asked the doctor to tie my tubes in order for this not to happen again, but he says he can't do that on the same visit. That procedure will be in a few weeks. We've scheduled it. I'm on some medicine to help with the pain, but it may be pretty intense for a day or so. Jeff and I think it may be best for me to stay at his house."

Cayleen thinks Jessica is waiting for an objection. *How can I object when I don't know what's going on?*

Jessica says, "Cay-K, I'm fine—or going to be. There's no need for you to worry. Are you supposed to work this afternoon?"

Stunned, Cayleen says, "Yes." She hadn't thought about work.

"Well, why don't you go ahead and try to go to work. It's just like I've had bad heartburn and gone to the doctor. Work will get your mind off of things. You can call me at Jeff's when you're done. Sound good?"

"Okay. Love you, bye." Cayleen hangs up. *A miscarriage is like bad heartburn? Mom was pregnant? What is going on?*

CHAPTER 5

Cayleen plops down on the couch next to Hunter and snuggles her way under his arm. *This is nice,* she thinks. *Just sitting here, watching TV.* It doesn't bother her that she is in no way interested in the show; just being with Hunter is nice. Cayleen has not told Hunter about the episode with her mother from several months ago. Hunter didn't ask where she went from school that day. She didn't tell him about the other procedure her mom had to make sure no more pregnancies would happen. Cayleen had to drive her mom to that one too. That time, Jessica had stayed at home rather than at Jeff's. She had been staying less and less at Jeff's lately.

Cayleen doesn't worry about that. What she does worry about, or is shocked by, is that Jessica had gotten pregnant in the first place. Cayleen and Hunter had not been bashful about making up for lost time once they started being sexually active, but Cayleen had made sure they did not get pregnant. Cayleen's the teenager—why have both her parents gotten pregnant without meaning to? Isn't she supposed to be the irresponsible one?

Hunter did ask about Cheyanne, Cayleen recalls, and Cayleen told him she moved to New Mexico to be with her boyfriend. Cheyanne had been in a long-distance relationship with Cyrus in New Mexico for years, though not exclusively. Cayleen wasn't sure if she mentioned the circumstances leading to Cheyanne's sudden change in scenery, which happened just after Jessica's recovery.

Cheyanne and a distant cousin had been high on cocaine for

days—something about doing an eight-ball between the two of them within twenty-four hours or less. Cayleen can't remember the details, and her knowledge of drugs is a little rusty. The distant cousin's mom had gotten worried when the kids called professing newfound knowledge of God at one in the morning. Her worry increased when, within an hour, she went by the apartment in which the "revival" was taking place to find the kids nearly passed out. The cousin was raced to the hospital, and after medical approval, Cheyanne was taken home by Jessica. Jessica didn't want the rest of the family to know. The ensuing conversations included Cheyanne leaving town to make new friends in New Mexico.

Cayleen looks up at Hunter's face and touches his dark hair. "Your mom's wedding is this weekend?"

Without looking away from the TV, Hunter says, "Yep."

"Where is it going to be?"

"The Golden Leaf—on the west side of town." Still no eye contact.

Cayleen doesn't mind. This is practically a deep conversation for them. "You know, they've known each other for less time than you and I have been going out."

Hunter's gaze shifts from the TV to Cayleen's face. "Yeah, I know."

Cayleen can sense Hunter is not comfortable with that fact, but she doesn't know why.

"Is that weird for you?"

Hunter shrugs and turns his attention back to the TV. Conversation closed.

> But while they were gone to buy oil, the bridegroom
> came. Then those who were ready went in with him
> to the marriage feast, and the door was locked.
> —Matthew 25:10

Cayleen looks at herself in the mirror and beams. "Jazi, look at this hair! She did such a good job! I love it. Thank you!" Cayleen stops admiring her hair, stands, and turns to Jasmine's chair to look at her friend's updo. "Wow. You look so nice with your hair that way." Cayleen can't help but giggle with excitement. "Can you believe it? Senior prom. I'm so impressed they're getting a limo. Sure beats last year."

"What, your Wendy's dinner for junior prom wasn't worth repeating?" Jasmine teases.

"Hunter's mom was out of town. She left him money, but … he just doesn't know about those things," Cayleen says. "It was the corsage that wasn't worth repeating. Stopping at the grocery store for a single long-stemmed rose because it was across the street from the dance … it was just difficult to pose in those pictures."

"Well, you better figure it out. How else are you going to hold your wedding bouquet?"

"Jazi, I've told everybody he gave me the ring as a thank you—nothing more. He made that very clear." Cayleen remembers the day he gave her the ring. It was her birthday, and he had stopped by for a minute. With all her family present, Hunter did not want to join the party, but he showed up, which was an improvement. As he walked in the door, he had the ring between his thumb and first finger and nudged it in her direction. "Here," he had mumbled. "It's a thank-you ring. For all the stuff you've done for me. You know."

Cayleen carefully plucked the ring from his fingers and admired it before placing it on her finger. It slid perfectly onto her finger.

"I used the size from your class ring so it should fit," Hunter explained.

Cayleen was in shock with the forethought he had put into this gift. Elated, she wrapped her arms around his neck.

Two weekends later, Hunter and Cayleen were at a party in the woods. Cayleen was so excited about her new gift; she had not taken the ring off. Cayleen was talking with a few friends when Hunter stomped over and tugged her arm to follow him. They stopped several feet out of earshot from the rest of the crowd.

"I told you that was a thank-you ring!" Hunter yelled.

"I know," Cayleen replied with slight attitude.

"Then why does everyone keep thinking we're engaged? What are you telling people?"

"I'm not telling anyone anything. Maybe they're assuming we're engaged since we've been together so long! I don't know why people think that. I didn't tell them anything except it was a thank-you ring. Maybe they don't believe me." Cayleen threw her hands in the air. "I don't know what to tell you, but I did nothing wrong! You can't be mad at me about this." Cayleen marched back to her friends.

In the beauty salon, Cayleen looks down at the opal, double-band ring. She ponders what things the thank-you ring erased. The dance last spring that Hunter told her he wouldn't go to, so she had arranged to work? On the day of the dance, he had told her he was going with another girl because her date had backed out. Did the ring erase that? Last summer, they'd gotten into an argument in the laundry room of a house during a party because he hadn't told her he loved her. He told her four times that night—Cayleen had counted—just before he broke up with her on the grounds that he wanted to play the field. Did the ring excuse all the times they had broken up? Each time she had forgiven him without his asking and held no grudges—the ring was an added bonus.

Cayleen looks up in the mirror at Jasmine's reflection and smiles.

Jasmine is jabbering away, excited about the events of the evening. "Dinner is a surprise for all the girls. Do you know who all will be going with us?"

Cayleen places one hand out and starts counting. "For the boys, it is Bill, Zeb, James, Hunter, and … Caleb! That's right. Caleb's going! I don't know which girls those boys are taking … well, except James." Cayleen leans down so her face is near Jasmine's and gives her a hug from behind. Jasmine had been lusting after James for years and only recently had they started dating. "I can never keep up with the rest of them." Cayleen turns and walks to the counter to pay her bill. Jasmine thanks her hairstylist and is not far behind.

The girls go back to Cayleen's house to resume their beauty

rituals in preparation for the night. Makeup and dresses are all that's left. At six thirty, right on schedule, the doorbell rings.

"The boys are here," Jessica calls from the entryway. "We'll all be outside."

Hunter's mom is excited for the occasion, and Jasmine's mom is helping with the last zippers and shoes.

Cayleen turns to Jasmine. "You ready? I'm out!"

"I'll be along in just a minute. I need to fix my lip gloss one more time," Jasmine replies.

Cayleen gets to the doorway, and Hunter smiles. "Cay, you look beautiful."

It is her turn to do a once-over. "You don't look so bad yourself, Hunter." She gives him a small peck. "No ruining my lips until after Mom's pictures."

As they walk outside, they are swarmed by mothers handing out corsages and boutonnieres and snapping pictures. Finally, they are properly flowered and ready for yard pictures.

"Does everybody get this crazy for pictures?" Hunter asks under his breath while striking another pose.

Cayleen says "Just think, nearly all our graduating class feels this same way, grinning goofily at their parents." She straightens out of the frozen position from the freshly snapped picture and looks him in the eyes. "It only happens once. Then it's over, and you don't have to dress all fancy!" She smiles.

The paparazzi of mothers cease as the seniors climb in the limo and head to dinner.

With the bantering and laughing in the limo, it seems like no time passes before they are outside the fanciest Italian restaurant in town. Cayleen lightly slaps Hunter on the thigh and says, "You're kidding!"

The driver opens the door, and several couples get out.

"Only the best for you, Cay!" Hunter says.

"You know, I heard Wendy's is a great place too," Jason teases as he steps out of the limo. Hunter is mad, but Cayleen is happy that Jason got away so quickly.

The table is ready for the party of ten. Cayleen is impressed that the boys had thought ahead enough to make reservations and wonders which mom helped them out. While walking to their table, she passes her father and his wife.

"Hi, Dad!" Cayleen is surprised that they would pick this restaurant on this night. Cayleen bends down to hug her father. No matter how big it grows, Spring Forks is a small town. Minimal pleasantries are exchanged between Hunter and Luke, and they follow the small crowd to the table. Luke's opinion of Hunter changed when Hunter broke up with Cayleen for not having sex. Cayleen had never seen a prouder look on her father's face as the night he found up she and Hunter broke up. However, when she and Hunter got back together, Luke hadn't been the most supportive.

Dinner goes smoothly, and the girls end up being friends. As the meal comes to a close, the waiter brings the bills to the boys—one for each couple. He does not bring one to Hunter.

Hunter waves the waiter over.

The waiter leans in.

"I'll take the bill for the two of us," Hunter says.

The waiter stands up and says, "That has already been taken care of."

Hunter says, "You didn't charge anyone else, did you?" Hunter looks at the others at the table.

"No, no." The waiter shakes his head and points to Cayleen. "Someone wanted to pay for her meal and the meal of her date. That person left already."

"Dad," Cayleen whispers to Hunter with gratefulness in her heart. "Thank you."

Bill says, "Well, that's nice! I wish my dinner would have been paid for!" He counts out cash and leaves it with the receipt.

Hunter's angry gaze has not lifted from the candle on the table.

As the others leave the table, Cayleen and Hunter are the last to walk toward the door.

Cayleen says, "Are you mad that my dad paid? Why?"

"I took you somewhere nice. I can pay for it. I don't need him to pay for it."

"I don't think that's how my dad sees it. I think he thought it was nice for you to take me here, and it was a kind of gift from him to both of us." They stop walking just inside the door so the others can't see them. Cayleen touches his arm. "I know he didn't do it to make you mad."

"Let's go." Hunter leads Cayleen to the limo.

"Next stop: prom!" Jason says as the last couple steps into the limo.

Pictures seem to take forever—with girls' pictures, boys' pictures, individual pictures, and any other pictures they want to remember from their last school dance. Cayleen finally gets a chance to look around after the group is done. She's sure the photographer's made a profit for the evening off of their group alone.

Celeste, one of the group of girls, comes over to Cayleen. "There's punch over there." She gestures over her right shoulder with her glass. "Did you get your favors when you walked in?" Celeste holds up the favors in her other hand.

Cayleen smiles warmly and shows her the favors she is holding behind her back. "They got me."

"We're at the table over here." Celeste gestures in front of her. "You and Hunter joining us?"

Cayleen looks around for Hunter, searching the dark areas until she finds him several feet away, talking with a group of people. She gets his attention and gestures to Celeste, pointing to the table. He waves in acknowledgement. Cayleen turns to follow Celeste. *An entire conversation using only gestures? It's my own fault Hunter and I never talk.*

The dance portion of the evening seems to drag on for Cayleen. Hunter doesn't dance, and sitting there with people she barely knows is not her idea of fun. Hunter is talking with his friends or doing something. She can't keep track. At one point, he asked her to dance, but that was one slow song and was at least an hour ago. Sheesh, she hasn't seen him in what seems to be an hour.

Suddenly, hands are on her shoulders and a face is dangerously close to her left ear. "You ready to go, my Cay?" Cayleen feels Hunter's breath on her cheek.

"Please!" Cayleen makes eye contact.

"All right, guys. We're outta here." Hunter stands and waves to the others at the table.

"Where's everyone from the limo?" Cayleen asks.

"They're on their way to the limo," Hunter says. "I think Jasmine had to go to the bathroom, and Nicole went with her. Bill and James are waiting, but they'll be there soon."

The after-party is at a house. As the limo pulls up and the couples start piling out, they hear the blaring music and see nearly every light is on.

"Are we late?" Cayleen asks.

"What do you mean?" Hunter puts his hands up. "The party doesn't start until we get here!" Hunter grabs Cayleen's hand, pulls her in for a quick smooch, and leads her inside. *He is right,* she thinks. Hunter Blake is the life of the party—always funny, crazy, laughing, making others laugh, rowdy, and—the part she likes least—never one to leave a party. Once inside, they go their separate directions, like usual.

Several hours later, Hunter finds Cayleen and pulls her into one of the smaller rooms. The stereo is playing George Jones, though Cayleen does not recognize the song. Old country is something that Hunter exposed her to, which she now enjoys. He stops her at the chair and has her sit, gesturing for her to stay there as he moves to the stereo. He starts playing a song and moves back to where Cayleen is sitting. She can tell he has had quite a bit to drink.

"You tell me that I don't tell you I love you. Well, I don't talk much, but this song pretty much sums up what I feel about you.

Listen to the words." If Cayleen hadn't known already he'd been drinking, his slurred speech now gives him away. She opens her mouth to speak, and Hunter raises a hand to silence her. "Just listen!" As the intro ends, the words begin.

"He said I'll love you till I die," Hunter sings most of the words, slightly lethargic, with eyes closed, concentrating on the music, seemingly feeling every line of the ballad. "He stopped loving her today, they placed a wreath upon his door, and soon they'll carry him away, he stopped loving her today."

Cayleen respects Hunter's request and remains silent through the song, listening carefully to absorb all the words.

Hunter is very intent on the song, not looking at Cayleen, and closing his eyes or staring at his feet, as they sit on the oversized chair. When it is finished, she continues looking at Hunter. If he wanted the song to be for and about her, it seems to Cayleen that he would have at least looked at her. He's so drunk. She really wants to laugh, but she knows it will hurt his feelings.

"I love you, too," she manages to choke out. "I don't know what to say."

Hunter's eyes are nearly closed, and he has a drunken smile. He presses his lips together and stands, walking to the stereo. "Just wanted you to know," he explains as he walks back to Cayleen, grabs her hand, and leads her back to the party.

Don't be fooled by those who say such things, for
"bad company corrupts good character."
—1 Corinthians 15:33

CHAPTER 6

Cayleen takes another shirt from her closet, folds it, and places it in her laundry basket.

"I can't believe you're already going." Cheyanne sighs on Cayleen's bed. Over the summer, Cheyanne and Cyrus had moved back in with Jessica. Luke had offered Cyrus a job at the construction company since he had completed his business associate's degree at a community college in New Mexico. "I won't have you here to talk with!"

"I'm just a phone call away," replies Cayleen. "We knew this was coming."

She is right. Cayleen had applied to the engineering college on the other side of the state early in her senior year. By Christmas, she had been accepted and submitted her intent to attend.

"I'm just nervous! I don't know what to expect, living in a dorm. And they say the school is tough." Cayleen makes a puckered face, picks up another shirt, and starts folding. High school had never really been that difficult. It took work, but Cayleen works hard and earned a 4.0 grade point average. "I can't believe I'll be so far from Hunter." She plops down beside her sister. "I miss him already!"

"Where is Hunter? I expected him to be here today—of all days!"

"He is working out of town. You know that construction company he's been working for?"

Cheyanne nods.

"They took a job out of town, and he won't be back until the weekend. I have to leave for orientation today." Cayleen sighs and lifts herself back off the bed. "I guess I'll be home next weekend to see him."

Cheyanne taps the edge of the full laundry basket. "And do laundry." She smiles up at Cayleen.

"Yes, and do laundry. I'm not sure about those washer-dryers in the dorms. You have to pay for them, and you never know what the guy before you put in there!" Cayleen makes another face in disgust.

Jessica pokes her head in the room. "You ready to go? It'll take four hours to get there, longer if we stop. I'd like to get there before dark so we can find your room!"

"Yeah, Mom. Just about ready." Cayleen grabs the bear Hunter gave her years ago for her birthday and sets it atop the clothes in the laundry basket. "You know that room at the Day's Inn that I booked you? I might stay with you tonight."

"I thought you might. Let's go!"

> Listen to me, O royal daughter; take to heart what I
> say. Forget your people and your family far away.
> —Psalm 45:10

Cayleen had saved campus maps of exactly how to get to her dorm, and they had no trouble finding it. By early afternoon, Jessica and Cayleen are outside the building with two octagonal towers and a walkway between.

Gesturing to the tower closest to where they had parked, Cayleen says, "Mom, this one is marked the West Tower." She glances at the email on her phone. "West Tower, 4-D. I'd guess that's the fourth floor."

"Okay, let's find it!"

The two take off toward the tower. Inside is bustling with new freshman arriving and unpacking. The tower is open on the lower level. There are four separate areas—the guidebook calls them *suites*—that are connected by a walkway. The walkway is open on each side. From the bottom level, Cayleen can see all five floors.

Each suite has five rooms: three with double occupancy and two with single occupancy. Cayleen read all about them before signing up. Each suite also has two separate bathrooms, which is the real reason she signed up for that type of housing. She doesn't know what to think of the dorms where all the bathrooms have lines of stalls. All she can remember is sharing a bathroom with her sister and being able to close the door. In each level of the building, there are three male suites and one female suite. Cayleen looks up and counts the windows in her head. *One, two, three, four ... that's it.*

As Jessica and Cayleen walk across the open area, says, "Oh, look! Here's the laundry area!"

"Yep. Probably won't be using that," Cayleen mutters under her breath.

"Oh, and there is the kitchenette! How quaint!"

Quaint is not the word Cayleen would use to describe the single oven so narrow only two burners fit on top. *At least there's a sink,* Cayleen thinks.

"Oh, and here's the elevator!" Jessica's excitement, which other students hear, is beginning to get on Cayleen's nerves.

As the elevator doors open and the other college student and parents step out, Jessica says, "This is my daughter, Cayleen. She's just arriving!"

Luckily for Cayleen and the other family, the elevator doors close quickly. "Mom, I bet everybody is just arriving. I don't think it's something to brag about."

"Oh, honey. I'm just so excited you're here—that's all!"

"Yeah, I gathered that," Cayleen mutters.

On the fourth floor, the elevator doors open to reveal a well-pierced, bleach-haired older student by the nearest door.

"Hi, I'm Trevor. I'm the RA for this floor. Are you on the fourth floor?"

"Uh, yeah ...4-D?" Cayleen says.

"Oh, you're the RA? That's great! This is my daughter, Cayleen.

I'm Jessica. We're from Spring Forks. Cayleen isn't used to the big city here. What year are you?"

Cayleen rolls her eyes. *This isn't a big city, Mom. It's a suburb.* She knows correcting Jessica just makes things worse. Jessica's excited chatter makes Cayleen wonder if she's flirting.

Trevor smiles and says, "Don't worry. I'll keep a close watch to make sure Cayleen doesn't get into trouble … 4-D is just across the walkway on your left. Oh, and I've been here for two years, so I guess that makes me a junior, but we really don't talk too much about that here." He makes eye contact with Cayleen and smiles. "You'll see."

"Oh, I like him already," Jessica says.

In the suite, Cayleen is hit with the realization this will be home for at least a year. There is bustling of unpacking going on all around her. One girl stops and asks, "Are you Cayleen?"

"That's me," Cayleen replies. *Is this my roommate?* Cayleen had gotten paperwork with her roommate's information on it several weeks earlier—someone by the name of Katrina.

"Hey, Trina. Cayleen showed up!" the girl calls down the hallway.

A thin girl, at least six inches shorter than Cayleen, saunters in from the hallway. Her hair is chopped short, framing a European-looking face. "Hi, I'm Trina." Trina offers her hand. "We were beginning to think you weren't coming." Trina seems a bit disappointed she won't get her own room.

"Orientation doesn't start till tomorrow morning, right?" Cayleen asks.

"Yeah, but most of us got here yesterday. Dorms have been open for a few days now," Trina says while walking to a room just off the door to the suite. "This is us." She waves to show the meager room with two beds, two desks, and two dressers. "Since you weren't here, I took that side." Cayleen couldn't really tell there were sides; the room was shaped more like a T.

"Okay. Thanks. I'll grab my stuff."

Jessica and Cayleen head back toward the cars; they drove separately so Cayleen could use her vehicle to drive home on the weekends. At this point, she doesn't know if she will make it to the weekend.

Unloading Cayleen's car took some time with the three flights of stairs. The elevator was booked with students coming and going. Cayleen looks around at the meager furnishings of her new home. *Nothing on the bed.* Jessica said they would buy that when they got here rather than lugging it over in the car.

Jessica sees what Cayleen is thinking. "Ready to go shopping for sheets?"

Cayleen nods. She doesn't have the energy for any more of a response.

They drive to the store and find the necessary items. Cayleen is happy she gets to pick some things that will make it feel more like home.

Several hours later, their work is done. They sit down with fast-food meals on their beds at the Day's Inn.

"My baby's going to college." Jessica sighs. "What do I do?"

"What do you do? What do *I* do? I'm sure Cheyanne and Cyrus will keep you busy, Mom."

"I'm sure you'll find some friends very quickly, Cay-K. Trina seems like a nice girl."

Cayleen sighs. "We'll see."

Stay alert! Watch out for your great enemy, the devil. He prowls around like a roaring lion, looking for someone to devour.
—1 Peter 5:8

It turns out Trina is a nice girl—and not a nice girl. Trina is bipolar. Unfamiliar with the disease, all Cayleen knows is that at one point, she is Trina's best friend. The next day, Trina flies off the handle at Cayleen, throwing things, cussing, and screaming loud enough for the entire floor to hear. One day, Trina went to one of Cayleen's friends and told him Cayleen hated him. Simultaneously, Trina told Cayleen lies about her friend. Before Cayleen knew not to trust Trina, Cayleen's friend was no longer speaking to her.

Jessica was right about Cayleen finding friends quickly. After Cheyanne's suggestion to put herself out there, Cayleen went to the sorority rush events and pledged Pi Omega. Cayleen wasn't sure about a sorority, but she knew the statistics: a daunting four-male-to-one-female in the classrooms.

Cayleen wants to at least have some female friends, so she attends all the events. Since Cayleen has to be in town for the weekend for sorority functions, she asks Hunter to come and see her rather than driving back home to see him. She had gone home several weekends already and tried to track him down for phone conversations.

Hunter's new job was taking him out of town. With Hunter's lack of phone skills, Cayleen feels the strain on their relationship. It feels like they are going in different directions. Putting her doubts and fears aside, Cayleen is excited for the visit.

Trina is sitting on her bed. It's one of her good days. "When will Hunter be here?" Trina plans to sleep at a friend's house while Hunter is in town.

"I'm not sure. They left Spring Forks already, but I'm not sure what they have to get done before they come by. Jason is bringing Hunter."

"Ooh, who's Jason?" Trina asks. "Maybe I should stay for this!"

Cayleen replies, "If you want, but Jason is ... different ... with girls. He doesn't like to be tied down much."

"Oh, noncommittal, huh?" Trina says. "Noncommittal can be fun, but I'm much more interested in the Ryan guy I've been seeing." Trina checks her watch. "Speaking of him, I gotta go! I'll see you later. I'll make sure I sleep elsewhere for the weekend. If nothing else, the guys next door have a comfortable couch."

"See ya," Cayleen calls as Trina walks out the door. Ryan is one of the guys from the suite next door. Most of the guys in their suite are sophomores, which doesn't really matter since nearly no one graduates in four years. Cayleen found out what Trevor had been talking about during orientation: 15 percent of freshman graduate in four years, another 20 percent graduate in five years, and another 25 percent graduate in six years. They didn't talk about the remaining 40 percent of the freshman class. Cayleen doesn't want to think about it.

The phone rings.

"Hello?"

"Hey, Cay." It's Hunter. "We've got to go run some errands for Jason. We made it to town, so I wanted to let you know."

"Okay."

James and Hunter had visited once before and knew where Cayleen lived. "I'll give you a call when we're headed back your way."

"Okay, bye."

"Bye."

Grrr ... her insides fume. Why does she always find herself sitting and waiting for him? It's after seven now. *By the time they "run errands," with the traffic and distances between the city and here, it will be hours.* She picks up a magazine and walks out to the suite. *There's no use staying mad. Do something to get over it.*

In the suite, Michelle is watching TV. Cayleen joins her. Michelle is a kind and witty girl with mothering tendencies that Cayleen had been privy to on several occasions. Her medium frame is at most five foot three and is currently distributed between the coffee table, which holds her feet, the couch, which holds her apple-shaped midsection, and the wall, on which she has placed her head. Her short blonde hair is pulled back. On the TV is a soap opera that Cayleen had never gotten into. Cayleen doesn't care—she just needs a distraction. She opens her magazine.

"Is your boyfriend coming tonight?" Michelle asks. "I thought I heard Trina talking about it."

Cayleen looks up from her magazine. "Yeah. He is in town, but I'm not sure when he'll be here."

"Oh, that's fun! My boyfriend is going to school back home in Minnesota. We don't get to see each other as much as we'd like. He's coming down next month. Finally!"

"Oh, I see," Cayleen says. Michelle has pledged the other

sorority on campus. They had gotten to know each other a little during that first week of school, but since then, both girls have been busy with school and sorority life. Cayleen finds it weird that Michelle has a boyfriend. She is always hanging around Joe and Josh, two other freshmen who have often been in their suite. *To each his own,* Cayleen thinks, and turns back to her magazine. Seconds later, she finds herself laughing hysterically at the embarrassing moments on the page.

Michelle looks over. "Share!"

They giggle over the magazine and talk like they've known each other for years. After two episodes, Cayleen finds herself wanting to watch the soap opera. Growing tired, Cayleen eases over to look at an alarm clock. *Eleven o'clock. Isn't that great?* Her anger rises again. *When he does get here, it's going to be nothing but a booty call.* She turns to Michelle and sighs. "Well, good-night."

"Isn't your boy coming?" Michelle asks.

"Yeah, but I'm not sure what time. If I stay up, I'll keep getting more and more mad that he's not here yet."

"See you tomorrow then."

"Night."

Cayleen walks into her room and closes the door. Making sure the phone is within reach, she falls asleep.

She awakens to a loud knock on the door.

"Cay?" James whispers. Maybe the knock wasn't as loud as she thought.

Cayleen stumbles to the door and opens it. Rubbing her eyes, she asks, "Where's Hunter?"

"Oh, he's passed out in the truck out front." James gestures toward the parking lot and then leans in to give Cayleen a hug. "Speaking of sleeping, where am I at? It's been a long day."

Cayleen points to a pillow and blanket on the floor. "You can either be there or you can sleep on the couch in the suite." Cayleen points to the couch that is probably three feet too short for James.

"The floor it is!" James makes his way into the small room.

Cayleen moves past him to the doorway. "I'm going to try to wake Hunter. If you need the bathroom, it's either of the two doors on the left."

Cayleen stubs her feet into her slippers and makes her way downstairs to the parking lot. The truck doors are unlocked. Hunter has his head bowed in an uncomfortable position. *He's going to wake up cramped everywhere. I should take him inside.*

Carefully, Cayleen slowly opens the door.

Hunter's shoulders slump even farther forward, which Cayleen didn't believe was possible. She stares for a minute, wondering how she's going get him out of that position. She puts a hand on his thigh, wishing he would wake up. Nothing. She slides a hand under his knees and pulls them toward her. Hunter's feet are sticking out of the truck. The position of his upper body is still slumped. *Maybe I can give him a piggyback ride,* Cayleen thinks. She snuggles her backside between his knees and starts to lift.

He grabs her forehead and pulls, and she starts screaming at him. She hears a pop and unbearable pain in her neck. Her back arches to alleviate the stress on her head, she ducks, bends her knees, and forces her hips out, finally struggling free. She turns with fire burning from her soul through every inch of her body.

Hunter is slumped in the same position. She wants to hit him, kick him, and cause as much pain as she can, but he's passed out and doesn't hear her screams. With a feeling of helpless realization, she starts to cry.

Not knowing how long she has been crying next to the truck, Cayleen finally finds her strength to get back upstairs—alone. She goes into the bathroom to clean her swollen face, grateful James is in the bedroom rather than the couch.

After splashing her eyes with cold water and silently thanking Michelle for taking care of them by putting extra hand towels in the bathroom, she returns to her room. She opens the door without making a creak.

James is snoring. Loudly.

Cayleen stops worrying she'll wake him and climbs over him and into her bed. Numb, eyes tired from crying, she falls asleep.

Later in the night, Hunter stumbles to her room and falls into bed with her. Because she doesn't know what to say to make it stop, he gets what he wants. As has happened many times in the past, her tears stain the sheets even after he falls asleep.

> Why do you continue to invite punishment? Must you rebel
> forever? Your head is injured, and your heart is sick.
> —Isaiah 1:5

The next morning is a blur for Cayleen. Hunter and James are up and gone early for more investments and adventures James is looking into. Cayleen doesn't pay attention. She is in shock of the previous night's events. What Cayleen finds even more frightening is the realization that this feeling of betrayal by being physically hurt by Hunter—it is not the first time.

Several years earlier, at a friend's house, there was a conversation going on in the kitchen. Hunter was talking with another guy, and Cayleen was talking with her neighbor who was sitting at the table. Hunter started getting heated in his conversation, and Cayleen feared it might escalate, which happened quite often. Cayleen moved to flank Hunter and said, "Calm down."

Hunter responded, "I've got this." The subject of his interest was not Cayleen. He pushed Cayleen with the back of his hand, and she tumbled Cayleen to the floor, flailing as she went. Completely knocked flat on her backside, she attempted composure and quickly headed out. She left the house, and Hunter never noticed what he had done. Bill, a mutual friend whose house was the setting for the party, stopped her in the driveway.

"Bill, I don't know what he's going to do next. He knocked me down without even noticing he did it. He put no effort at all into it, and it knocked me completely over!"

"Hunter was just trying to look out for you, Cay. He didn't want you involved. He's not like that. You know that."

"Yeah, but is anybody like that or not like that? I saw him mad near me—I mean close enough that he could have hurt me—when we first were going out. You know how much he fights when he's been drinking, and you know how bad the other guy gets hurt." Cayleen looked Bill in the eyes and asked, "What if it's me?"

Bill says, "Cayleen, don't even talk that way. You know Hunter is not like that. Come on. He probably doesn't even know what he did. We'll tell him, and he'll apologize." Bill lowered his voice and smiled. "Then we'll have a good time and drink beers."

Several minutes later, they were back inside. Hunter was listening to Bill prep him for an apology. When Bill was done explaining the situation, Hunter waved in Cayleen's direction. "She shouldn't have been that close to me."

Apology? That's no apology! Cayleen stormed to the entryway with Bill close on her heels. He got his arm in front of her with an unopened beer can.

Bill said, "Have another beer, Cay!" His tone lightened, and he shrugged. "It's a party. You know you're going to forgive him in the morning anyway."

Cayleen's heart sank; she knew Bill was right. She paused, wanting to have fun rather than feeling empty. Swallowing her pride and letting her anger go, she smiled and took the beer.

Back in her suite, Cayleen wants space. *No. I need* space. *I've got to think my way through this.* She demands logic from her brain rather than the ache in her heart. *Think, think! Is it worth it?*

All the love they've shared over the past four years—well off and on. All the good times … suddenly Cayleen can't think of very many good times. It's been yelling and fighting and drinking for so long. Were there ever any good times?

His drinking hasn't changed. There was one season he decided to play football and chose not to drink for three months. Hunter Blake was the most gentlemanly man she'd ever known that season.

But the season ended. At a party at the end of the season, she talked to his mom while he was outside drinking and partying with friends. The drinking began once the season ended.

What about the physical danger, the most recent event? This is what scared Cayleen the most. She is strong enough to lift him and carry him when he passed out, which had happened on several occasions. She smiles as she thinks of the time she carried Hunter inside his house, his mother standing with a look of shock as Cayleen walked in the door and plopped Hunter on the couch after he had passed out in the car. But she had no way of defending herself against him. Hunter had never intentionally hurt her, and Cayleen had no fear of him intentionally hurting her. What frightens Cayleen is what he would do unintentionally. He would never remember what he'd done and never apologize for it. Once is a mistake. Twice is a pattern. Cayleen thinks of the grown men Hunter put in the hospital from his drunken fights. *I'm not sure what he'd do to me if I let it happen a third time. It's not worth it.* Tears stream down her face.

Violent people mislead their companions,
leading them down a harmful path.
—Proverbs 16:29

CHAPTER 7

One of the perks of Cayleen's sorority life is that it keeps her active. With one meeting a week and usually at least one function to attend a week, she stays busy. There are eighteen freshmen entering the sorority with her, which is huge for the school and the sorority. Trina has also joined the same sorority. Cayleen has gotten close with several of the girls, especially when they start to see through Trina's variety of behaviors. Trina successfully managed to turn a few girls away from Cayleen, yet there are still enough girls that Cayleen feels comfortable and has some friends.

School also keeps her busy. By second semester, she knows what happens to that remaining 40 percent of students who weren't accounted for in orientation. The first round of tests, Cayleen found she had actually failed a test by half a percentage point. *Half a percent? What teacher would fail a student by half a percent?* Cayleen realizes that, though she did well in high school, she never had to study. She had never learned to study. Her graphing calculator only holds a certain amount of notes; the rest she has to know. Freshman year is the biggest intellectual challenge Cayleen has faced.

Since her breakup with Hunter, Cayleen only goes home every now and then. One of the times she did go home, she went out to a party in the woods. It didn't feel right. And Bill had been drunk enough to hit on her. That was the last party she had been to with her friends from home.

Michelle has been a constant support for Cayleen. They study together, go to the gym together, and giggle together when either of them needs it.

One night after sneaking a bit of vodka into their slurpees, the girls sit on the couch in the suite. The conversation turns to girl talk. Michelle starts talking about her first time, giggling and laughing about the uncomfortable situation. Her story is so animated.

Cayleen laughs right along with her.

Michelle asks, "What about your first time?"

Cayleen stops laughing, makes a funny face, and looks down at her straw. "My first time wasn't that funny."

Michelle says, "Oh, come on! I did!" She smiles. "They're usually more awkward than funny."

Cayleen shakes her head. "No, my first time was more unwanted than awkward. I didn't want to, and he did. I like to think of it as unwanted sex." Cayleen looks at Michelle and smiles. "Maybe I should tell you about the first time for Hunter and me. That was funny! We were at his friend's parents' house, and the mom walked in … Hunter grabbed the sheet and pulled it around him, leaving me totally exposed!" Cayleen notices Michelle isn't laughing. "Not funny?"

Michelle says, "Cay, you said your first time. You call it unwanted sex?"

"Yeah, so?"

"So, that's what they call rape."

Cayleen shakes her head. "No. That's not. Rape is when someone hits you over the head and ties you up. Or someone breaks into your house and threatens you with a gun. That's rape." Cayleen slurps the rest of her drink with large sucking noises, making sure it is all gone. "Well, I guess I'm done! I should go to bed!"

"Yes, dear, you should," Michelle says.

Cayleen makes her way to her room. "Tomorrow, we can talk sober about what you just told me."

> Gone are the joys of wine and song; alcoholic
> drink turns bitter in the mouth.
> —Isaiah 24:9

"What did you do to me last night?" Cayleen whispers while holding her head and stumbling out of her bedroom.

Michelle is watching the soap opera again. "Uh, I didn't—"

"Sh. Not so loud. Please … I'm dying over here."

"Uh, dear, that's all your doing," Michelle whispers.

Cayleen sees the nearly full slurpee cup on the coffee table. "Is that yours?"

"It sure isn't yours. You made sure to finish every drop."

"Oh." Cayleen cups her mouth and nose with one hand and steadies herself to sitting with the other. "Can you throw it away? I think the smell is making me sick."

Michelle chuckles. "Sure." She dumps the contents of the cup down the bathroom sink and pitches the cup in the trash. "I think we need to talk."

"Really?" Cayleen says. "Okay, but can we wait until my coffee's ready and the Excedrin kicks in?"

"You bet," Michelle replies. "I told you that Midol works better than Excedrin for hangovers. Why didn't you take that?"

"Ugh … just give me ten minutes, okay? No thinking, no talking … ten minutes."

"Okay."

The coffee maker starts making sputtering noises, and Cayleen slowly moves in the direction of her bedroom. She closes the door.

Several minutes later, Cayleen reemerges with a fresh change of clothes and a giant cup of coffee. "Better."

Michelle glances up from the TV. "Did you drink any water?"

"Yeah, I downed a big bottle of water when I took my Excedrin. I don't know if my stomach could take much more. Now it wants coffee." Cayleen walks to the couch and sits next to her friend. "What's bothering you?"

Michelle looks around the suite. No one is out of their room, but it's only nine in the morning. Soon enough, the room could be bustling with other Saturday hangovers or people coming and going for different things. "I'd like to talk in private. Will you come down to the study rooms with me?"

"Sure. Let me put on my slippers." Cayleen jams her slippers on her feet.

"Elevator or stairs?" Michelle asks.

"Oh, tough call." Cayleen considers each option. "Stairs. Less motion."

Down in the study rooms, Cayleen feels better. The stairs must have made the water kick in, and the coffee is working wonders. She pulls up a chair, places her elbows on the table, and rests her chin in her hands.

Michelle says, "Do you remember what we talked about last night?"

Cayleen thinks for a minute and smiles. "Yeah, boys! Who we like! Trevor will have to watch out for you if you do what you say!" With a wink, Cayleen looks up. "And most embarrassing moments … and our first times." Cayleen studies her coffee mug. It was from high school and had everyone's name on it from her graduating class. She looks for Hunter's name.

Michelle says, "I don't know if you remember, but you told me about your first time. You referred to it as unwanted sex. Do you remember that?"

"Yes." Cayleen is hollow with her response, frightened and scared of being judged. If she allowed unwanted sex to occur, she is weak—and Michelle can see that weakness.

"Let me explain something to you," Michelle says. "When one person does not want sex, then sex shouldn't happen. It doesn't matter if you've been dating that person, if you are on a first date, are friends with someone, or if it's a complete stranger. If one of the two people involved don't want sex, then it shouldn't happen. Period. If it does happen, there is a word for that: rape."

Cayleen allows her gaze to drop from Michelle's intense stare back to her coffee mug.

"It's not something to be ashamed of, Cay. Do you know why?" Michelle pulls Cayleen's hands in hers. With Cayleen's eyes locked in hers, she says, "Because it's not your fault. It was never your choice. He didn't give you a choice."

Cayleen breaks their eye contact by looking at the ceiling, tears welling in her eyes. She pulls her hands back and buries her face in them.

Minutes pass slowly.

Cayleen doesn't know whether to continue with her breakdown in the study room or bolt and run. She's been running for so long … running from the truth … hiding from what's happened to her. "I'm sick of hiding. I'm sick of running." Cayleen sobs into her hands. Cayleen finally looks up, hands drenched in tears, face red and splotchy. "What do I do?"

The next thing Cayleen knows, Michelle is at her side, pulling her head onto her shoulder. She whispers, "You see someone way more qualified than me."

Cayleen pulls back, fear in her eyes at the thought of her friend abandoning her to someone else.

"I'll help you, dear." Michelle pulls her back in close. "I'm here."

I myself will strip you and expose you to shame.
—Jeremiah 13:26

Michelle, true to her word, encourages Cayleen to see the school counselors. Without a strong Christian presence on campus or a close church family, neither girl has ideas of faith-based options for Cayleen. The girls look up the location on the campus. On Monday, they decide Cayleen should go. Michelle offers to go with her.

"No, thank you," Cayleen says. "I think this is something I need to do on my own."

"Have you told Mike?"

Cayleen had been seeing Mike for a few weeks. Mike lived across the walkway and had hung out in their suite several times. Cayleen hadn't noticed he had come over to see her, but Michelle did. Cayleen chalked his visits up to being one of Ryan's friends, and Ryan was over occasionally to see Trina. Things had fallen into place between Cayleen and Mike shortly after her breakup with Hunter. Mike had helped Cayleen understand the calculus that she found herself struggling to comprehend. He was a physics major, and Cayleen thought he was very smart. Mike had a teasing manner, with piercing blue eyes and a strong build, and was only slightly taller than Cayleen. All things about Mike were different from Hunter, which made him even more desirable to Cayleen.

"No, I haven't told Mike. I did tell him my first time was unwanted, and he looked at me funny, but that's it." Mike pressed her into talking about many things, but luckily for both of them, he had not pressed her about that. Looking back, Cayleen is relieved; his teasing may have been too much for her to handle. She says, "See ya, Michelle."

With a deep breath, she heads down the stairs. *I'm just walking on campus.* She does not let it sink in where she's headed. She's not sure she has the courage.

Standing in front of the building, Cayleen pauses and looks up. *You've made it this far.* She starts up the stairs.

The receptionist asks if she has an appointment.

"No," she says.

"Who are you here to see?"

"I'm not sure." Cayleen says. *What do I say?* "Uh, I was raped."

That got the receptionist's attention. She quickly stands, asks Cayleen to sit in the waiting area, and moves to another room. When the receptionist reemerges, another woman follows.

The new woman puts out her hand. "Hi. I'm Dr. Helen Turner. Why don't you follow me." Dr. Turner rotates back in the direction she came, making sure Cayleen follows. She leads Cayleen to a small office with cushioned chairs on one side and a desk on the other.

There are windows on two sides of the room, letting in the light from outside.

Cayleen thinks, *I would rather be out there right now.*

Dr. Turner gestures to the chairs and closes the door behind them. "Feel free to call me Helen or Dr. Turner, whichever is more comfortable for you. And you are?"

Cayleen realizes she forgot to introduce herself in the waiting area. "Oh, sorry. I'm Cayleen Jamison."

"It's nice to meet you, Cayleen. Is it okay if I call you Cayleen?"

Cayleen nods and takes a seat.

Helen positions herself in the other chair. "Ruth, the receptionist, tells me you have been raped. Did this just happen this weekend?"

Cayleen's nervousness causes her words to come out more quickly and harshly than she expects. "No, no, it happened more than four years ago."

Helen is quiet.

More controlled, more slowly, searching for the right words, Cayleen says, "I just didn't think it was rape until now." Feeling like she's done talking, Cayleen waits for a response from Helen.

Helen says, "Would you be comfortable telling me what happened?"

Cayleen looks nervously down at her hands, her knees, and her feet. Her thoughts race from the only time she had ever thought about the details of the event. She wrote about it in her diary on the plane ride home the next day. Cheyanne had been sitting next to her and read what she had written. The sympathy from Cheyanne had been immense, which is why Cayleen didn't want to tell the rest of her family. She knew the devastation they would feel. She hadn't told anyone, as if not voicing it would somehow erase it from memory. But the dreams reminded her.

"I've never really told anyone what happened that night."

"Would you like to go into that now?" Helen asks gently. "There are some meditation techniques I can use if you'd like to be in more of a relaxed state. If you'd rather not, you can tell me more about yourself, where you're from, what you're active in school."

Helen is amazing. How does she do that? Make you want to just open up like that? Her posture, tone, non-judging face, and welcoming eyes. Cayleen didn't realize God had been preparing her to release the pain and grief she had been holding onto for years. Helen happened to be the person in the room with her.

Cayleen shakes her head. "No, I think I'm ready now." Cayleen tells Helen every detail she can remember, which is nearly all of it. Cayleen is amazed by how much she does remember since it's been four years. Tears fall down Cayleen's face. She never pauses, steady and thinking of each word, each detail, her voice monotone. At one point, Helen hands her a box of tissue, silently listening. Once her account of the night is over, Cayleen looks up at Helen.

Helen holds Cayleen's gaze with a pleasant expression that surprises Cayleen because she expects judging, patronizing looks. Helen says, "I think you've done wonderfully today, Cayleen. I would like to continue this conversation. Would you like to continue today—or do you want to wait until next week?"

Cayleen whispers, "Next week." She licks her lips, not noticing until now how dry her mouth is.

Helen stands slowly and bows in front of a small refrigerator. She opens it and pulls out a bottle of water. Slowly, she offers the bottle in Cayleen's direction.

Cayleen opens the bottle and takes small sips.

Helen sits and says, "I'd like to make an appointment with you for next week before you leave for Christmas break. Does this time work with your schedule?"

Cayleen nods, still sipping water.

Helen gracefully rises and moves behind the desk. She picks up the phone and schedules the appointment with the receptionist.

Cayleen is trying to figure out how she will face the sunlight outside she so desperately wanted when she first walked in this room.

The freedom she longed for when she entered is now a frightening prospect with the numbness and sorrow that has washed over her.

Would the entire world be different? Would people look at her differently? Would her secret show on her face? In her walk?

Helen is back in front of her, perched on the edge of her chair. She has a card in her hand. Helen presses the card toward Cayleen. "Here you go. These are my numbers. Why don't you put them in your phone so you don't lose them? You can call me whenever you need me. There's a cell phone number on the back if it's after hours."

Cayleen does as she's told. Helen rises.

"I'll walk you to the door."

Once outside, the sun hits Cayleen's face. *Is that nice or does that burn?* Cayleen's not sure. She feels unsure about everything right now. Raw, tenderized. She's not even sure if the burden of her experience has been lifted or if it just got even heavier.

We are filled with fear, for we are trapped, devastated and ruined.
—Lamentations 3:47

Over the next weeks, Cayleen continues meeting with Helen. Cayleen feels comfortable telling Helen about her research of rape in the Bahamas online. Unlike the United States, Cayleen found out that rape is not a crime in the Bahamas. In addition, Colorado classifies rape as an age-based, crime; even if someone under a certain age has given consent, they are still not old enough to have sex with someone over the age of eighteen. In the United States, there is grounds for rape based on him being the bartender, knowing how much she had to drink while he remained sober. Had the situation occurred in her hometown, there would have been grounds for rape of three different types, but since it happened in the Bahamas, it wasn't even a crime. Cayleen tells Helen how glad she is to live in the US where rape is a crime. God is leading Cayleen to slowly let go of any form of hatred for the man.

Cayleen's meetings with Helen allow her to recognize that the drugs and boys before Hunter were a way of coping with the pain she did not allow herself to recognize at the time. The unhealthy eating habits could also be an attempt at control when she felt she had none. Though Cayleen did not find this an excuse for her behavior, she did allow acceptance of what she'd done.

Helen told her that acceptance is the first step to forgiving yourself.

Cayleen wants to forgive herself, but she isn't sure how.

During one of their weekly conversations, Cayleen tells Helen that smoking is a vice she has not been able to kick. She tells Helen that, for Lent, she is giving up smoking. Though Cayleen is Episcopalian, she still believes in sacrifice to feel closer to the sacrifice Jesus made for humanity.

Helen says, "Cayleen, what is your relationship with God? What role does he play in your life?"

With each session, Cayleen gets more comfortable. "Well, I go to church most Sundays, which for college students, I think is saying something. I'm active in a Bible study, or maybe it's a group. We don't study the Bible that much, but we study other books. I'm not a part of the church groups on campus. Is that what you mean?"

"Sort of," Helen says. "You never lost your faith. How do you explain that? Why do you not ask why? Where was God in your life during the *incident* as you've termed it?" Her questions weren't demanding or confrontational, merely rousing discussion and thought.

Cayleen purses her lips and raises her eyebrows. "Well, that was never an option for me." Cayleen shrugs. "I've never known life without God being a given. He's just there and always has been. Mom brought us up that questioning why God has things happen to us is not acceptable because that would be an expression of not trusting in God, and that is being mean to God." Cayleen pauses and looks toward the window. "God is the reason I walked back to my family rather than drowning myself in the water that night." She pauses and looks Helen in the eyes. "I believe God is in people and that he's a loving God. It's been hard for me to realize, but over the past weeks and months we've met, I've prayed for understanding so I can accept what has happened to me. I think I have gotten a little of that. See, I think God is in people, or he can be if we want him to. He's the good things we do for others. There was no God in that man that night." She shifts her gaze back to Helen. "God didn't do that—one man did."

Helen returns her gaze with a questioning look, prompting Cayleen to continue.

Cayleen says, "There's God in Michelle for encouraging me to come here. There's God in you for helping me cope. We can choose to take actions based on what we want or what God wants, but true good in people is when what we want is exactly what God wants us to do. But what do I know—I'm only eighteen."

As Cayleen walks back into her suite to grab her books for her next class, she notices a large package by her door. She smiles. It is another package from Jessica. *Mom is so sweet.* Cayleen grabs scissors and opens the box. The first package had come the end of September, the end of the first full month at school. It had been filled with candies, school supplies, cookies, and granola bars. When the second package came, Jessica admitted she had signed up to have packages delivered by the school. Jessica didn't have to do anything. They changed with the holiday. In November, the package had fall colors. For February, the package had been red and filled with hearts. In addition to the school packages every once in a while, Jessica mailed her own. Since it is April, this package is filled with springtime goodies.

Cayleen is still discovering newfound treats when Mike walks in. "Another package from your mom?"

"Yeah," Cayleen says. "This one has flower lollipops and cookies! Want one?" She takes a lollipop and tosses it on the couch next to where he's sitting.

"A flower-shaped lollipop. Are you in the third grade?"

"I think it's kinda cool my mom did all this," Cayleen replies, quietly stung by his words.

Mike says, "So have you signed up for the short summer session?"

"Yeah, I'm taking Physics II and Calc III. I figure it'll be easier if I take those two over the summer rather than with everything else." Cayleen had a difficult time with Physics I. She thought being able to focus on just a few classes at once would be good—even if they crammed all the material from an entire semester into a six-week course.

"Yeah, you and physics don't get along very well," Mike says, laughing.

Cayleen stops going through the package and looks at him.

His laughing stops. "So, one more month—and you're moving into the Pi Omega house! You excited?" Mike asks.

"Yeah. It'll be nice to have my own room." The girls had picked rooms several weeks before. Priority was based on years in the sorority and then grades. Luckily, Cayleen had done better than several of her classmates. "Travis from upstairs said he'd give me his bed so I can have a bed and put a desk under it."

"You're taking Travis's bed?" Mike laughs sarcastically. "Do you think it will make the move?" Travis had put his bed on stilts and had a couch under it in his dorm. Cayleen's new room would be about the size of her dorm room if not a little smaller, and she wanted to use his bed to have a study space below it.

"Yeah, I do!" Cayleen packs her goodies back in the box and heads inside her room.

Mike follows her and plops down on her bed.

Cayleen starts putting things away and then takes things out that she needs for class. "Mike, I've got to go to class. Aren't you supposed to be in class?"

"Not for another fifteen minutes. Hold on a minute. I'll walk with you." Mike gets up and saunters across the hall to get his things. Lately, it seems like Mike is always picking on her. He didn't so much when they first started hanging out, but now every conversation seems to have a sarcastic remark directed at her. He talks that way to all his friends too. She wonders how he keeps friends, talking to them so rudely.

"Ready, slowpoke?" Mike yells from the hallway.

Cayleen rolls her eyes, grabs her backpack, and follows him out the door.

> Some people make cutting remarks, but the
> words of the wise bring healing.
> —Proverbs 12:18

Think, think! Cayleen tells herself. She studies the problem she has reworked three times already without getting the right answer. Frustrated, she throws her pencil onto her desk. *I need a break!*

Cayleen opens the front door to the Pi Omega house and steps outside into the warm summer afternoon. It's Saturday and not busy around the sorority house. In the summer, not many girls stay around for the summer classes. Most of them are out shopping or visiting family or boyfriends. Cayleen needs to study. Everything builds on the two classes she's taking this summer.

She settles into her normal spot atop an empty planter box in front of the commercial office next door to the sorority house. There is no smoking on the Pi Omega grounds, Technically, she's not supposed to have nicotine on grounds either. Most of the other girls keep alcohol in their rooms and drink out back, so Cayleen cuts herself a break. Besides, who is going to yell at her? Her? She smiles.

When room choices were handed out, Trina was elected house organizer. She got the big single room with the oversize jack-and-jill bathroom to share with another girl. Then when grades came out, Trina failed the last semester, which deemed her unable to hold that office. Cayleen was next in line.

Cayleen would have loved to have the bigger corner room with windows coming on both sides rather than her dinky space with one small window. Knowing Trina and the horror that Cayleen would have to put up with, possibly for the rest of her life, Cayleen opted out of changing rooms. That left Cayleen in charge of enforcing all the rules. No boys, no drugs, no alcohol? Right.

Cayleen takes another puff and looks up the street. One direction is campus, and the other is a small downtown area. The Pi Omega house is the farthest housing from the rest of campus. With such a small sorority, the organization rents an old house. Stories say that the building used to house people renting rooms and then the wrestling team for the school before Pi Omega signed on.

Cayleen looks at the church across the street—her church. She smiles, knowing this is just where she is supposed to be. Tomorrow at eight, the first set of church bells will ring. Her service will ring them again at eleven. If she doesn't get out of bed by the time the bells chime for the second service, she knows she's in trouble.

Cayleen stubs out her cigarette and puts it in the can, not wanting to be a messy smoker. She walks up the steps and back into the house. *Maybe I'll make a little snack*, she thinks as she's washing her hands in the sink.

There's a knock at the door. The front door is glass with a small wood frame around it. As she walks toward the door, her heart skips a beat. Excited, she opens the door. "Hunter!" She welcomes him into the house and gives him a hug. "What are you doing here?" She hasn't spoken with him since Christmas break when they had shared some not-so-sweet moments. Still, it always makes her heart smile to see him, and she always thought he was incredibly hot.

"I thought I'd seen you sitting outside, so I've been walking up and down the street, trying to find where you went." He smiles. "Luckily for me, this was the first place."

"Well, how have you been? Do you want to come in and sit down for a while?" Cayleen doesn't understand why, but she's ecstatic and doesn't want him to leave. "You shaved! It looks great on you!" For most of high school, Hunter thought that since he could grow facial hair, he should in all forms: goatee, full beard, mustache, anyway it would grow. At the time, Cayleen couldn't convince him to shave.

"No, no, I can't stay. James is in the truck. I think he thought I was a little crazy."

"Oh, well, I'd love to go say hi!" Ca

The truck is parked just in front of the planter.

James steps out of the truck and saunters over to Cayleen. He reaches down and gives her a hug.

"Are you in town long?"

James answers in the negative, and Hunter in the affirmative.

James bows slightly and turns back to the truck. "It was good to see you, Cayleen."

"You too, James." Cayleen turns back to Hunter. "So how long are you here?"

"Well, we should be going pretty soon, I guess." Hunter looks at James in the truck and scratches the back of his neck. "Will you be coming home for the summer at all?"

"Yeah, I'll be coming home next weekend or so. Finals are next week. When I get done with those, I'm housesitting for a night or two—and then I'll be coming home. Why?"

"Uh, I was wondering if you'd like to go out to dinner or something with me … while you're home."

Somehow all the bad memories are gone from Cayleen's mind, and all she can think of is the love she's felt for so long for Hunter … and how great he looks. "Yeah. I'd love to, Hunter."

"Okay. I'll give you a call after next week, then."

"Sounds good." Cayleen moves in to give him another hug. "It's been really good to see you, Hunter."

"You, too," he replies and gets back in the truck.

Cayleen walks back to the porch and watches them until she can no longer see their truck.

She goes back inside, more motivated to finish studying if that will lead her closer to home … and Hunter. On her last study problem for calculus, her phone rings. It's Mike. She groans. *That's going to be a problem.*

It has been weeks, if not months, since she and Mike had fun together—or at least Cayleen has not been having fun. His biting remarks are no longer tolerable. They have had breakups multiple times over the past weeks. Now she has a reason to end things for good.

"Hi, Mike."

"Hey, Cayleen. Do you want to get together tonight?"

"You know what … we'd better not. I have a lot of studying to do." She needs to think about how to do this. *Is a breakup over the phone okay?* It felt like she should do it in person—at least he could see her face.

"I can come over and help … if you want," Mike says.

Maybe this would be the time for the breakup discussion. I would rather do it in person than over the phone. Mike deserves that. "Okay."

Mike doesn't live far from Cayleen's sorority house. Waiting for Mike, Cayleen tries to figure out what she's going to say. She doesn't have much time, and before the conversation is worked out in her head, there's a knock at the door.

Mike has pillow in his hand and his glasses on. He is so vain. He never wears his glasses except when he's sleeping over. Cayleen doesn't wear contacts, and whenever Mike sleeps over, he's told her it's just easier to wear his glasses rather than to sleep in his contacts. Mike is also carrying his pillow. Cayleen is broke. It's college, and Mike knows there is only one pillow on her bed. *He looks so cute,* Cayleen thinks as she reaches for the door. *Can I do this? I have to.* Her internal conversation ceases as she opens the door, standing aside for him to come in.

"Hi." Mike leans in for a kiss, but Cayleen turns her head, and he gets her cheek.

"Hi," Cayleen says, leading the way to her room, quickly, wanting this to already be over.

Mike sighs—or was it a moan—behind her. At least she's not leading him on, right?

In her room, away from eavesdropping ears, they sit and face each other. There are only two chairs in Cayleen's room—one to her desk, which she gives Mike, and the other for her junk, clothes, papers, and books. She's cleaned it off so they can sit face-to-face.

"I can't do this anymore," Cayleen starts.

"What?" Mike's glare pierces through Cayleen.

"I can't do this. I need to do other things. We've talked about it before, and you and I are just not alike enough. I have faith in God, and you don't—that's huge for me. I don't know how to relate to someone who is not a believer. It's been fun, and I do care about you. I just need this to be over right now."

"What do you mean? Is this because you're going home next week?"

His words feel like thousands of needles.

He leans forward slightly. "Is this because of Hunter?"

Cayleen is too young and innocent to hide things from anyone. "He stopped by today. I really think he's changed. I have to try this with him. This summer is our opportunity to do that."

Mike shakes his head, looking at the floor. "You've got to be kidding." He looks up at Cayleen. "Well, I'll be here next year when things don't work out." With that, Mike walks out the door.

Cayleen is relieved things went so well with Mike. Her relief only lasts through her second and last final test—when he calls.

"How did finals go?" he asks.

"Fine. I'm pretty sure I passed both classes." Cayleen had figured out what her final grade needed to be in order to pass and was confident she had passed both with an A or a B. She is elated things went so well and confident she would not have done as well during the regular semester, but she didn't want to show Mike any excitement for fear he'd get the wrong idea.

"When are you going home?"

"I'm housesitting for the Wilsons for two nights. I'll be leaving Friday," Cayleen says. She could have lied to make things easier on herself.

Mike says, "I'd like to cook you dinner before you go. I've already got everything to make dinner. Why don't I meet you there about four? How long has it been since you've cooked and had a good dinner? You don't cook much at the Pi Omega house."

It has been weeks since she has actually cooked dinner. His logic seems so sound. "Okay." Cayleen doesn't know what else to say. It is so hard telling him to go away, and she doesn't have the energy to keep doing it. Cayleen hangs up the phone. The Wilsons were Jessica's friends from growing they up, and lived in the same town as the college. Mike had been with Cayleen to the Wilsons' house on several occasions; they were friendly and often invited her and her friends to their house for dinner.

Mike is prompt, and by four-thirty, they are both standing in the Wilsons' kitchen. Mike is in charge and doesn't let Cayleen do anything: no cutting, no cleaning, just talking. They banter back and forth—just light conversation about school. Mike has also just finished his intensive summer session. He chose to double major; every major has an intensive summer session that only lasts six weeks but is required for graduation. Mike has to complete two of these and chose to take his first after his sophomore year and would take the other after his junior year. He is in an engineering discipline and tells Cayleen about the surveying of a hillside they had to do— trekking up and down, fighting with his other team members, and working late to complete the project. Cayleen thinks about how anal Mike is about having things just right and smiles as her sympathy goes out to his teammates.

Dinner is a feast of chicken, pasta, vegetables, and a wonderful roux. He even brought wine, which Cayleen thinks is amazing. *He was so thoughtful about the whole thing.*

The wine dulls Cayleen's senses, and they have done this many times before, which seems normal.

Cayleen shoves him. "You just got me pregnant!" She is mortified and angry.

"What? You're crazy. You'd never know that. We just finished. There's no way you'd know."

"I want you to leave." Cayleen doesn't even look at him.

Mike hesitates, lying next to her.

"Leave," she says.

Mike does as he's told, hesitating for a moment at the door and looking at Cayleen.

She meets his gaze with the same steely glare.

Without words, Mike leaves.

The following morning, Cayleen looks up the closest distributors of the morning-after pill. She calls one facility and makes an appointment.

Once there, they take a pregnancy test. The doctor, whom she is not sure actually is a doctor, looks at the test and then back at her. "It's negative."

"We just had sex last night." Cayleen knows pregnancy tests only work after several weeks. "That's why I'm here for the morning-after pill." She also knows that each hour that goes by without taking the pill will reduce her chances of it working.

The doctor hesitates and pulls out a packet of pills. They look similar to the pills Cayleen was taking until a few weeks ago when she and Mike broke up. "Take these pills first." He gestures to several pills in the top row. His fingers go down. "Then take these pills eight hours later. Finally, take these pills the following morning. Make sure you don't need to do any driving. Be sure to eat before taking your first set of pills—and try to eat with each subsequent set."

Numbly, Cayleen takes the packet and finds her way out of the clinic. Before returning to the Wilsons' house, she stops by Taco Bell, an extravagant treat for her college budget. She gets several items so she will have food for the upcoming doses.

Mike calls, and Cayleen answers before thinking about dodging the call. The first dose of pills make her feel funny and a little queasy. *Maybe that's why the doctor said to eat first*, she thinks. "Hello?"

"How are you?" Mike says with a laugh.

"Fine."

"Do you still think you're pregnant?"

"I'm taking the morning-after pill."

"Did you just say that right? You said I'm taking it—wouldn't you have taken it or not? It's a pill. Can you figure it out or not!"

Cayleen says, "I'm taking it. It's not one pill. It's a series of pills—or at least that's what the doctor gave me. Look, I don't feel well. I'm going to go now."

"Do you want me to come over?"

"No," Cayleen says. "Bye." She hangs up before he can persuade her otherwise.

The next twenty-four hours are a blur for Cayleen. She's sleeping, then watching TV, not moving off the couch for fear she'll be sick. She doesn't get sick, for which she's relieved. She hates being sick, and she's scared the pills won't work if she throws them up. The only thing Cayleen is sure of is the time between taking doses of pills, and she doesn't let that leave her mind. Thanks in part to the alarm on her phone, she takes her doses right on time.

On Friday, Cayleen's stupor has not lifted. She packs her things, cleans up after herself, and drives off. Her full laundry basket and several other items for the eight weeks at home are already in her car. Two hours into the drive, Cayleen sees a red car with sirens in the rear-view mirror. She looks down: eighty-five miles per hour. Ten over.

Cayleen has only been pulled over once. She was sixteen, and Jessica had given her an envelope and said, "Put this on the car." Cayleen had thought she said put this *in* the car, which she did. Several months later, she was driving from work to Luke's to have dinner when a policeman about her father's age, pulled her over. He said something about registration. She opened the glove box and showed him the envelope with the colored sticker still sitting inside, unopened.

"Do you mean this?" Cayleen had asked. "Mom said to put it in the car." She shrugged. "I just didn't know what to do with it!"

Cayleen thought the policeman must have seen something across the street as he looked the other direction for a minute. Was he grunting or laughing? When he looked back, he was a little less stern, but still commanding. "Miss, where are you going right now?"

"I'm going to have dinner at my dad's house," Cayleen replied.

"Once you get there, give this envelope to your dad and tell him

I stopped you. He'll know what to do. Have him show you so you don't have this happen again." The officer had handed her back the envelope and strode back to his car. Since then, Cayleen had been very diligent to place her registration sticker on her car whenever it came in the mail.

As she slows her car to a stop on the side of the interstate, she knows this will not be as good an outcome.

The young police officer approaches her car. He is yelling at her. Cayleen wants to cry, but she doesn't. She's numb.

The officer comes back with the paperwork and says, "We don't drive that way in this part of the state." He leaves her for good, and she thinks, *Yes, we do. I've lived here all my life. I would know.* All the same, Cayleen sets the cruise control for ten miles an hour under the speed limit for the rest of the drive.

> While you were doing these wicked things, says the Lord,
>   I spoke to you about it repeatedly, but you would not
>   listen. I called out to you, but you refused to answer.
>   —Jeremiah 7:13

CHAPTER 8

Cayleen looks at herself in the mirror of her childhood bedroom. *I'm ready,* she thinks. Hunter is coming over to pick her up for dinner in a few minutes. She giggles, thinking of how they never really went out on dates during high school. They were always with a group rather than going out places as a couple.

She walks out into the living room to visit with Jessica, Cheyanne, and Cyrus. Cheyanne and Cyrus are getting married in less than a week, which is one of the other reasons Cayleen came home. The wedding details have had the house humming for the past two days since her arrival.

In addition to planning the wedding, Cheyanne and Cyrus are buying a home from Luke's construction company. Cyrus is still employed by Luke, and while Cayleen was home, Luke had also given Cayleen a job cleaning houses for Jameson Construction.

Cheyanne and Cyrus are looking at house amenities. "If we purchase the washer and dryer, that's another $1,500 we would have to bring to closing," Cheyanne says.

Cyrus says, "We're going to have to have a washer and dryer. What else are we going to do? Come over here to your mom's house to wash our clothes?"

"I just don't know how we're going to get that in addition to our closing amount." Cheyanne looks up at Cayleen. "You look nice. Is Hunter on his way?"

"I think so," Cayleen answers, sitting on the sofa next to Jessica. "Is Paul in town?"

Paul is Jessica's latest boyfriend. Jessica and Jeff hadn't made it through Cayleen's senior year, and Jessica had been dating Paul for several months. He was a childhood friend of Jessica's and lives in Los Angeles. Paul had recently divorced his wife of twenty years. His mannerisms with Jessica made Cayleen slightly uncomfortable with how attached her mother had gotten to him so quickly, but she reasoned herself out of saying anything. She's the daughter—what does she know.

"Paul's coming into town on Thursday—just before the wedding." Jessica smiles. "Did I tell you about my latest trip to LA?"

"The one where he took you rollerblading on the beach?" Cayleen asks with a smile.

Jessica nods.

"Yeah … you mentioned it. It sounds great for you!" Cayleen is careful with her words. The entire experience didn't seem great to her. Half-naked people flaunting themselves on the beach, and everyone worried about how they look rather than what they're doing. Cayleen had never been to LA. Jessica's stories paint the picture in Cayleen's mind that the people who are slightly overweight in LA stay at home—locked in their rooms. It all sounds so superficial to Cayleen: the extravagant homes, the nice cars, the adventurous outings. It makes Cayleen's head spin. She grew up in the same house all her life, driving the same car that Jessica bought when Cayleen was ten. Her house, her car, it all works, and Cayleen doesn't understand why there needs to be more than that. Cayleen thinks about the similarity she sees between what Jessica has described and some of the people she sees in church. There are often people who come in with energy through the roof, helping in various ways and talking about the work God has done in their lives. Then they disappear. Cayleen doesn't feel like she had seen God work in her life like the stories she's heard from people at church.

The knock at the door interrupts her thoughts. "Well, I'll see you all later," Cayleen says over her shoulder as she walks toward the door.

Jessica says, "Not so fast! I haven't seen Hunter in so long! I want to at least say hi."

Cayleen grabs the knob, Jessica close behind, and opens the door. Cayleen can't help but stop for an instant and stare at the image of the man on the other side of her doorstep.

Hunter is dressed as he normally does in jeans and a T-shirt, yet his appearance causes her to lose her breath. He's recently gotten a haircut, and his brown eyes are even more striking against his clean-shaven face. The energy he exudes, his presence, Cayleen finds stunning. She takes in a breath and says, "Hi."

Hunter does not have a chance to respond before Jessica is pushing her way past Cayleen to welcome him into the house. "Hunter! It's so great to see you! Come in, come in!" As Hunter walks through the door, Jessica grabs him in a hug.

"It's good to see you too, Jessica," Hunter says.

Cayleen is slightly confused. *She didn't like him this much in high school.* Jessica leads Hunter inside, and Cayleen follows them.

Soon, there's a welcome party in the kitchen with Cheyanne and Cyrus joining them. Questions surround Hunter about what he's doing now and what he's been doing for the year they haven't seen him. Cayleen finds out that Jessica has seen Hunter since Cayleen has been at college here and there. Cayleen thinks it is odd, but not alarming that Jessica didn't tell Cayleen when it happened. Cayleen's nervousness for a dinner with Hunter gets the best of her, and she has to use the bathroom … again. When she comes out, she's ready to break up the little reunion.

"Are we ready?" Cayleen asks.

"Sure, whenever you are," Hunter says, meeting her gaze with his stunning brown eyes.

Leaving the kitchen with variations of "Good to see you" following them, they exit the house for Hunter's truck.

"Sorry about all that," Cayleen says. "I didn't realize they would hammer you like that."

"It's fine," Hunter says with a smile and a glance as he opens Cayleen's door. "It's good to see everybody too." He shuts the door behind her and walks around the truck.

"So, where are we going?" Cayleen asks.

"I was thinking the Steakhouse. Does that sound okay to you?"

Wow, Cayleen thinks. He's not even making her decide where they have to go for dinner, and the Steakhouse is a nice restaurant with a less formal atmosphere where they'll fit in perfectly with their jeans. "Sounds great."

Small talk is easy on the drive over. Hunter catches her up on the happenings of Spring Forks. During dinner, Cayleen catches Hunter up on her life at college and the sorority ladies with whom she's had the pleasure of making friends. Hunter doesn't even call her sorority the pyros as he's done in the past. His attempt at humor had always rubbed Cayleen the wrong way; she took it as a form of disrespect.

Nearing the end of the meal, Cayleen says, "Cheyanne and Cyrus are getting married next weekend." She looks down at her napkin. "Would you like to go with me? I'm the maid of honor, so I'm not sure how much I'll be sitting. I'll have to stand for the ceremony, and I'm not sure what they're doing for the reception."

"I'll go to your sister's wedding with you," Hunter says.

Cayleen looks up, relief on her face, and says, "Okay."

> But my people would not listen or turn
> back from their wicked ways.
> —Jeremiah 44:5

The next few days are a blur for Cayleen. She tries to balance working for her dad with planning a bridal shower, which she has no experience for, in addition to her calls and short visits with Hunter. Her excitement for their renewed relationship fills her with a giddiness that doesn't go away.

Cheyanne asks, "What's up with you?"

"Oh, I just got off the phone with Hunter," Cayleen nearly sings.

Cheyanne smiles and shakes her head. "Is he coming to the wedding?"

"Yes."

"How do you think that's going to go? We don't have any friends of his invited."

"I think it'll be fine. I've asked him not to drink. As long as he's not drinking, he doesn't fight. It'll be fine."

"Good. Now, what are we doing for my bridal shower?" Cheyanne's distractions take over their conversation.

> Smooth words may hide a wicked heart, just
> as a pretty glaze covers a clay pot.
> —Proverbs 26:23

"I can't believe this day is here!" Jessica exclaims while admiring her oldest daughter. They are in the basement of the church, getting ready. It's July, and because of the heat, Cheyanne hesitates to put on her dress until the last minute. The air-conditioning is hardly felt in the room. Instead, they have the windows cracked. Outside, the groomsmen can be heard. It smells like they are smoking and sounds of passing a flask seep through the open windows.

Cheyanne peeks out one of the windows. "Hey, can I have some of that?" she asks Noah, the best man.

"Of course—whatever the bride wants," Noah says with a laugh, handing Cheyanne the flask.

Cheyanne sticks her arm out the window and takes a pull off the small metal container. "Can I have a drag of that too?"

Noah hands her his cigarette. "You can have the rest if you want it." Cheyanne's arm is now fully out the window. She tries to blow all the smoke out the open crack, somewhat unsuccessfully.

Cayleen is mortified at the scene unraveling in front of her and turns to Jessica. "Isn't there some rule that you can't smoke in church?"

Jessica, also shocked, merely shakes her head in disbelief.

Luckily, Cheyanne is finished by the time the priest walks in the room. "People are starting to fill the pews, and we have about ten minutes until we start."

"Time for the dress," Cheyanne tells all the ladies in the room. As a group effort, they hoist her dress over her beautifully done hair, making sure not to touch her makeup, and carefully fasten her in.

"Two minutes." Jessica is keeping an eye on the clock. "We should make our way upstairs now. Oh, I just can't believe it! My baby!" Jessica grabs Cheyanne by the shoulders and pulls her close. "My oldest baby is getting married!" Jessica pulls away and wipes at her eyes and nose without smudging her makeup. Quickly, seemingly not to cause another scene, Jessica leaves the room heads for the stairs.

"You ready?" Cayleen asks.

Cheyanne nods.

Cayleen grabs her for a quick hug. "Let's go then—you first. I gotta grab your dress."

> Does a young woman forget her jewelry, or a bride her wedding dress? Yet for years on end my people have forgotten me.
> —Jeremiah 2:32

With all the commotion of the wedding and being the maid of honor, Cayleen doesn't catch up with Hunter until the reception. The bridal party is seated at a head table with the bride and groom flanked by the best man and maid of honor. Cayleen doesn't see when Cyrus points Hunter out to Noah. Cayleen is oblivious to Noah buying Hunter drinks at the bar—in a very steady fashion. Cayleen only sees Hunter with a drink in each hand as she approaches him to say hi.

Cayleen looks momentarily at the drinks with a narrow gaze. "Thanks for coming," she says.

Hunter sets one of the drinks on the nearest table. "Yeah, this is great!" he yells over the music.

"Did James come with you?"

"Yeah. He was my ride. My truck broke down. I figured that, with you doing your maid of honor thing, that it would be fun to have James here. He was really excited to come, knowing it was Cheyanne."

"Are you drinking because you don't have to drive?" Cayleen words are icy, but she can't help it. She specifically asked him not to drink, and here he is double-fisting.

"No, I …"

Cayleen doesn't hear the rest of Hunter's excuse. She is tired of him always having an excuse. She rushes toward the courtyard, throwing the doors open for the fresh air and peace from both people and noise.

"Is everything okay," Noah says from behind her.

She turns.

"I saw you run out here. Are you okay?"

"Oh," Cayleen says. "I didn't mean for anyone to see me. It's just my … oh, never mind." Her gaze goes back to the plants in the courtyard.

"I don't think anyone else noticed." Noah moves closer to Cayleen and puts a comforting arm around her. "You can talk about it. I don't mind."

Cayleen pushes away from Noah and says, "I asked him not to drink! He does that too much, and then it gets out of hand. We just decided to try this again, and that was the thing. He drank too much before, and I wasn't going to put up with it again!" She takes in a breath and tries to calm herself. "Well, enough. This isn't my night. It's for Cheyanne. I guess we should get back in there, huh?"

Noah grabs her by the waist and looks her in the eye. "You deserve better than that, you know?"

"What do you mean?" Cayleen asks. *What does Noah know about my relationship with Hunter?*

Noah continues holding Cayleen with one hand and tugs the other through his blond hair. "Cyrus told me a little about what has gone on with you and Hunter. You deserve someone who will listen to you when you ask them to do something, that's all I mean." Noah drops his hand from her waist.

Cayleen holds her position for a moment longer. She is slightly taller than he in her three-inch heels, and she looks at his face as he looks away. Once he looks back, their eyes hold for an instant—and then she is gone.

A good person produces good things from the treasury of a good heart, and an evil person produces evil things from the treasury of an evil heart. What you say flows from what is in your heart.
—Luke 6:45

Space, Cayleen thinks, *I just need space. The cabin is a good place to get space.* After the wedding festivities, she makes the trip to the family cabin for a few days. During the summer, the cabin is their vacation place. Jessica, being a teacher, had the summers off with her daughters and often took them to the cabin in the mountains, several hours from their home. Jessica's grandmother and grandfather had built the cabin decades earlier. Now the cabin is shared by all the grandchildren and great-grandchildren, though the creators of the home away from home had since passed away. With running water, electricity, and five bedrooms, the cabin is hardly a cabin. It has enough space for Cayleen not to be bothered by other family members.

Cayleen had brought Hunter up to the cabin years before for a weekend. There were strict rules about no cohabitation between couples who aren't married, and they had not shared a room. Cayleen's thoughts make their way to that weekend while she gets ready. On that trip, Hunter had been drinking a little more than he needed to, and with the altitude being higher than he was used to, he had passed out soon after dinner. It hadn't been much of a weekend from Cayleen's memory.

She splashes water on her face and wipes it clean with a towel, trying to wipe away the embarrassment of the memory. It had been so embarrassing to try to explain to her grandma why he had fallen over on the couch and literally passed out drunk in the living room.

After breakfast, Cayleen sets out on a small walk around the property to clear her head. It is here that Cheyanne and Cyrus met. Cyrus's family owns a cabin just down the road. Cheyanne and Cyrus had met as teenagers; now, six years later, they are married. Cayleen smiles at the hope of Cheyanne and Cyrus having many happy years to share together.

Cayleen's thoughts then move to Noah. Cayleen smiles at the thought of how attractive he is. When they shared a few words at the reception, it seemed Noah was always around her. The next morning, Jessica had hosted a breakfast. They had talked briefly several times. Cayleen doesn't know what to think of the situation and turns her attention to the beauty around her.

God in all things, right? I see him in the beautiful wildflowers and the running river. Well, Lord, I sure could use a little help here.

And since we know he hears us when we make our requests,
we also know that he will give us what we ask for.
—1 John 5:15

After two days in the mountains, Cayleen returns to Jessica's house. She has to get back to cleaning houses. Arms loaded with clothes and gear from her trip, she stumbles inside to see a beautiful arrangement of flowers on the entry buffet.

"Wow. Those are nice," Cayleen says on the way to her room.

Cheyanne and Cyrus are sitting on the sofa. "Glad you think so … they're for you," Cheyanne says.

Cayleen runs out and positions herself so she can see the flowers and the sofa. "They're for me?"

Cheyanne laughs. "Yeah. Why don't you read the card?"

Cayleen reaches for the small card among the multicolored long-stemmed roses. She reads the card aloud: "I hope you got the space you need. Welcome home. Noah." Surprised, Cayleen looks at Cheyanne and Cyrus.

"Noah called while you were gone. Why don't you call him?" Cheyanne asks with a smile.

"I don't have his number," Cayleen says, looking at the flowers and wondering how she'll be able to thank him without his number.

"Well, that's no excuse." Cheyanne gets off the couch, grabs her phone, and thumbs through screens. Cheyanne hands her sister the phone.

Cayleen is nervous and doesn't know what to do, but she hears the ringing coming from the earpiece and grabs the phone.

"Hello?" Noah answers.

"Uh, hi, Noah. This is Cayleen, you know, Cheyanne's sister."

"Yeah. I know, Cayleen," Noah says.

Cayleen smiles. "I wanted to thank you for the flowers."

"Well, I'll be honest, Cheyanne helped me a little with that," Noah says.

Cayleen moves away from the sounds of the TV Cheyanne and Cyrus are watching and walks outside.

Once their phone conversation is done, Cayleen comes back inside. As she shuts the door, Cheyanne says, "So?"

"So what?" Cayleen says, a smile still on her face.

"You can't give me a so what after you've been on the phone for two hours!"

"Oh my goodness. Has it been that long?" Cayleen asks.

Cheyanne insists Cayleen tell her every topic they discussed, and Cayleen complies. They talked about families, ex-boyfriends/girlfriends, even Noah's ex-wife, the fact that there was an eleven-year age difference between the two of them, what college was like for Cayleen—and she mentioned her grandmother was paying for nearly all college expenses—and cleaning houses for spending money. They discussed what Cayleen wanted to do after college and Noah's job as a truck driver.

"So, do you like him?" Cheyanne asks.

"I think so," Cayleen says with a smile.

"What are you going to do about Hunter?" Cheyanne asks as Cyrus comes in the kitchen to join them.

Cayleen is stunned into silence. She hasn't thought about it.

Cyrus says, "You know, he was taking shots while you went in the bathroom that night of your date."

"What?" Cayleen asks.

"Yeah, you were going to the bathroom—and he was out here taking shots with me. And did you see him at the wedding? He had two drinks every time I turned around!"

Cayleen stares at the floor. *Not good,* she thinks.

"Yeah, Cay. I don't think he's changed like you thought he did," Cheyanne says.

"What do I do?" Cayleen asks.

Cheyanne says, "You gotta break it off with him."

"Oh, no." Cayleen thinks of when she tried to break things off with Mike and how things just got complicated. "I don't want it to turn out like Mike."

"So just call him," Cheyanne says. "I know you think it's a respect thing to break it off face-to-face, but it's never as clean as things are in your head, Cay."

After an hour of looking at the phone, Cayleen finally pushes enough of the buttons to connect to Hunter.

"Hello?"

"Hi, Hunter." The enthusiasm is gone from Cayleen's voice. She hopes he notices. It would be easier if he knows what's coming.

"Hey, Cay. How was the cabin?"

"Good … it was good. Look … I don't think this is going to work."

"What do you mean?"

"I thought you said you weren't drinking like you used to … then, at the wedding, you were having more than one drink at a time. Even after I asked you not to drink."

"I know I messed up that night, Cay, but please give me another chance."

"Hunter, how many second chances do I need to give you? I don't like the person you turn into when you're drinking. I've told you that. You do things that you wouldn't do normally."

"I'll change!"

"Hunter, I'm not asking you to change. I don't think relationships are about people changing each other. They're about whether or not people fit together, and from what we've had together, it just doesn't seem like we fit."

"What can I do to have you with me?" Hunter asks. "Antabuse! I'll go on Antabuse. It's this thing they give you so you can't drink when you're on it."

"Hunter, I really don't want you going on some pill just to be with me. That doesn't seem right."

"Do you love me?" Hunter asks.

Cayleen doesn't know what to say. She loves him, but she can't be with him.

He says, "If you're breaking things off with me, just tell me you don't love me."

"Hunter, I can't tell you I don't love you," Cayleen says softly.

Cheyanne peeks in; she and Cyrus have been eavesdropping on the entire conversation.

Cheyanne whispers, "If you're going to break it off, don't have any loose ends. Cut it off completely. Don't leave him hanging."

Hunter says, "Well, then why can't we be together? Why can't you give me a chance to change?"

Cayleen feels his pain in her own chest. It's breaking her heart to have to speak the words to him. Tears silently roll down her own cheeks. She thinks about the times he has been too drunk to know he hurt her and whispers, "I can't."

"Can't we at least be friends? Then you could see that I'm serious. I'll stop."

"Friends between us would always be wanting something more. Hunter, you'd always be waiting for something more from me. I don't think that would work." Cayleen's voice grows softer with her words. She didn't know it would be this hard.

"Then you don't love me. If you don't love me, then tell me you don't love me!"

The tears sting her cheeks, and her voice shakes. "Fine! I don't love you." Cayleen closes her eyes and wails, crumpling to the floor.

The phone goes dead.

Don't befriend angry people or associate with hot-tempered people, or you will learn to be like them and endanger your soul.
—Proverbs 22:24–25

Cayleen does not get much time to mourn. The next day, Noah calls, making her giddy with the excitement of a new relationship. With houses needing to be cleaned, Cayleen doesn't physically sit still long. The cleaning helps, she thinks. The quiet helps clear her head, and having cleaned houses so many times in the past, the familiar tasks allow her to think things through.

She is cleaning a bathtub and thinking about the upcoming camping trip, which is her next chance to see Noah. Cheyanne and Cyrus are going, and Noah's family will be camping as well. Cayleen is thinking about how nervous she is to see Noah's family again in the light of now being his girlfriend. Suddenly, she begins coughing.

Oh, no! She thinks, seeing the bleach and ammonia she had just used to try to get the stains off the tub. Holding her breath, she hastily gets to her feet and runs out of the room, switching on the fan as she leaves. Once out of the room, she feels a little better. The constricting in her chest subsides a bit. She steps into the open garage for fresh air. Once she catches her breath, she thinks she should stay clear of the room for a while. As she left bathrooms for one of the last things to be cleaned on a house, she lit a cigarette, not wanting to be known as *milking*. She had heard the term used to refer to workers who stood around doing nothing.

Cyrus walks up. "Hey, Cayleen. How's it going?" Cyrus is the purchaser for Jameson Construction and walks the houses to check the amounts of materials. Cayleen doesn't really know what he does on the jobsites, but Cayleen is up for conversation.

"Good. I think I just made the bathroom a little toxic though."

"What'd you do?" Cyrus asks with a smile.

"I mixed bleach and ammonia. I didn't want to scrape the stuff of the side of the tub, and when the ammonia didn't work, I tried the bleach."

Cyrus starts laughing.

Cayleen says, "When I started coughing, I realized what I'd done and booked it out of there."

Cyrus gets his laughter under control. "Do you need someone to go in there and air it out for you?"

"Oh, I think I'll be okay, I turned on the fan on my way out of there. I figured I'd give it a few minutes to work before I went back in."

"Okay. Well, let me or Rod know if you need something." Rod is the superintendent on this house and, technically, Cayleen's supervisor.

"Okay, thanks."

"See ya later!"

Cyrus and Cheyanne's house is not yet finished, and they are still living with Jessica.

"Bye." Cayleen puts her finished cigarette in an empty can on the floor and heads back inside.

> We know that we are children of God and that the
> world around us is under the control of the evil one.
> —1 John 5:19

Several days later, Cayleen finishes her dinner: a Wendy's burger. Jessica doesn't cook much, and neither does Cheyanne. Cayleen likes to cook, but they often don't keep much in the house. Suddenly, knots start forming in her lower abdomen. Cayleen doubles over in the living room chair.

Cheyanne looks over from the television. "Are you okay?"

"Uh, yeah. I think I must have PMS cramps or something. Or maybe it was the burger. I think I'm going to go lay down." Bent over at the waist, Cayleen makes her way to her bedroom and plops on the bed. The pain is excruciating.

Cheyanne comes in the room and kneels next to the bed. "Can I get you anything? Midol? Tums?"

Cayleen forces a slight smile. "No, thanks. I'll be fine, I'm sure." Cayleen doesn't know what is wrong and doesn't want to take the wrong thing. She can imagine taking Midol when her stomach is upset from the burger and having it hurt that much more.

As a child, Cayleen often had stomach pains. When she was seven, the doctors diagnosed her with a milk allergy that she grew out of by thirteen. No matter the diagnosis, her stomach was just not happy. Cheyanne had been cursed with dramatic PMS cramps, but Cayleen hadn't had much of a problem. The family was unaware of any spiritual reasons for chronic sickness or stomach pains and never thought to look in that direction.

Cheyanne puts her head next to Cayleen's.

Cayleen strains a smile. "I am supposed to start my period sometime, and with taking the morning-after pill, my period has been a little weird." Cayleen hadn't thought much about her period since taking the morning-after pill. She had a period just after taking it, but she didn't track how long ago that was. *Just a few weeks,* she thinks.

Cheyanne says, "Maybe you're stressed about starting back at school?"

"I can't think of what I'd be stressed about there. I like it. Hey, you should go back and watch TV. I'll be fine. I'll read a magazine or a book or something." Cayleen grabs a book from the top of her nightstand. As usual, there's a pile of books for her to finish when she has time.

"Okay, I just feel bad!" Cheyanne hesitates as she walks out the door. "Holler if you need anything."

"Okay."

> Dear friend, don't let this bad example influence you.
> Follow only what is good. Remember that those who
> do good prove they are God's children, and those
> who do evil prove that they do not know God.
> —3 John 1:11

Two days later, Cayleen is still having lower abdominal pain. Her period has started. *My cramps always come before my period— not during my period. Maybe I'm getting an ulcer. Maybe I'm worried about seeing Trina and what mood she'll be in.*

Cayleen gets up to go to the bathroom. She's been trying to drink fluids since she doesn't feel like eating. Luckily, she cleaned some houses in advance and she hasn't had to work for a few days. Cheyanne, Cyrus, and Cayleen are scheduled to go camping with Noah this weekend and are set to leave that night.

Sitting on the toilet, Cayleen's gaze naturally shifts down toward her knees. Her heart skips a beat. In her underwear, there are two quarter-sized things that look like they have horses' heads in them. Cayleen starts sweating. Her thoughts jump everywhere. *What's wrong with me? Is that a disease? What do I have in me that would make that happen?*

Then it dawns on her. Cayleen remembers reading somewhere that the morning-after pill can prevent pregnancy from occurring, but it cannot stop a pregnancy. Horrified, she calls Cheyanne. *She'll know,* Cayleen thinks as the phone rings. *She'll know what to do.*

Fortunately for Cayleen, Cheyanne is already on her way home from work. Once home, Cheyanne barges in the bathroom where Cayleen is still frozen. Cheyanne confirms Cayleen's worst nightmare: twins.

"He is the stone that makes people stumble, the rock that makes
them fall." They stumble because they do not obey God's
word, and so they meet the fate that was planned for them.
—1 Peter 2:8

The plan for camping had been for Noah to drive to Spring
Forks and pick up Cayleen and drive in tandem with Cyrus and
Cheyanne. Because of the events of the day, Cayleen wants to ride
with her sister, and she insists on still going camping.

"I'm fine," Cayleen says. "I just don't want to talk to Noah quite
yet." The drive is three hours from Spring Forks, and Cayleen can't
imagine not talking about what happened. Cheyanne and Cyrus
are complacent, and when Noah arrives, Cyrus tells Noah the new
plans to make it sound like Cheyanne wants it more than Cayleen.

"Cheyanne won't get to see her sister for a while once she gets
to college, and with you in the picture, she'll probably be spending
her time with you rather than Cheyanne. They just want to have a
little girl time before she goes."

Noah quickly agrees.

Once on the road, Cheyanne says, "What are you thinking?
What are you feeling?"

"I don't know exactly," Cayleen says. She feels numb more than
anything else. "I want those kids, you know?" It is difficult to
swallow, and she is on the verge of tears. "Not with Mike, but I
know now that I want kids. It's different for you, Cheyanne. You've
always known you want kids. But me, I didn't think I wanted kids.
I've never been sure."

"Did you want kids when you were with Hunter?" Cheyanne asks.

"I don't know. I guess I always thought we would have kids one
day. I had dreamed of marrying him and moving to Montana—you
know that."

Cheyanne smiles. "Yeah, and you being Cayleen Blake and
living on a farm in the country." Cayleen had dreamed of taking
Hunter's last name since she was seventeen.

"Yeah, but that didn't work out." Cayleen looks out at the scenery, and her thoughts grow sad. "Besides, cows take a lot of work."

"Noah's a good guy, Cay," Cheyanne says. "He's really close with his family."

"Yeah, that's a good thing." The girls grow silent, and Cayleen turns to the thoughts in her head. She really does want kids, she realizes, shocked. Her heart feels empty now that she knows she had the chance and threw it away. *But not with Mike,* she thinks. *Maybe with Noah?* Noah is close with his family, which Cayleen likes. He's got a steady job and has always been nice to her, Cayleen continues on that track of thought. *He's handsome,* she thinks. *Not the tingles-down-your-spine kind of handsome that Hunter is, but he's definitely a good-looking guy.*

"How do you know that you've met the one?" Cayleen asks.

Cheyanne thinks for a moment. "I don't know. You just know. Why?"

"Maybe Noah's the one," Cayleen says, looking out the window.

"Cay, you haven't even slept with him yet."

"I know. We've talked about that too, and we're waiting until we love each other. That's what I wanted, and he said okay. He's monogamous. His first wife cheated on him, and he said he could never do that to anyone. I've never cheated on anyone either, so I could show him how someone could be monogamous back. He's not an alcoholic, and he believes in God." *With those things combined, couldn't things work out between them?*

"That's a great thought, Cay." Cheyanne smiles. "But don't you think it's a little premature?"

Premature or not, Cayleen thinks, *why not? Marriage is a decision, right? A promise? So why not chose it?*

The godly give good advice to their friends;
the wicked lead them astray.
—Proverbs 12:26

CHAPTER 9

Cayleen lies in the middle of the living room floor, arms spread wide, eyes gazing at the ceiling, and thinks about Noah's words: "You wasted six years of my life!" Cayleen sighs. She thinks of the six years she and Noah were together. Noah had moved to be with Cayleen about a year after they began dating. Cayleen had graduated college in an unheard of four years, and they had moved back to Spring Forks. They both started working for Cayleen's dad's home-building company. Noah was unhappy in his role at the family business, and Cayleen supported a career move for him to do what he'd always dreamed. During that time, things were weighing on Cayleen's mind and making her doubt whether she and Noah could do life together. Noah is more than ten years older than Cayleen, and their interests did not mesh. At the age of twenty-five, Cayleen returned from a weekend of business training, realizing their life paths were not the same. Those three days were the longest she had been without Noah in five years. She spent an entire day meditating on her situation, journaling and reading old diary entries, and listening to the voice inside her. When she pulled into the driveway, she told him she didn't want to be with him anymore.

Now Cayleen wants quiet. She has promised herself three months of quiet. No TV, no music. It is a time of reflection, to center herself and listen for that inside voice she had been suffocating for so many years. She considers the last six years an incredible learning experience and wants to make sure all the lessons sink in. She paints, writes in her journal, writes poetry, and exercises, but she does not allow herself to become as distracted as she had been. Cayleen still attends church every Sunday, but she doesn't lean back into God and use her Bible to stir her faith and center herself.

Looking back on her relationship with Noah, Cayleen sees how many times God tried to steer her path. Cayleen's parents had opposed the relationship from the start. Cayleen tried to break up with Noah, but she allowed him to move to be with her to fix their relationship. Within a week of getting engaged, she nearly cut off her ring finger. On the day of their engagement, she had lost her voice entirely—without being sick. Years later, Cayleen would realize that—even though they went to church and were active in their church community—the damage had been done. Her emotional tie to Noah had been made the first time they slept together.

For you ignore God's law and substitute your own tradition.
—Mark 7:8

Cayleen shakes her head, sits up in the middle of the floor, and allows the change in position to change her train of thought. She sees the empty room and thinks about the division of assets in their separation. It was all surprisingly civil—all but the two days Noah came to get his things. On the first occasion, he left something in every room where it couldn't be missed: a shirt on the foot of the bed in the spare room, a belt in the middle of the floor in the office, a jacket hanging in the empty closet. Everything was purposely positioned where Cayleen was sure to find it. Noah got the small rental home they had purchased, and Cayleen got the larger home. Cayleen made more money and was in a better position to afford the home with larger payments. Nearly all the furniture was Noah's. When he came by to pick up his furniture, he had uttered those words that brought such remorse from Cayleen. She doesn't want to be accused of wasting someone's life again.

Cayleen feels a fuzzy stroke against her leg and looks up at Bella. Cayleen scoops up the small cat, holds her against her chest, and strokes her head. "Hey, Miss Pretty."

Cayleen allows her thoughts to drift to what Noah had gotten out of their relationship. She had bought him a new Harley-Davidson, which he kept. And two trucks they purchased. Then there was the rental house. Oh, the rental house. Cayleen and Noah had bought it from Jessica. Jessica bought it for Cheyanne to live in when Cheyanne was going to college, and then Jessica kept it as a rental. When Noah and Cayleen sold their first home, they rented the small home near the college from Jessica for a few months while Cayleen's house was being built. Once they moved out, Jessica complained about how difficult it was being a landlord and finding good tenants. Cayleen and Noah offered to buy the house. Jessica agreed, stating she would accept $75,000 for it and not one penny less. No closing costs, no realtor fees—Jessica wouldn't pay one cent. Jessica told stories of how she and Luke had been the bank for other rent-to-own options early in their marriage, and Jessica wasn't willing to do it again—not even her own daughter. Cayleen had cashed out some financial accounts she had stashed away to cover the down payment of $15,000, a larger down payment since they were not living in the home at the time of purchase, and the house was theirs. Now it's Noah's. And Noah's retirement account … since they worked for Luke's company the retirement advisor said, if Luke is contributing to his retirement account and Cayleen is heir to the company, she cannot contribute. *No worries. We'll contribute the maximum to Noah's account! Well, Noah, you sure got a lot for your waste of six years!*

Cayleen's cell phone rings, and Cheyanne says, "Sista, how goes it?"

Cayleen hadn't heard from Cheyanne in six weeks—since she told her she and Noah were separating. Cheyanne and Cyrus had moved to Saint Croix several years earlier. They had sold everything, taken their dogs, and moved! Cayleen thought it was crazy in a wonderful kind of way. She had made it out to see them once and had realized firsthand that Cheyanne had her hands full with Cyrus's alcohol abuse and drug use.

"Cay-K." Relief overflows in Cheyanne's voice. "Cay, I've made it off the island. The dogs and I had to leave everything. I rented a car in Miami, and we're driving to Spring Forks." Cheyanne sounds scared, but steady.

"Do you want to tell me what happened?" Cayleen knows Cyrus and Cheyanne's relationship is rocky, but she didn't realize she was leaving him.

"Cyrus came at me in my sleep with a hammer."

The silence seems excruciatingly long to Cayleen.

Cheyanne's voice shakes slightly. "He put it through the wall above my head. The noise woke me, and pieces of drywall hit my forehead. He was standing over me and so drunk and drugged up. Then he said, 'Aren't you glad I didn't hit you? I thought about it. And I really wanted to, but didn't.' Cay, I knew I had to leave or he'd kill me. I waited until morning, found as much cash as I could find in our apartment, packed a backpack and the dogs, and went to the airport."

"Are you okay?" Cayleen wants so badly to be physically next to her sister, holding and comforting her.

There is a strained laugh on the other end. "Yeah, as good as I can be! I have barely any clothes. I had to go to the Walmart by the airport to buy kennels and dog food. I don't know what is going to happen. I don't know if Cyrus is coming after me—or if he even knows I'm gone yet—but I'm alive."

"Come home, Chey. You can just stay here. Then you don't have to deal with Mom's questions."

"Thanks, Cay-K. I hadn't gotten that far yet." A small laugh at the other end. "Can you call Mom for me?"

"Yes, I'll call her. You drive safe. Check in with one of us along the way. Love you."

"Love you too."

Turn away from evil and do good. Search
for peace, and work to maintain it.
—1 Peter 3:11

"Are you ready to go?!" Cheyanne pops her head into Cayleen's office. Cheyanne unsuccessfully looked for a job outside of the family company, but when the receptionist went on maternity leave, she was able to fill the vacancy.

"Just … one … more … minute …" Cayleen finishes typing and shuts down her computer, looking for unfinished business on her desk. Finding none, she looks up at Cheyanne. "Denver, here we come!"

It is the Wednesday before Thanksgiving. Neither girl wants to spend Thanksgiving with family—fearing the questions about their failed relationships and judgmental glances made in polite conversation over a prim and proper place setting. Instead, Cayleen booked them a room at a downtown hotel, and they planned to get away for a long weekend.

"So, are you still on your dry spell?" There was no beating around the bush with Cheyanne.

"Chey!" They'd had this talk several times in the few weeks Cheyanne had been back. Cayleen wants to be in a place where she knows, in her heart, whether a relationship is right or wrong and wants to make the choice from there—and not some physical attraction or emotion. Cayleen also knows Cheyanne doesn't respect this about her or feel the same way.

"If something happens this weekend, it happens. I'm not sure I want to date anyone yet, but it would be nice to know boys still find me attractive." Cayleen was feeling the blow to her self-confidence without having someone in her dating life. Her body had not changed significantly, leaving no reason for a lack of confidence. Regardless, it was there. Cayleen, unknowing it was the thoughts of the enemy in her head, recently added kickboxing to her morning workout routine to fight back at the weaknesses she felt on the inside.

"So, like a what-happens-in-Vegas-stays-in-Vegas-type of weekend?" Cheyanne's excitement shows as she accelerates from five to fifteen over the speed limit.

"I've never been to Vegas, but I guess so!" Cayleen looks out the window, glad Cheyanne likes driving. "What about you? You're always giving me such a hard time about not dating. What happened with you and … the guy you met at that book thing …"

"Thad," Cheyanne says. "Yeah, Thad and I didn't work out."

"Well, that was quick. What happened?"

"I kinda wigged out on him." Cheyanne steals a side glance and smile at Cayleen. "We were really close to having sex one night, and I started balling."

"Why is that wigging out on him?"

"I don't think you understand. I was balling, like in a ball, tears streaming down my face, complete mess. Balling." Cheyanne looks through the window at the road. "And you know it wasn't about him. It was about me not wanting to be there. So, I said I'm sorry—and then I left."

"Have you talked to him since?"

"No. I really don't see a need to. We were only dating a few weeks, and he's so much older than me. I don't really feel it. Besides, do you know Clay Thomas from work?"

"Is Clay the one who is our trim contractor? I think I know him."

"Yeah, that's the one. Did you know we graduated from high school together? We didn't really hang out together then. He asked me out this weekend. Of course, I told him no since we're going to Denver, but he's taking me out next week."

"That's exciting, Chey!" Cayleen says.

Cheyanne was always jumping from relationship to relationship. She had filed for divorce, which was a bit complicated since Cyrus was still in the Virgin Islands, but it still would take several months.

Cayleen sighs and thinks, *I have no room to judge. I'm the weird one for not dating anyone. The rest of the world waits until they cheat or have someone waiting in the wings before they leave. Not me. On my own. Maybe my whole life, but that's a choice I had to make to survive. Had I stayed in that relationship with Noah ... his needs, wants, and desires would have ruled my life. I cannot allow that to happen again. And that is the real reason I'm not dating yet. I don't trust myself not to make the same mistakes again.*

Cayleen doesn't realize the thoughts she is listening to are enemy thoughts. There is no reason for her to need to do anything. There is someone more powerful and wiser looking out for her own future: God. Cayleen needs to tuck into him and trust him rather than herself, allowing him to keep her from making mistakes rather than taking it on herself. Cayleen still doesn't know to think this way ... yet.

"Do you want me to tell you about the places I found?" Cayleen is sick of her own thoughts. Just a few more hours of small talk, and they'll be in the city. "There's a few restaurants and three nightclubs we have to hit!"

Before long, the girls pull into the hotel's valet area. They check in and check out the room.

"Wow. This is great!" Cayleen looks down at the walking mall of Sixteenth Street.

"Yeah." Cheyanne looks over toward the window then jumps on the bed. "Wanna go to dinner? It's only six. We could wait and get ready and go about eight or nine and then go out to the clubs you wanted to go to after."

"I'm not sure how long I'm going to make it tonight. You know me—I worked out this morning at five. Can we get ready and have dinner about seven?"

The crisp November air nips at the girls' cheeks as they briskly walk toward their first destination: the Cheesecake Factory. They settle in at the bar, after denying the kind hostess' offer to put them on the sixty-minute waiting list.

"Their portions are enormous, but this menu is huge! I think its twenty pages," Cayleen exclaims.

Cheyanne says, "I don't remember it being this big."

"Hey, Chey sister?" Cayleen says with a silly smile.

"Yes, Cay sister?" Cheyanne matches the silly smile.

"Thank you for coming with me this weekend."

"Thanks for having me! And, technically, you came with me since I drove." Cheyanne winks.

Cayleen raises one eyebrow and smiles. "Uh, you drove my car."

They both go back to the menus.

Several hours and two stops later, the girls enter the dance club without having to pay the cover. The four guys from the Irish brew pub who have befriended them are not as lucky. Cayleen smiles and looks around at the vast club.

"I've never been anywhere like it!" Cayleen says.

"I can tell!" Cheyanne laughs. "You're doing good, little sister. You're out much later than we thought we would be."

"What happened to our friends?" Cayleen slurs slightly.

Cheyanne laughs. "Don't worry. Those kinds of friends come and go." One of the three jobs Cheyanne had on the island was as a bartender. As such, she was much more familiar with the bar scene than Cayleen. "Oh, I take it we're dancing?"

Cayleen feels the music. It moves her shoulders, body, and hips. She's dancing at the side of the crowded dance floor. Cheyanne joins. Soon enough, they move toward the center of the dance floor. Songs change, time passes, and both girls are having too much fun to notice.

"Thirsty?" Cayleen asks.

"Yeah." Cheyanne grabs Cayleen's hand, and they maneuver to the bar.

"Wanna get some fresh air?" Cheyanne yells above the music, just inches from Cayleen's ear.

Cayleen nods, and they grab hands, heading for the door. After sweating, the cold air is refreshing.

As they stand near the door, the bouncer announces, "Last call."

The girls share a dumbfounded look and grab their phones. Cheyanne pulls hers out first. "One forty-five."

"Hey, there you are," a man says playfully. "We've been looking all over for you."

Cayleen thinks, *It's the guy from the Irish Pub. They're still here?* "Oh, hey," she stammers. She is embarrassed for claiming them as friends at the Irish pub and now realizing he's probably ten or fifteen years older than she is. *This trip is about figuring out if I still got it, right?* "We were just going to get our jackets from the coat check downstairs and then get something to eat. Did you want to go with us? I'm sorry." Cayleen flashes her bashful smile. "I forgot your name."

"Kirk."

"Did you and your friends want to get a bite to eat with us, Kirk?"

"Yeah, sure."

"We'll run down and get our coats then meet you back here." Cayleen and Cheyanne bump their way back into the crowded club.

"Do you really like that guy?" Cheyanne asks. "Or are we going to try to ditch him out the back door?"

"Eh, I don't know. He seems nice enough. But if he likes me, that means I still got it, right?"

"What does it tell you? He tracked you down! So, yes, sister, I'd say you still got it." Cheyanne smiles. "I heard someone talking about a pizza joint being open. Let's go find it."

Now, what I meant was that you should not associate with people
who call themselves brothers or sisters in the Christian faith
but live in sexual sin, are greedy, worship false gods, use abusive
language, get drunk, or are dishonest. Don't eat with such people.
—1 Corinthians 5:11

On Saturday, the girls slowly load themselves and their bags in the car.

"Oh, boy. I'm not looking forward to the next few hours," Cayleen mutters, not opening her mouth too much for fear of it making her stomach feel even worse.

"You had a good weekend, I'd say!" Cheyanne exclaims with a sideways glance and a smile. "Sleep if you want. It'll make you feel better."

Cayleen closes her eyes and thinks about the weekend, drifting in and out of sleep. Dining, dancing, and drinking—maybe too much drinking. Not only had she not allowed herself to date, she hadn't allowed herself to have any alcohol since she and Noah separated. Oh, and the boys? Cayleen cringes at the thought. Somehow, now that it is over and she is going home back to real life, she doesn't feel any better about herself. The voice, or feeling the inside her chest seems to gently say, *You got what you asked for—now was it what you really wanted?*

Cayleen's thoughts immediately change to church. "When you talked to Mom, did you tell her we'd meet her and Grandma at church tomorrow? Are you going to church tomorrow?" Sunday church was a tradition. Cayleen is comforted by routine. Every Sunday when Cayleen is in town, she goes to church with her mom and grandma. They went to church with Jessica growing up. Now it just seems like part of the week to go to the Episcopal church four generations of women in their family have attended. Even in college, Cayleen would go most Sundays.

Cayleen doesn't feel connected to the church itself, though she and Noah had volunteered in the youth ministry, and she had gone to some Bible studies at her church in college. She goes because it's tradition—a way of showing respect for her mom and grandma. Cheyanne doesn't feel the need to always attend church, but it generally comes with a free lunch at a restaurant—and Cheyanne is always up for the free meal. Since Cheyanne sometimes only goes to lunch, Cayleen wants to clarify her sister's plans.

"Yeah. I'll pick you up," Cheyanne answers. After living with Cayleen for several months, Cheyanne has moved into their grandma's home. Their grandma had moved into an assisted living home. Their grandma is in good condition, though her eyesight is bad. She can still drive, but she has gotten in a few fender-benders lately. When she came into some money that allowed her to afford going to an assisted living facility, she moved in.

Cheyanne is still driving Cayleen's personal car, which Cayleen had offered when Cheyanne moved back since Cayleen has a work car. Weekends are difficult, but Cayleen has friends to pick her up. Luke told her he doesn't mind if she drives the work car on the weekend since it's free advertising for the company. Cayleen is still uncomfortable using the work car for personal use. Cheyanne doesn't understand it but accommodates her occasionally by picking up her sister.

"Grandma asked about me needing a car last week," Cayleen says.

"Oh, yeah?"

"Yeah, after I drove the work car to church. She was wondering if I needed a new car and was giving you this one."

"We agreed I'm borrowing it until I can buy my own car." Cheyanne says.

"I know, dear sister, but when will that be?" Cayleen says gently. "Right now, you're filling in for the receptionist, but she comes back after the New Year. What are you going to do after that? You haven't given me an answer on my offer to be my assistant." Cayleen had not told Cheyanne that Luke had already told Cayleen he didn't have a place for Cheyanne after the receptionist came back. Cayleen had asked Luke if Cheyanne could be her assistant. Luke, just as much a realist as Cayleen, had pointed out the difficulties Cayleen would face being boss of her older sister. In the end, he agreed that her department could use an administrative position. If Cayleen chose to fill that with Cheyanne, Luke would support it.

"I know. I just feel like working for Dad's company is giving up. Cyrus had such bad things to say about Dad as a boss."

"I worked with Cyrus at Jamison Homes for over a year before you moved to the islands, and I know why Cyrus said bad things about Dad as a boss. Cyrus didn't do any work!"

Cheyanne thinks for a moment. "I guess I can see that. After we moved to the islands, he bounced from job to job. He couldn't even hold down a job as a busboy at the steakhouse. He hadn't worked for six months before I left, and I was working two and sometimes three jobs." Cheyanne sighs. "It just seems like I'm giving up or not trying hard enough to find a job if I go to work for Dad."

"How are you giving up? It's potential you have the opportunity to be a part of. I've been there for nearly four years and have moved up based on merit. Dad may treat us a little more harshly than the other employees, but that's because he doesn't want anyone thinking we get favors for being family. It's hard, but I went from being a land planner to running the entire land development department. If you were to accept my offer and be my assistant, I'd like you to look into whether or not you'd like to be a land planner and move from there." Cayleen took a breath. "You could use your experience you gain under me to take with you—either at Jamison or another land-planning agency or even do it on your own. It's not giving up, Chey. It's taking advantage of the opportunities that are presented to you."

Cheyanne smiles and takes her eyes off the road for an instant to make eye contact with Cayleen. "You sound a lot like Dad, you know. I'll think about it. That's the best I can do for you right now. I'll think about it."

"Okay, well thinking about it isn't going to buy you a new car." Cayleen realizes talking is making her hangover better. "And I can't afford to buy my own car right now. I just had to refurnish my house. I'm not asking for this car back, but if Grandma offers to help me buy a car, I'm going to take her up on it."

"I've got it! Grandma should buy *me* the car!" Cheyanne laughs. "I'll give this one back to you, and Grandma can just by me a new one."

"I'll be sure to mention that, Chey." Cayleen shakes her head and smiles.

A peaceful heart leads to a healthy body;
jealousy is like cancer in the bones.
—Proverbs 14:30

CHAPTER 10

Cayleen opens the door to Jessica's home and yells, "Happy birthday, Cheyanne!"

They find each other in the kitchen and embrace.

"Long time, no see, boss," Cheyanne jokes. Cheyanne had left the office a few hours earlier in light of her birthday. Cheyanne had taken up her sister on the job offer and is working as Cayleen's assistant.

"How was the celebration Clay created for you?" Cayleen asks playfully.

"Good! Good." Cheyanne smiles. "Clay is out back. Do you want a drink? I was hoping we could sit outside. It's still a little cold. Do you mind?"

"It isn't that cold for March, and I have my jacket. Yes, let's sit outside for a minute! Grandma should probably stay inside."

Grandma is happily eating the appetizers Jessica had put out. They look dreadfully unappealing to Cayleen. Grandma had moved back into her house when she realized the money she thought would be a monthly income for life was going to stop after one year. Cheyanne had moved in with Clay rather than living with Grandma or Cayleen.

"Mom, we'll be outside. Let us know if you need us to do anything," Cayleen says as she opens the back door.

From down the hallway, Jessica says, "We're all set. Lasagna should be ready in half an hour."

The girls walk outside onto the wooden deck that had been a part of the home since they were young. Clay is sitting in one of the folding outdoor chairs that are arranged across the deck. Cheyanne sits in a chair next to Clay, lacing the fingers of one hand with his. Clay's other hand cups his beer.

Cayleen sits near them and asks, "Why don't you have a drink, Chey?"

Clay and Cheyanne share a small smile and glance. "Cay, there's something we want to tell you! We're pregnant!"

Cayleen's face freezes in utter shock. Luckily, her frozen face masks the horror in her mind, which is nothing close to the excitement Cheyanne has in her face and voice. *They've been dating for less than three months! They're not married or engaged! When we were in Hawaii with Dad over New Year's, Cheyanne didn't say anything about a long-term relationship with Clay. Cheyanne didn't flirt heavily with boys, but she didn't say anything to me about Clay. Chey drives my old car, they live in an apartment, and smoke marijuana day and night. She works for me for slightly over minimum wage—how will they raise a baby?* Forcing a smile across her face, Cayleen says, "Congratulations! I'm sorry to be caught off guard, but is that what you were trying for … a baby?"

Cheyanne says, "Yes! Do you remember when I was late last month? Well, when we thought we were pregnant, we realized how badly we wanted a baby. So, we got a fertility monitor and got pregnant! We're about five weeks now."

"Cool." Cayleen gulps down half her drink.

"Tell her the other part." Clay says. Judging from his face, his excitement matches Cheyanne's. His gaze is on Cheyanne, not making eye contact with Cayleen.

"About the house?" Cheyanne's eyes widen, and their foreheads nearly touch.

Clay nods. "You need to."

"I bought the house from Noah," Cheyanne says.

Cayleen gulps the rest of her drink.

"Noah wanted to move back home, and it was a good deal. Clay can fix up the inside to be just what we need for us and the baby." Cheyanne smiles at Clay.

Cayleen's shoulders slump. "Can I ask how much you paid for it?"

"Noah sold it to us for eighty thousand."

Cayleen does the math in her head. *Noah walks away with another twenty thousand—fifteen of which came from my accounts.* She takes a deep breath, allowing the air to fill her lungs, and exhales audibly. The voice inside her presses on her heart. *Let it go. What's done is done. Easier said than done!* Cayleen fumes silently.

Jessica peeks her head out the door and yells, "Lasagna's ready. Come and get it!"

Cheyanne looks at Clay and then back to Cayleen. "We haven't told Mom or Grandma yet. They're gonna flip. Can you keep it quiet for now?"

Yes, they are gonna flip! And I sure don't want to be messenger, Cayleen thinks. "I won't tell them," she says. All three walk inside.

But I wasn't talking about unbelievers who indulge in sexual
sin, or are greedy, or cheat people, or worship idols. You
would have to leave this world to avoid people like that.
—1 Corinthians 5:10

Cayleen pushes opens the garage door and is greeted by the barks and then skidding paws of two large dogs—one is a fifty-pound black mutt, and the other is a hundred-pound boxer. They bound down her hallway, slide on the tile floor, and knock themselves against the wall and the door. "I'm home," Cayleen mutters under her breath. "Hi, doggies." Cayleen heads upstairs to put her things in her bedroom.

"We're in here," Cheyanne calls from the dining room.

When Cayleen comes back downstairs, Cheyanne and Clay are looking on Cheyanne's computer. Cheyanne is sitting at one of the tall black chairs from Cayleen's new black dining room set, which she specifically ordered to be counter height. Cayleen has always been tall and loves the feeling of sitting in a chair that is so tall her feet can't touch the ground.

Clay is looking at the computer over Cheyanne's shoulder—barbeque tool in one hand and the other on Cheyanne's belly.

Cheyanne and Clay have moved back in with Cayleen. Jessica was not happy about the new baby, but the idea is growing on her. Her initial reaction had more nasty than nice. Cheyanne and Clay had gutted the small house and were not able to finish before Clay's apartment lease was up. Cayleen had offered for them to stay with her for minimal rent so they could spend their money fixing the house. After they moved in, she realized the amount she was charging them didn't even cover the additional utilities they incurred. The large dogs forced Bella to stay in her room all day—only to be let out at night. *Family helps each other out,* Cayleen keeps telling herself.

"What are you looking at?" Cayleen asks.

"We're just looking at the baby website to see about what's going on with the baby." Cheyanne is glowing when she looks at Cayleen. "Do you want to see?"

Cayleen forces a smile and says, "Sure." At work, Cheyanne makes paper babies based on the dimensions of the baby listed on a website. Sometimes Cayleen walks into Cheyanne's office to find the earphones on Cheyanne's belly so the baby hears music. Cayleen is not at the point of wanting to know everything about the baby Cheyanne is carrying, but she tries to be supportive and not ruin Cheyanne's excitement.

Cayleen looks over Cheyanne's shoulder while Clay walks out to the grill. "Isn't it so exciting?" Cheyanne's excitement and glow fill the room.

Cayleen smiles. "I'm so glad you're so excited. How's the house coming?"

"We're having trim delivered tomorrow and painting it if you want to come help." Cheyanne looks up with a smile.

You work for me, live in my house, and want me to help you fix your own house? Cayleen holds back her thoughts. "I have some studying I need to do. Maybe I can bring by pizzas."

Cayleen had started taking online courses for her master's degree before her breakup with Noah. Now that her mind is better able to focus, she has taken it up again. Cayleen's undergraduate degree had nothing to do with what she is doing for work. With the promotions Luke has allowed her to earn, she is managing millions of dollars of budgets, crews, and middle managers with little formal training. Taking the online courses allows her to be more confident in the job she is performing.

"We'd appreciate dinner. Thank you!" Cheyanne exclaims. "Clay's cooking steaks, and we have some rice for dinner tonight if you want some."

"Thank you. I'll think about it."

"Hey, you never told me about Hunter this weekend? How did that go?"

"Well, he called me a week—no, wait it was longer ago—I don't remember, but out of the blue. He said he had talked to Mom, and she had given him my number."

"Right, you told me that."

"We had coffee the weekend before last. It was a Sunday afternoon at Starbucks. I usually do lunches with a first date, but since Hunter and I know each other … and I didn't want to do cocktails with his drinking history."

"Yeah, you told me about coffee. He spent the past five years in the marines after serving his time in Denver for that outrageous bar fight that got him hospitalized just after you broke up? Does he still blame you for that?"

"I'm not sure how he could since that was long after we broke up. He had been working in Denver on skyscrapers and all sorts of things. We didn't talk about that. We talked about what we've been doing for the past few years. As a sergeant, it was very difficult for him to counsel his guys—like nineteen-year-olds who are getting divorced. The only relationship he had to base it on was ours."

"Oh, heavy. Go on."

"I think I told you everything else about coffee. Just light conversation. Hunter wanted to see me again and asked if he could call. I said yes."

"And?"

"He wants to get together on Friday night. I agreed to ice cream. I'm not willing to commit to dinner."

"Seriously, Cay? Dinner is a commitment?" Cheyanne laughs. "Go on."

"Well, yeah. Dinner is a commitment. Dinner means we're dating. Dinner leads a guy on. Dinner means we may hang out after, which may lead to another hangout spot and driving together and a lot of things I'm not ready for with Hunter right now!"

Cheyanne laughs even more. "Okay! Now, go on ... you're at ice cream."

"We get to ice cream, and Hunter says he hasn't eaten dinner. He asks if we can go to the burrito place next door first."

Cheyanne giggles. "He got you to dinner anyway!"

"No! I didn't eat at the burrito place! You know how big the ice creams are." Cayleen smiles. "I don't think Hunter had ever gotten one because, after his burrito, he couldn't finish his ice cream."

Both girls laugh.

"So ... how was it?" Cheyanne asks.

"Nice." Cayleen smiles. "It was nice. Friendly conversation. Hunter asked if I wanted to go anywhere after, and I told him no. He asked to see me again the next day, which was last Saturday, and I told him we could go to lunch or something."

"Wasn't last Saturday your massage appointment from your birthday that you were so excited about?"

"You do listen!" Cayleen says. "You're right. I had my massage. I told him that Friday night and said I'd call him when I was done."

"So ... I didn't know you met him on Saturday too. I miss working on that house so much! Do tell!"

"I never ended up meeting him." Cayleen's face darkens as she looks down at the table.

Clay walks in the house, announces that the steaks are almost ready, and walks back outside.

Cheyanne says, "Why didn't you meet Hunter for lunch?"

"My appointment was for an eighty-minute massage. I didn't know when I would get done, so on Friday, we'd left it that I would call Hunter when I was finished so we could grab a bite to eat." Cayleen takes a small sip of her fresh drink. "I left my phone in my car. I didn't really mean to leave my phone in the car, but it's not like I needed it in the spa anyway. Hunter texted four times, called five times, and left two voice mails." Cayleen looks up at Cheyanne. "I was only in the spa for two hours at most. When I called him back, he was frantic, practically yelling at me for not calling him sooner. I explained that I had been at the spa, left my phone in the car, and then I wonder why I am explaining myself to Hunter. It felt just like it did in high school. I told him I'd call him later and hung up."

"Have you called him back yet?"

"No." Cayleen has no intention of ever calling Hunter back.

"Eh, well, win some, lose some. How about that handsome boy who has been stopping by the office?"

Clay walks in, and the aroma of freshly charred steaks fills the room. Clay shoos the dogs out the back door. "Dinner!"

"What handsome boy at the office?" Cayleen thinks of the men at their office. "Uriah?"

Cheyanne bursts into laughter. "Not Uriah, silly." They both consider Uriah as more of a brother than a dating prospect. "Though Uriah would be a good candidate. He's handsome and funny and adventurous." Cheyanne has clearly not thought about this prospect before.

"And a fellow employee!" Cayleen giggles. "Uriah is great, but what if things didn't work out between us. How awkward would that be?"

"Good point." Cheyanne moves on. "The handsome boy I was

referring to was that Cline boy … the tall one with dark hair. all, dark, and handsome—isn't that what you're looking for?" Cheyanne raises her eyebrows. "Don't you serve on a committee or something with him? Go to those early-morning meetings?"

"I'm eating," Clay announces. He grabs a plate and starts to dish up.

Cayleen looks at her drink and takes a sip, knowing just who Cheyanne is talking about. "Gavin Cline."

"Yeah! Gavin! What about him?"

"He is really handsome and smart, and he is in his family's business. I'm not sure if he likes me."

"You never know unless you put yourself out there," Clay says. "Are you guys gonna eat?"

> Walk with the wise and become wise; associate
> with fools and get in trouble.
> —Proverbs 13:20

CHAPTER 11

Put myself out there, put myself out there, put myself out there, Cayleen thinks. She and Gavin are meeting on a jobsite. He pulls up behind her before she switches out of her four-inch heels and into her closed-toe boots. *If the opportunity comes up, I'll do it.* Cayleen steps out of her car. The moment her feet hit the ground, she realizes her knees are weak.

"Nice outfit," Gavin teases. Cayleen didn't think about how her skirt and sweater combination would look with her lace-up Uggs, which are still dirty from the last jobsite. Her outfit looked great with the heels.

"Safety ... set the example ... you know," Cayleen explains.

"Where's your hard hat?" Gavin flashes a smile Cayleen's sure would win him millions if he were on a movie screen.

"It's in the car. Luke says, since I'm in land development, there should be no risk to my head—unless I'm underground. And if I'm underground, I'm fired." Cayleen laughs at her dad's protective nature.

Gavin smiles. "Do you always call him Luke?"

"Yes, I do. Some people don't know he's my dad, and I don't want people thinking I'm using my dad's business to my advantage. What do you call your dad? Bob? Robert?"

Gavin laughs a hearty laugh. "No one calls my dad Bob except people who don't know him. I know what you mean. I call my dad Robert too."

Cayleen smiles. "Thank you for meeting me here today.

Luke—uh, Dad—just bought that partially finished subdivision to the west, and I have no drainage plan to go off of to develop the property just south of yours."

"Yeah, the previous owner was not very pleasant to deal with when I was developing this property. I can see him just selling it and leaving. Did you know we bought this land from a church?" Gavin raises his eyebrows and smiles.

Cayleen is impressed conversation is so easy with him. "Actually, I did know that," Cayleen says. "I've been watching property in this area for quite some time."

"You own the property just across the street there, don't you?" Gavin points to a large piece of vacant land between the road and an older subdivision.

Cayleen nods with a slight smile, impressed that Gavin has done his research. *So, he's not just eye candy after all.*

Gavin smiles and puffs out his chest slightly. "I thought so."

"I'd like to know how you got the church to sell," Cayleen says. "Does your family know people in the Denver area?"

Gavin laughs. "No, no, but you knew it was from Denver, good research. No, our family has been active in the Catholic Church for generations. Grandfather Cline made a few phone calls, one thing leads to another, and here we stand. Do you want to drive to the end of the road so I can show you where the irrigation starts—or do you want to walk?"

"I'm up for a walk if you are."

Gavin thoroughly reviews the irrigation layout and drainage for both subdivisions. His knowledge is a huge help to Cayleen, and she is deeply appreciative. *Put yourself out there,* she thinks. "I can't thank you enough for taking the time to come out here and tell me all this. Can I buy you lunch to say thank you?" Cayleen is shaking on the inside.

Gavin smiles and raises an eyebrow. "Sure. I have lunch plans for today. How about tomorrow?"

"Whatever works for you. I appreciate you doing all this." Cayleen hopes her voice is steady.

"Okay, tomorrow then. What time and where?"

"I'm flexible and hardly ever take a lunch out of the office." Cayleen checks the calendar on her phone, relieved her hands aren't visibly shaking. "Tomorrow I need to be back by two, so any time before then."

"Let's go to Red Robin. How about eleven forty-five? Beat the rush?"

"Sounds good. I'll meet you there." Cayleen reaches out to shake Gavin's hand. "Thank you, Gavin." Cayleen turns back to her car.

"See you soon, Cayleen," Gavin calls after her.

For from the heart come evil thoughts, murder, adultery,
all sexual immorality, theft, lying and slander.
—Matthew 15:19

Cayleen walks into Cheyanne's office, fidgeting with her skirt. "I changed my outfit three times this morning, and this is what I ended up with. I never change my outfit. I'm so nervous. Do I look all right?"

Cheyanne looks up from her computer screen and smiles. "You look fabulous! When do you leave?"

Cayleen looks at her phone. "Three minutes. I didn't know it was possible to be this nervous! I present projects in front of politicians and don't get this nervous. I thought butterflies were only supposed to be in your stomach! I have butterflies from my feet to my arms—not to mention my knees get wobbly whenever he's around."

Cheyanne giggles. "You're fine. Take a deep breath and just be yourself. It's just lunch."

"Easy for you to say. You're not the one walking into a restaurant with wobbly knees." Cayleen looks at her phone. "I'm out. Back after lunch."

"Good luck!" Cheyanne calls out. "I'm awaiting juicy details when you get back!"

Cayleen arrives at the restaurant a few minutes early. When she opens the door, to her surprise, Gavin is already there. He looks up from his bench, his forearms resting on his thighs.

Why hasn't Hollywood found him yet? They're missing out.

When he sees her, he comes over to greet her. "Hey, Cayleen." He reaches out to shake her hand. "I haven't put in a name yet. I figured I'd wait."

"Thank you," Cayleen answers. She finds the fact that he waited for her to be considerate.

They are quickly shown to a table. Conversation flows between them. Cayleen is amazed at how easy it is to talk to Gavin, considering how nervous she is. Gavin has jokes and stories; they talk about mentors who inspired them and how they organize themselves in their jobs. Before Cayleen realizes much time has passed, lunch has been taken away, she has her box of leftovers, and she's taking out her credit card.

As they stand to leave, Gavin asks, "Thank you for lunch. Now I owe you. Can I repay you the favor?"

Cayleen leads the way to the door. "You can." As they approach the door, she looks Gavin in the eyes. "But I'd like you to buy me dinner." Cayleen smiles. "If it works for your schedule, let me know. See you, Gavin." Cayleen strides to her car, shaking and cheeks burning.

"Thanks for lunch, Cayleen," Gavin calls out to Cayleen's back.

When you follow the desires of your sinful nature, the results are very clear: sexual immorality, impurity, lustful pleasures.
—Galatians 5:19

The doorbell rings, and Cayleen calmly walks to the door, thankful for the peace and quiet of no dogs barking and scurrying across the floor.

Jessica is carrying a large box. "Hi, Mom. Is that the cake?"

Cayleen had wanted to throw Cheyanne's baby shower. Cheyanne was grateful since Cayleen's home had the largest entertaining space. Cayleen still feels badly about pushing Cheyanne and Clay to move into their new home, but she also still can't see why they were living with her for weeks after the carpet was installed. Cayleen remembers the uncomfortable conversation she brought up with her sister.

"What stage is happening at the house?" Cayleen did not visit to help very often. It was frustrating to see the lack of progress and lack of work being done. She realized it was difficult to work all day long and then go to a house for even more hours of work, but it was a choice they made. In Cayleen's mind, six months of living with her, after starting the renovation a month or two earlier, was excessively long for an eight-hundred-square-foot house. Jamison Homes built a house from start to finish in sixty days.

Cheyanne replied, "They installed carpet two weeks ago, but the electrical outlets aren't done yet."

"Have they hung doors and trim?"

"Yeah." Cheyanne was distracted by the magazine she was reading on the couch.

"And the counters were installed?"

"Yeah. Oh! And I got my washing machine and dryer last week! They're front loading!"

"Chey, you know I love having you stay with me, but do you think maybe you should be getting your house ready for a baby? I love you, sister, but I really don't want a baby in my house."

"We are getting our house ready for a baby! I see what you mean." Cheyanne got off the couch and left the room.

Cayleen felt terrible. Before the next weekend, they had moved out of Cayleen's house. They even left Cayleen's car since they had purchased two newer cars. Clay moved their things while the girls were at work.

Jessica bumps Cayleen's arm, jarring her back to the present, and sets the cake on the dining room table.

Cayleen giggles. "Think it's too much of a hint to have a Noah's ark cake and decorations?"

Jessica is still upset that her oldest daughter is not married. "It's not too much of a hint if they're not married." She walks to the other bags of goodies to place on the table and starts arranging for the guests.

Cayleen is still staring at the little animals and little boat made out of cake. "It sure is cute!"

Cayleen grabs a bag of decorations and begins hanging them around the room. She thinks about how different her family is for being so strict about marriage. In some families, it doesn't matter if people are married. It's not really religion that keeps their family that way—it's tradition. Even church isn't really a religious experience. It is a tradition. Cayleen feels that people should be married to have a baby, but she's not sure why. She decides to pray, not realizing how powerful her prayers are. *God, next time you want me to be married, let me be pregnant! Then I'll know it's right.*

"Honey, I'm home." Cheyanne's joyous voice fills the house, interrupting Cayleen's prayer. Cayleen is amazed at how being pregnant has given Cheyanne a glow and joy that she's never seen before in her sister. It makes Cayleen smile. She turns from her decorations to greet Cheyanne.

The girls embrace.

Cayleen asks, "Can I get you anything before people really start coming?"

"Yeah, what do you have?"

Jessica answers, "Fruit punch, Sprite, water, and lemonade."

"Lemonade sounds delicious," Cheyanne answers. "I've found my love of it in the past few months."

All three giggle.

"We know," Cayleen and Jessica say in unison.

Jessica gets the drink.

"How many people do you expect to come, Cheyanne?" Cayleen asks.

"You sent out the invitations!" Cheyanne teases, accepting the drink from Jessica.

"I know I did, but I figure you'd have a better idea of who actually will show up. None of Clay's family RSVP'd."

"Surprise, surprise." Cheyanne rolls her eyes. "They'll be at least twenty in his family alone."

"Oh, boy. Do you think there are enough seats? I can sit on the floor."

Cheyanne looks around the room, scanning the two couches and eight chairs placed around the space. She takes a loud drink of her lemonade. "I think it'll be fine. People can stand or sit on the floor." Cheyanne walks to look at the cake and then glares at the back of Jessica's head. "Mom, seriously? A Noah's ark cake?"

Jessica is busying herself with party preparations and doesn't even look up. "Your sister picked it out."

Cheyanne sends Cayleen a look and starts giggling. "Well, it is what it is. But I'll tell you before anyone else finds out—Clay and I married ourselves last night."

"What?"

"Yep, in Colorado, you can marry yourselves. You don't need a witness. We chose to marry ourselves in the bathtub. I love that bathtub!"

Cayleen starts to laugh in utter shock, shaking her head.

Jessica stops her preparations. "Praise the Lord. They're bringing my granddaughter into this world in wedlock." She runs over to Cheyanne and kisses her multiple times. "Thank you, thank you, thank you! Thank you for doing that!"

"Mom, we didn't get married for you." Cheyanne pushes away.

The doorbell rings.

"And the fun begins," Cayleen exclaims as she briskly walks to the door.

Several hours later, Cayleen loads the last of the gifts into Clay's truck.

Cheyanne leans out of the window. "Thank you, sister! What time is your date?"

Suddenly, Cayleen is nervous. She's been distracted all day and hasn't thought about her date with Gavin. "He's picking me up at seven."

"Do you know what you're wearing?"

"Malea is coming over to help me pick something out," Cayleen says.

Malea also works at Jamison Homes. Malea has told Cayleen that Cheyanne takes advantage of Cayleen, and Malea doesn't respect Cheyanne because of that. Cayleen respects both women and respects that they might not get along.

"Thank you for hosting all this, sister. See you Monday!"

"Are you coming to lunch tomorrow?" Cayleen asks.

"I think I've done my duty of being friendly to the family for the weekend. I'm going to rest tomorrow."

"Okay. See you Monday." Cayleen turns and goes back in the house.

Jessica is in the kitchen, tidying up the remnants of the party.

"Thank you, Mom. I can get the rest—if there is anything left to get. You've done so much!" Cayleen smiles.

Jessica turns. "Thank you for hosting! It's so nice not to have to clean my house."

Nice for everyone, Cayleen thinks.

Jessica keeps piles of junk on every surface until the piles seep onto the floor. Anytime Jessica is hosting, Cayleen, Cheyanne, and Jessica help clean the house. Jessica generally spends the entire party worrying about one thing or another rather than enjoying her guests.

"I guess I'll be going." Jessica turns toward the door.

Cayleen follows Jessica to the door, giving hugs before opening the door. "See you at church tomorrow, Mom." She heads upstairs to pick a few outfits.

Malea lets herself in when she arrives. "Hello?"

"Hey. I'm up here," Cayleen calls from her walk-in closet. Malea was once a resident of this home—though not as frequently or for as long as Cheyanne. Malea and her two sons stayed with Cayleen for a few weeks after she and her ex-husband separated and before she started renting a home from Luke down the street.

"Hi!" Malea is the same age and about the same body size as Cayleen—tall and thin—but their lives are very different. Malea has two children in elementary school. Malea had her first child at sixteen. Cayleen empathizes. After all, that could have been her. Malea fought her way through high school and professional school and design technical drawings for Jamison Homes. Malea pushes a stray blonde hair back behind her ear and pokes her head into the closet.

Cayleen emerges from the closet, partially dressed, with clothes in each arm. "What do you think? First, black pants or jeans?" Cayleen motions with her arms.

"Black pants." Luckily for Cayleen, Malea is decisive.

"Okay, tight or not so tight."

"Tight. Put them on—and let me see the tight ones."

Cayleen puts on the tighter pants. "These are a size four, and the ones I just had on were a six."

"Turn around, Cay. I gotta see you from behind!" Malea giggles.

Cayleen turns slowly in a full circle. *I've never had someone come over to help me get dressed. I've never felt this nervous. Is this how it's supposed to be?*

"Those are the ones!" Malea says.

"Okay, now which top? Black sweater with white underneath or …" Cayleen gestures to her closet. "I've not come up with anything else so far. I wore my other cute clothes when we met on the jobsite and when we had lunch. I'm running out!"

Malea laughs. "With a closet full of clothes, you're running out?" She shakes her head. "Put on the sweater."

Cayleen complies, modeling her black and white outfit.

"Perfect. That's what you'll wear. It's beautiful, dear. What time is Gavin going to be here?"

Cayleen continues fidgeting with her outfit. "Uh, seven."

"Well, then, I guess I'm going to go. You've got less than twenty minutes. Remember to relax and be yourself, and if he doesn't like you for who you are, he's the one who's missing out." Malea leans in to hug Cayleen and lets herself out.

"Thank you!" Cayleen yells before hearing the front door slam.

Cayleen rushes to finish touching up her makeup and hair, putting on jewelry to accentuate without being too much. Gathering her purse, phone, wallet, and jacket, she checks the time. She's nearly ten minutes early.

As she slowly walks downstairs, she thinks, *I've never really done this before. Noah and I were a long-distance relationship and never really went on dates. Mike lived on the same floor as I did. Hunter, well, that was a different story. Is a girl supposed to be ready when the guy arrives? Is she supposed to make him wait?*

Cayleen takes a deep breath. *Be myself, be myself. If I'm myself, I'm nearly always on time. I don't like making people wait for me.* She sits on the arm of one of her couches and looks at her phone. Two minutes.

She jumps up. *Malea and I didn't pick shoes!* She bounds for the entry closet where her shoes are kept and looks down at the options. *Flats? I like that he's taller than me.*

When the doorbell rings, Cayleen is standing at the door. She takes a deep breath and unlocks the door, smiling that Malea locked it on her way out. She looks up at Gavin. "Hi."

"Wow. You answered the door really quickly! You look nice." Gavin does a full once-over of Cayleen, making her slightly uncomfortable. "You ready to go?"

Cayleen tries to make her once-over of Gavin not as obvious. *Wow! He sure does clean up well!* Gavin is in dark jeans, a polo shirt, and lightweight black jacket. His blue shirt creates a shimmer in his blue eyes. His dark brown hair is slightly long on top, though still cut short, and is still wet from a shower. Cayleen can imagine what it feels like under her fingers. Gavin's frame is similar to Luke. He seems to fill the doorway, but he is not overweight. Cayleen hopes she's not drooling and has the weak feeling in her knees again. Cayleen's insecurities kick in, and she wonders if she's overdressed. She wonders if she's supposed to be on time for a date, and she wonders if she's waited too long to respond to his question.

"Yes," Cayleen says, and then realizes she doesn't have her jacket. "Oh, wait just a minute." Cayleen walks toward the dining room where she left it on the back of a chair.

Gavin follows her into her house. "Wow, what were you doing before I showed up?"

Cayleen is confused and self-conscious, thinking about how childish she feels for having a friend come over to help her pick an outfit. "What do you mean?"

"I mean this house looks show ready—like there's nothing out anywhere. No magazines, no computer, no papers." Gavin's eyes get big and he looks down at Cayleen, causing her to smile. "Nothing."

"Well, I had already cleaned up. I'm ready now if you want to go, unless you want to stay and have a cocktail or …?" Cayleen wasn't sure how these things were supposed to go.

"We can go to dinner." Gavin follows Cayleen out of the house and opens the passenger door to his old red pickup. "So, what did you clean up from?"

"Excuse me?" Cayleen asks.

"You said you already cleaned up your house. What did you do today that you had to clean up from?"

The easy conversation flows through dinner. When Gavin asks if she wants to stop by and get a drink at a pub, meeting up with some of his family, she easily agrees.

To Cayleen's surprise, James walks past to the bathroom. Cayleen does a double take. James's beard was so full she barely recognizes him. She tries to say hi, but he does not even acknowledge her presence. Soon enough, she sees another one of Hunter's high school friends. Ryan stops and smiles with a partial wave, almost like Cayleen had forced him without touching him. *Wow—they're being incredibly rude tonight. I wonder what I did to them.*

Gavin asks if she'd like to sit at a small table on the side—without the large crowd.

Cayleen nods.

It is so loud that speaking does not have much effect.

As Gavin leads them to a small table, Cayleen recognizes a large table comprised mainly of Hunter's friends from high school. Cayleen raises her hand to wave at them all. Suddenly she recognizes Hunter in the middle. His beard is so thick she that she barely recognizes him. He glares at Cayleen. Even in the darkened room, she knows he would rather have her dead than standing near him. Cayleen stares at Gavin's back and wonders why they are all so mad at her. Suddenly she realizes the date.

November 4 is Hunter's birthday. *Why would they be mad at me? I haven't talked to Hunter in over six months. The phone works both ways.*

Gavin finds an empty table, and Cayleen sits across from him.

"Do you like bowling?" Gavin asks.

Cayleen nods.

"Would you like to go bowling—or would you like to stay here and have another drink?"

Cayleen is enjoying the time with Gavin and doesn't want it to end. She also doesn't want to make the wrong decision. "Yes!"

Gavin raises his eyebrows and says, "Really? Let's get out of here then!"

On the way to the bowling alley, Cayleen admits she's a terrible bowler. "If I break sixty, it's a good game for me."

Gavin laughs. "Well, you're a perfect partner for me because I'm so competitive."

Over the next two hours, and four games of bowling, Cayleen somehow scores two turkeys. She's flabbergasted, and so is Gavin.

"I thought you weren't going to beat me," Gavin says.

"I think your total score has to be higher to actually beat you, right?" Cayleen asks. Even with turkeys, Gavin still has the higher score.

"I think you're just being nice to me. You can't score two turkeys and still lose," Gavin replies.

Cayleen laughs. "I wish that were the case! You're just my lucky charm!"

On the ride home, Cayleen says, "Over the course of tonight, you bought me an amazing dinner, took me out to socialize at the pub, went bowling, and convinced me to take the risk of owning an investment property and finishing my master's degree ... did I miss anything?"

"Nope, I think that about sums it up. Except that I won bowling." Gavin pulls the pickup into Cayleen's driveway.

Cayleen laughs. "Yes, you did. And I didn't let you win. I really tried and probably played the best I've ever played in my life! All in all, I had a great evening, Gavin. Thank you."

Gavin stays in the same spot with the engine running, looks at Cayleen, and says, "Yep! Good night!"

Considering Gavin has opened her door when they got to the pickup every time and is now not making a move toward kissing her or getting out to open her door and walk her to the door, Cayleen quickly takes the hint, looks at the door handle, and opens her own door. "Good night, Gavin." She quickly walks to the door and lets herself into the house.

Cayleen slumps into the couch, feeling conflicted. *I had such a good time. It was a great conversation. He's so handsome. I like how I feel when I'm with him, and we have so much in common.*

Then the voice inside her answers: *Let him go. He's on his way somewhere else right now. Its only eleven. He is on his way somewhere without you.*

But why would he be going anywhere else? Where would he be going?

The voice says nothing, leaving the same feeling in her chest. *He's somewhere else right now. He's not with you. Let him go.*

The realization that he is somewhere else brings a wash of emotion, leading to the same spot Cayleen has been so many times in her life:

feeling not good enough, not pretty enough, not fun enough, not enough. Cayleen drags herself upstairs and cries herself to sleep.

> He will wipe every tear from their eyes.
> —Revelation 21:4

CHAPTER 12

Over the next several months, Cayleen is conflicted. She and Gavin see each other several times a week in their professional circles. In addition, their friendship has grown based on working together on the development projects they own next to each other. Even in social settings, they often see each other, having mutual friends.

The voice on the inside of Cayleen's chest remains the same. She wonders if it is still there. She hasn't heard it say much. In her mind, Cayleen has fantasized about having a relationship with Gavin. She sees the girls Gavin brings to social settings and wonders why he would pick them over her. Cayleen is smart, better built than several of the women Gavin's chosen, and is as pretty—or prettier—than several of the women as well. *Why didn't Gavin choose me?*

He's somewhere else right now. He's not with you. Let him go. The longer Cayleen goes on wondering about Gavin, the weaker the voice inside her gets, allowing her thoughts to cycle around Gavin with even more strength.

Cayleen doesn't realize all the distractions she could be focusing on because her mind is so focused on Gavin. Cheyanne and Clay have a beautiful baby girl, Lily, the birth of which Cayleen feels blessed to witness. Though the birthing process made Cayleen shy away from ever having a baby, holding the tiny baby brought forth a yearning she'd hidden for so long—the ache to be a mother. After becoming a mother, Cheyanne decided to stay at home full-time rather than working part-time as Cayleen's assistant.

The vacancy caused by Cheyanne is difficult to fill. Cayleen's workload has changed, and she needs someone who can really do anything Cayleen can do.

Cayleen says, "Dad, with Cheyanne leaving, I'd really like to hire someone to replace her."

"Yes, Cay. Your department is successful, and you have the money to hire a replacement."

"No, what I'd really like is someone who can *be* me, someone I can hand anything and can do anything. Not someone that I constantly have to give direction to."

Luke turns in his office chair toward Cayleen. "Who do you have in mind?"

"Gavin's sister-in-law, Bethany, is graduating school next month. She has gone to the exact same schools I did."

Luke smiles. "That's a pretty good resume!"

"Well, not the master's part, but she's gotten her undergraduate degree in civil engineering. She doesn't necessarily want to go into that field," Cayleen says. "I talked to her about it a little bit, but she wants to know how much we can pay. She's looking at working for her grandfather's company if not ours."

Luke smiles and says, "What do you think we should pay to get her?"

"Graduating materials from the school say they generally make fifty thousand after graduating," Cayleen says. "I think, to get her on board, we need to offer her that much."

Luke scratches some numbers on a piece of paper and taps the keys to his calculator.

Cayleen has no idea what he's figuring. She's already run the numbers for her department and is ready to prove where she will get the funds if asked.

Luke looks up with pursed lips. "Okay. Let's see what she says."

Cayleen excitedly leaves Luke's office for her own office

downstairs. As she looks up the information to call Bethany—whom she's met several times for interviews in addition to on her date with Gavin—Cayleen is conflicted. Her longing for Gavin is difficult to control and hide. By hiring Bethany, will it get even harder—or will Gavin finally see he's in the right place to be with her?

Cayleen doesn't allow the thoughts to settle. She doesn't allow herself to be still often at all anymore. She still attends church regularly, but she has no prayer life or time for reading her Bible. The voices on the inside are often emotional ones that she has to stifle.

No time to think now. We have work to do. Cayleen grabs Bethany's contact information and makes the call.

Be still in the presence of the lord, and wait patiently for him.
—Psalm 37:7

Over the next year, Cayleen is conflicted with her decision to hire Bethany. Bethany is a combination of cute and wholesome with her short brown hair, medium-tall build, and sometimes-awkward mannerisms. Bethany is pleasant, which is always good to be around, but her life focus is very different than that of Cayleen. Now that Bethany graduated college, which took a year longer than Cayleen, she and her husband are trying to start a family. Bethany told Cayleen in February their efforts had been successful; they were expecting a baby later in the year.

Cayleen is torn between her excitement for her friend and work that needs to be done. Cayleen remembers what happened with Cheyanne when she had Lily. Cayleen does not voice her thoughts to Bethany or Luke.

Cayleen has learned from being a manager to Bethany—with the help of Luke. Several times, Cayleen has walked into Luke's office, closed the door, and plopped into his guest chairs, ready to vent her frustrations when Luke finishes his current task.

"What's going on?" Luke peers over his reading glasses, looking up from a document.

"I just don't know what to do." Cayleen looks at the ceiling. "It takes Bethany a *lot* longer to do things than it does me!"

Luke chuckles. "Yeah."

"It's frustrating! I want to be able to give her something and have her get it done and not have to check. I want her to start a new project or tell me when she's done so I can give her the next task. I walk into her office, and she's doing other personal things."

Luke sets the paper down on his desk and peels off his glasses. "You need to give some time for personal stuff."

"I know." Cayleen looks at him. "I do! She doesn't remember to finish things, and she is working on personal things instead. When I walk in, I redirect, but it takes me walking in and checking on her to get her on task."

Luke chuckles. "Cayleen, not everyone is made like you. In fact, not *anyone* is made like you!"

Cayleen says, "I know, but with her being from all the same schools, I thought …"

Luke smiles. "Well, darling daughter, everybody is different. Is Bethany's position still penciling out?"

"Yes. The number of projects she's helped me subcontract through the engineering division has already paid her salary." Cayleen's voice expresses her relief at the recollection that Bethany has already paid her own way with the company.

Jamison Homes also has an engineering division that subcontracts services to outside clients.

"Well, maybe you should chalk this one up to learning. Not many—if anyone—are as hardworking as you are and can work as fast and efficiently as you do!"

Cayleen smiles in defeat. This is not the first time Luke has talked her down from management frustrations. "Okay." Cayleen looks at the paper on his desk. "How are things in your world?"

Luke puffs out his chest and purses his lips. "Tough," he says.

Luke had left his most recent wife several months before—or

was it a year? Cayleen couldn't remember. With Luke's decision to leave his wife, his entire world is crumbling.

Outside of Spring Forks, the entire country faces an economic downturn. The home-building industry in major cities has taken a nosedive. Spring Forks has historically been twelve to eighteen months behind the rest of the country in everything from music to fashion to economics. Luke and Cayleen renounce rumors about the economic downturn's effect on Jamison Homes to the employees. Luke claims that Spring Forks will remain unaffected, but Cayleen has taken a more realistic approach, evaluating the first round of layoffs and other ways to cut overhead expenses.

"I'm probably going to have to downsize," Luke says.

"Bethany's husband sells commercial real estate, and he could list the office like we've discussed. I've talked to my mortgage lender friend downtown. We could rent space from him in his building."

Luke wipes his eyes. "Yes, let's do that and see if it sells." Luke looks around the room while he's talking. "If we do that, we could have the sales staff move into a model home ... and we could allow some employees to work from home ..."

Cayleen doesn't know whether her entire department should continue. If they're not selling homes, they don't need inventory of lots for more homes. It doesn't make sense in her black-and-white mind to have a land development department.

Cayleen offers to take one of the first layoffs when they choose to do them, which Luke quickly shuts down. Luke reminds her that they had discussed her moving into a general manager position. As vice president of the company, she could function as an assistant to Luke.

Luke finally makes eye contact with Cayleen, bringing them both back from their thoughts. "Yes. Let's do it."

But if your heart turns away and you refuse to listen, and if
you are drawn away to serve and worship other gods, then
I warn you now that you will certainly be destroyed.
—Deuteronomy 30: 17–18

In an effort to reduce her own expenses, and the fun prospect of living close to a girlfriend in the same building, Cayleen purchases a small condo near downtown, renting out her larger home in addition to the rental she had built by Jamison Homes. Cayleen only has the courage to invest in a rental property after Gavin's witty encouragement.

She sits in her new-to-her condo on the couch, reading a book and drinking a glass of wine one June evening when her phone rings. Hunter is on the other end. All apprehension from their short previous encounter forgotten, she says, "Hey, Hunter. How are you?"

"I'm good, Cay. How are you?"

"I'm good! What are you up to?"

"Well, that's why I'm calling, Cay. I'm at the wedding of Chad and Micah Stetson. Do you remember Chad?"

"Of course! How are they?"

"It's great! We have Bill and James and Ryan and a bunch of other friends from high school here. We were just talking and really feel you should be here, Cay. Would you like to come out?"

Cayleen doesn't think—the fun and excitement of a wedding and seeing Hunter are all she feels. "Sure! Where are you at?"

Hunter gives her directions to the home where they're having the wedding, not knowing an address for her to look up. Cayleen is extra quick to get ready and out the door. By the time she pulls in the driveway, it's nearly nine. The sky is just now turning to dusk.

Hunter meets her as she's getting out of her car. "I'm glad you made it." He grabs her hand.

"Thank you for inviting me." Cayleen enjoys the grip of a man's hand. It's been so long since she's had a man interested in her. It's been so long since she's felt a man's touch on her hand. It feels so nice to have him gripping her hand. She loves the familiar feeling of being close to Hunter and how their hands click from the years of them being in this position. It feels right to Cayleen—or is it loneliness that makes it feel right?

Cayleen glows with excitement; everyone seems the same but

with kids or spouses—or both. Hunter dances with Cayleen, which she doesn't remember him doing often.

Bill talks excitedly and spills red wine on Cayleen's white shirt. The hostess, whom Cayleen went to elementary school with, is kind enough to give Cayleen a new shirt, waving a hand and telling Cayleen not to worry. Cayleen doesn't remember having a better time.

James's wife, Lisa, pulls Cayleen aside. "So, *you're* Cay," she says with a sway and a giggle. Lisa is so friendly and nice and constantly smiles. Her round, tan face is framed with bleached-blonde hair that cascades down to her waist. Lisa's frame is small with an extremely large chest. Cayleen thinks Lisa is beautiful and loves her style of baby doll dress with flip-flops.

"Yes, I guess I am," Cayleen answers. "Is there something I should know?" Cayleen smiles.

"No, not really. Hunter just always talks about you. Well, technically, he's always been hooked on you. You know, he was dating this one girl one time, super cute with fake ... you know." Lisa gestures toward her chest.

Cayleen giggles at Lisa's honesty.

"They were dating for a while. She had kids and was really into Hunter. Hunter flat out told her, 'I don't love you.' There's only been one person he's loved, and that's you, Cay."

Cayleen doesn't know if it's the wine or the fun evening, but that sounded like a sweet thing for Lisa to tell her. She smiles and toasts Lisa, taking another sip.

"So, I feel kinda like I'm meeting a celebrity right now." Lisa laughs and sways a bit. "I've heard so much about ya!"

Cayleen is embarrassed. "Oh, no, nothing close to a celebrity. So, how many kids do you and James have?"

Conversation is easy with Lisa. Cayleen finds Lisa's life interesting.

Lisa continues to ask questions about Cayleen and is so direct that she sometimes laughs at herself in embarrassment. Cayleen appreciates Lisa's honesty in her directness. Cayleen is not sure if it's the wine or that Lisa is so friendly, but she really likes Lisa. Cayleen finds out James and Lisa live just across the street from Hunter.

As the wedding festivities wind down, Lisa says, "We can't go to our house 'cause my mom's there with the kids. Let's go back to Hunter's house!"

Hunter peers at Cayleen without answering, waiting for Cayleen's response.

Cayleen says, "Yeah, I can drive." She has been careful not to drink too much to make sure she could still make it home. If she goes to Hunter's house, it seems safe to drink as much as she wants and sleep there. *Hunter's familiar and a friend, so it will be fine.*

The smaller party reconvenes at Hunter's house. Once there, Hunter turns on some music. The room is filled with laughter and conversations.

Lisa makes sure Cayleen's drink is set and takes her arm, directing her to the other side of the kitchen, making their conversation more intimate.

"So, what happened with you and Hunter? Why aren't you together *now*?" Lisa asks.

Cayleen says, "Well, in high school, he physically hurt me … and when he did some things when we saw each other more recently, he scared me into thinking he hadn't changed."

"What do you mean?" Lisa sways and takes a sip of her drink, eyes still intent on Cayleen. She steadies herself by grabbing the counter with the other hand.

"He seemed really possessive, calling and texting and really intent on things."

"Hunter? He's not like that. Maybe he was excited. I've never seen him be possessive with a girl."

"He used to get in fights a lot too. Does he still get in fights?"

Lisa pondered the question for a moment. "No. I think I've seen him and James wrestle a time or two, but the last bar fight was Bill." Lisa gestures to Bill standing on the other side of the kitchen.

Bill is very tall with a filled frame. Not heavy and not fat—but not someone you want to see on the other side of a fight.

Cayleen laughs. "In high school, my sister and I were fighting about something—who knows what now—and Bill stepped in. He just laid down on top of me until I stopped fighting back. It worked! I couldn't move."

Lisa laughed. "That'd do it!"

"I don't even know how he got me to the ground. I just remember realizing that Bill's face was like an inch from mine. That was uncomfortable. Hunter and James tackled Cheyanne."

The girls laugh.

The hours blink past, and soon enough, Cayleen realizes Bill has left. Lisa and James are also on their way across the street to their house. She feels slight apprehension on the inside of what is to come when she and Hunter are alone. She checks herself: no voice or feeling on the inside. That may be due to the amount of alcohol she's had or maybe it's been so long since she's felt that feeling or impression that she can't recognize it anymore. Cayleen doesn't care. She can't feel anything telling her being there is wrong. She also thinks about how long it has been since she's been with a man.

Hunter's safe. I've already been with him sexually—though it was years ago. I deserve this. Cayleen walks toward Hunter, her mind made up.

Their mother is a shameless prostitute and became pregnant
in a shameful way. She said, "I'll run after other lovers
and sell myself to them for food and water, for clothing
of wool and linen, and for olive oil and drinks."
—Hosea 2:5

CHAPTER 13

Three weeks later, Cayleen is cooking dinner in Hunter's kitchen. Her office is much closer to Hunter's house than her own apartment, and often they stay at his place. Hunter doesn't seem to mind, but it doesn't feel like her house—even though he's told her to make herself at home. Hunter doesn't say much, leaving Cayleen to make assumptions.

Hunter comes in the door from watering the grass.

"Hi, hon," Cayleen calls, hoping Hunter will come into the kitchen instead of sitting in front of the TV.

He doesn't get the hint and walks toward the couch. "Hey."

"Can you come in here a minute?"

Hunter walks the short distance into the kitchen. "Yeah, sure." He rubs his hands together. "Need some help with dinner?"

"No, I think I've got it. We'll just do chicken-bacon wraps tonight. I wanted to talk about our living situation."

"Yeah? What about it?" Hunter doesn't make eye contact with Cayleen. Instead, he busies himself with something Cayleen can't see on the counter.

"I've been staying here a lot lately."

"Yeah."

"If I'm staying here, it would make sense for me to rent out my apartment fully furnished." The first round of layoffs would occur next week. Fears of not knowing the future of the company—and paying her bills—circle through her head.

"Okay," Hunter replies with a shrug. Finally, he makes eye contact. "Good talk." Hunter claps his hands, smiles, and walks back to the couch.

Confused and unfulfilled, Cayleen turns back to the bacon on the stove. "Yeah, good talk," she mutters under her breath.

> Claiming to be wise, they instead became utter fools.
> —Romans 1:22

Cayleen rounds the corner to Hunter's house and pulls into the driveway.

Hunter is sitting on the front steps.

She walks around to sit next to him. "Hey, how was work?"

Hunter takes a deep breath. "I just got a call from my mom. My grandpa's really sick, and they say he's not going to make it through the night. She asked me to come up." Hunter's grandpa lives about forty minutes away in a smaller town.

"Oh, Hunter. I'm so sorry. Would you like me to drive you?" Cayleen places a hand on Hunter's back.

"Yeah, I'm going to grab a beer for the road."

On the drive, Cayleen asks questions about Hunter's grandpa and tells the stories she remembers about him from high school. Cayleen asks Hunter how he's doing, hoping that talking about himself will help him deal with his feelings.

"My grandpa's dying in the next day or two. My mom was given two years to live five years ago. How do you think I'm doing? I'm here, aren't I?"

Hunter decided not to reenlist in the marines because his mother, Dawnette, had asked him not to. She had been diagnosed with colon cancer and given only a few years to live. She had tried chemo, but she said the effects were not worth the fact that she would still die. She had made the decision to live fewer of her days enjoying them as much as possible rather than living only a few more days or months in pain.

As Cayleen sees it, Dawnette's existence is miraculous. She has already lived years longer than any doctor had hoped and without many drugs. In that time, she has seen her children and grandchildren more, vacationed with them more, and spent the quality time doing the things she loves.

As the headlights shine on the small trailer house that belongs to Hunter's grandparents, Cayleen spots Dawnette on the wooden deck, stealing a few puffs off a cigarette. Her hair that was once brown when Cayleen was in high school, is now highlighted mostly blonde. Her size seems to be the same as when Cayleen was in high school, not exactly fit but never a reason to fear a bathing suit. Dawnette's presence radiates enthusiasm and optimism—even in such a dark time. She embraces her son. "Hunter, thank you for coming."

"Of course, Mom." Hunter walks inside. Dawnette and Cayleen follow.

"Grandpa's in his room if you want to talk to him. He's a little out of it. He asked the neighbor kid for some whiskey this afternoon." Dawnette's eyes get big, making a silly face, and she laughs.

Cayleen smiles.

Hunter walks back toward the bedrooms.

Cayleen stands in the kitchen with Dawnette. "How is Grandma holding up?"

Dawnette's mother has been struggling with Alzheimer's for years. Cayleen has overheard stories of Grandma getting lost in grocery stores and department stores.

"Well, her mind's not so good. Dad has been taking care of her somewhat. In the past few weeks, his cancer got so bad. Cousin Sue Ellen has been coming over to help with Mom, and hospice has been here caring for Dad. Sissy is looking into a home in Spring Forks for Alzheimer's after Dad passes." Dawnette looks down at the table. "Do you want some coffee? Or water? I'm always drinking coffee—doesn't matter what time of day!" Dawnette gives a slight chuckle with a silly grin.

"I'll have coffee. Thank you. I can get it though. Are the cups here?" Cayleen opens a cupboard.

"Yep, you found 'em. Do you want some sugar?" Dawnette always has sweet coffee.

"Sure. Thank you." Cayleen puts a spoonful into her own mug of very black coffee. "And how are you holding up?"

"It's tough, Cay." Dawnette's eyes fill with tears, but none spill. "Watching Dad die. He was diagnosed with cancer after me." Dawnette's eyes meet Cayleen's. "Makes me think about how I thought I would go first. And that's *scary*."

Cayleen holds Dawnette's gaze. She feels emotion, which she thinks is empathy, wash through her body. Cayleen is unfamiliar with burden bearing or the fact that a person can actually feel another person's emotions. All she knows is that she has always been empathetic.

Dawnette says, "You know, when I showed you all that bank information and passwords, you know where all my stuff is in my house?" Several weekends ago, Hunter and Cayleen had visited Dawnette at her house for the entire day. During that time, they had talked about bank information, possible vacations, possible horseback rides for Dawnette, and the neighbors, and they even went for a drive in Hunter's truck. Hunter and Dawnette talked about possible hunting spots for the next season for Hunter.

Dawnette had made Cayleen promise she would be there for Hunter when Dawnette dies. Dawnette is leaving Hunter in charge of her estate. Hunter's older brother had used Dawnette's credit cards to purchase things and sell them for drugs and alcohol in the past; Hunter's younger sister lived out of state.

Cayleen had promised—empathy about Dawnette's circumstances overcome the small feeling on the inside of her making her wonder if she could keep the promise. The small voice resounded within her: *Don't do it!* It had been so long since she'd heard the voice that she didn't recognize it and dismissed it.

Dawnette continues walking to the other side of the trailer's small kitchen and leans against the counter, coffee cup cradled in her hands. "I don't know how Hunter's going to handle it. I don't know how he's going to deal with me passing and then have to do all the things for the estate. Of the kids, Hunter is the most responsible." Dawnette shakes her head. "I just don't know how he's gonna do it, Cay." Dawnette looks at Cayleen intently, gently touching her arm. "You gotta be there." Dawnette's grasp on Cayleen's arm intensifies, her eyes pleading.

"I will," Cayleen answers, promising for a second time with surety in her words and mind.

The voice inside says, *Don't do it!*

> So God's rest is there for people to enter, but those who first heard this good news failed to enter because they disobeyed God.
> —Hebrews 4:6

Cayleen opens the passenger door to Gavin's new Nissan pickup, placing two cold Snickers bars on the middle console. "Road food!" She puts her overnight bag in the back seat and climbs into the passenger seat. There is a two-day conference in a nearby community, and Gavin had offered to drive.

Gavin grabs the Snickers bar, rips it open, and takes a large bite. "It's cold!" He chews for a second. "But really good! I've never had one cold before."

"Mmmm … they're the best cold." Cayleen sips her coffee.

"You're not eating yours?" Gavin is done with his after three bites and is steering toward the highway.

"Not right now. I'm not hungry."

Gavin gives her a sideways glance.

"I ate lunch today, which is why I'm not hungry."

Gavin's gaze narrows. "I know you're not one of those girls who just doesn't eat when she's around a guy, but you gotta eat. Are you getting skinny lately?"

"I don't know." Cayleen struggles with the scale and chooses not to keep one. Her weight has only fluctuated by less than twenty pounds since she was in the eighth grade, but for some reason, she hates the number the scale points to when she steps on. Cayleen's backup for control in her life is her control of food, and lately, her world has been out of control. Still, she hates hearing the scolding from Gavin and says, "I'm eating, Gavin."

"Are you still working out in the mornings when the rest of us normal people are sleeping?" Gavin teases, the fatherly tone now out of his voice.

Cayleen giggles and fakes defensiveness. "Yes, I am still working out. It keeps me sane," she says. While looking out the window as they leave Spring Forks, she adds, "I need the stress release." Gavin could be right about Cayleen's weight loss; she tends to not get as hungry when she is stressed.

"How are things?" Gavin asks.

"When did we last talk?" Cayleen smiles as she looks at Gavin. He has been her professional confidant for some time. She easily got over her inner turmoil about their relationship since talking to Hunter was like talking to a brick wall. Every time she tried to tell Hunter about her work, Hunter would change the subject or say he had other things going and leave the room. Cayleen didn't talk to Gavin often, but when she did, she trusted what she said was in confidence and taken without judgment. Gavin gave sound, good advice and often pointed out perspectives she hadn't considered. Soon after moving in with Hunter, Jamison Homes did the first round of layoffs and sold their building. Cayleen found a smaller office space to rent in town, lowering their overhead and liabilities significantly.

"Did I tell you about the business plan I proposed to Dad?"

"The one about eliminating your entire department? Yes, you did. And he changed your title to be general manager now, right?" Gavin's eyes sparkle.

"Yeah." Cayleen's eyes widen. "For a home-building company when the market for homes has plummeted. Luke asked me to write a new business plan for investors, an investment proposal. I took all our liabilities and figured out how much we need to survive." Cayleen shakes her head. "I should email it to you! Maybe you would have some investor friends who could look at it."

Gavin says, "Yeah, email it to me!"

Without any enthusiasm, Cayleen says, "So, I'm buying another house."

Gavin doesn't take his eyes off the road.

Cayleen says, "Jamison Homes owns several rental homes. I pulled the mortgages Jamison has on them and figured out which would keep us going the longest. It's a home we built five years ago and has had the same tenant since it was built. I told Dad about it; he said he'd sell me the home for $225,000."

"What? Brand-new homes aren't even selling for $200,000 maybe $180,000. You're not actually paying that much for it, are you?"

Cayleen sighs. "I know. We're not selling our homes a thousand square feet larger for $200,000, but I can't bring myself to negotiate. Jamison is going to have to write the check for the down payment. I have no cash. Luke said he'll only charge me 5 percent interest like my other loan for the down payment I have for the first rental property." Cayleen forces a laugh. "But I wrote the loan document, so it's not a balloon payment like the last one. The payments start seven years from now."

Gavin allows a small forced laugh, knowing it's not a good deal for Cayleen, but allowing her to feel her victory with the payment plan. "How long does it buy Jamison Homes?" Cayleen has confided in Gavin that Jamison Homes is close to bankruptcy.

"I'm not completely sure, but with the settlement money from the lawsuit, we should be okay for a few more months. March? April? But if we have another closing, that would extend it." Cayleen and Luke had entered negotiations for a lawsuit in the previous months. Several weeks earlier, Cayleen had her first deposition with the opposing party's attorney. It had been a terrifying day for Cayleen. In the end, the parties settled outside of court, partially based on the records and testimony of Luke and Cayleen.

"Have you guys called the bankruptcy attorneys in Denver yet?"

"Not that I know of. Dad mentioned them to me, and I've been pressing him to call them, but ... he doesn't even come in to the office sometimes. He might be working from the model home, but I don't know."

"I don't know what I'd do in that situation," Gavin says. "What does Hunter say?"

Cayleen laughs. "Hunter doesn't say much. We don't talk about work much. We don't talk about anything much."

"How are things with Hunter?"

Cayleen smiles. "Hunter's Hunter."

"What does that mean?" Gavin asks. "You guys are living together, right? That seems pretty serious to me."

"Yeah, we're living together, but I still don't feel like it's my house. I feel like he's letting me live in his house."

Gavin says, "You rented your condo furnished, right? Maybe it's because you don't have much stuff there? Maybe you should take more of your stuff there?"

"There's no room for my stuff. And it's not that I don't like his stuff. I guess it feels like there's no room for me." Cayleen's voice drifts off.

"I've been to your house with Hunter," Gavin starts. "That house is big enough. There's room for you. What do you mean?"

Cayleen smiles softly. "Hunter is very rooted in his own ways. He does his own thing. If I can help, that's fine, but he won't go out of his way for me."

Gavin was silent for a moment. "They say you don't change people, right?"

"Yeah, well, I didn't think I wanted to change him. He just does nothing. When I talk about work, he gets stressed rather than letting me vent. He sits on the couch and watches TV in the dark. It's like pulling teeth to get him to go out of the house and go hiking, go out with friends, or do anything. I didn't know it was like that when we weren't living together because we would always be doing something when we were together."

"I'm not sure exactly, but it sounds a little like depression. Maybe it's a stage. Is that what he did when you were together a long time ago?"

Cayleen says, "We did go to his house and watch TV a lot, but then we'd party at night on the weekends with friends. I guess we did watch TV a lot during the week, but I don't know how much time we spent together during the week. His mom has cancer, and he talks about how difficult things were for him in the marines. He was happy that one fall he played football, which was great, but ..."

Gavin says, "Do you know what a guy told me at the office a while back?"

Cayleen smiles. "What?"

"He said I should make a list of the things I want in a person who I want to be with or marry."

Cayleen's smile slowly fades. She shakes her head and says, "Yeah, I already did that." She turns to look at Gavin with her eyebrows raised. "Did you make a list?"

"Yeah! I didn't write it down or anything. I'm not that formal, but I thought about it."

"Are you going to tell me what's on it?" Cayleen smiles even bigger.

"Oh, I put things like I want a girl who does stuff with me—like four-wheeling, hiking, and that kind of stuff. And I want someone who's not quite as much of a party girl like Stephanie. Remember Stephanie?"

Cayleen nods.

Gavin says, "But not quite as fuddy-duddy as Sadie. Somewhere in between."

Cayleen nods and looks out the window.

"Did you say you have a list?"

"Yeah," Cayleen says quietly.

"So ... does Hunter meet everything on your list?" Gavin asks.

Cayleen smiles and shakes her head. "I've never thought about it … but now that I do, no, he doesn't meet anything on my list!" Cayleen laughs.

"What? You didn't compare him to your list? What's the point of having a list?"

Cayleen looks at Gavin. "You met everything on my list, and that didn't work out. I haven't looked at it since."

In the four years she has known Gavin, she's never seen him so surprised. It amuses Cayleen, and she allows the silence rather than breaking it.

"Have you ever stopped to read those?" Gavin points out the window at a marker for some historic point of interest.

Cayleen smiles, appreciating Gavin's ability to quickly and abruptly detour around uncomfortable moments. "No, have you?"

"Yes, not on this road—but on another byway. It's a lot of fun and pretty interesting, just stopping and reading them all. You can't be in a hurry; it can take a lot of time."

With their conversation back on safe ground, the small talk continues. Cayleen can't easily forget her thoughts about a long-term relationship with Hunter.

Think carefully about what is right, and stop sinning. For to your shame I say that some of you don't know God at all.
—1 Corinthians 15:34

CHAPTER 14

" I don't understand why you're leaving me." Hunter's stare burns through Cayleen.

"It's not right, Hunter. It doesn't feel right. This isn't where I'm supposed to be." Cayleen can't find the right words to explain the screaming inside her that tells her that being together is wrong. She doesn't want to say the words she is thinking for fear of hurting him and stirring his anger even more. *I don't want to waste your life. I don't feel like this is my home. I feel like an inconvenience to you. I feel like I'm walking on eggshells to avoid making you mad. We don't ever talk. I don't feel connected to you. I can't be here anymore.*

Hunter had been out of town on a work trip to Alaska when Cayleen returned from her conference. Cayleen was glad for the space to think—but devastated by the result. She heard the voice for the first time in a long time: *This is wrong!* Cayleen knew before Hunter returned that she needed to move out, but she waited until he came home to move her things and talk with him.

"I thought about you every day I was gone," Hunter says.

"Why didn't you call?" Cayleen asks.

"Service was spotty," Hunter says.

"You only texted once in the week you were gone. If service was spotty, you could have sent a text or an email." Cayleen has been undergoing a major emotional overhaul, and Hunter barely made contact. Cayleen sees it as a sign.

"I didn't have service, and now you're going to blame you moving out on me not texting you?" Hunter's anger threatens to explode with every word. "You know, Cay, you always do this. You always leave me. Did you ever even love me?"

Cayleen says, "Of course I love you. It's just not right between us, Hunter."

"Explain that, Cay! Explain how it's not right!"

Shaking her head, Cayleen says, "I can't explain it, Hunter. It's a feeling. I wish I could explain it." If she could explain it, maybe she could reason it away. "I'm sorry. I'll be back tomorrow when you're at work to get my stuff."

"Where are you going? What are you going to do?"

"I'm moving in with my dad for a while until my condo opens up."

"Well, I guess this is goodbye then." Hunter walks to the other room.

"Goodbye," Cayleen whispers and walks out the front door.

Do not let my hope be crushed.
—Psalm 119:116

The gym is quiet as Cayleen stumbles through the door. At five o'clock in the morning, the gym has a lot of people, but no one says much. Cayleen looks for Malea on the cardio equipment. They have remained faithful to their morning workouts through several years of drama in each of their lives. The morning workout is their connection to each other and serves as a method of venting small frustrations that need go no further.

Malea took a career opportunity outside of Jamison Homes, which Cayleen completely understands. Cayleen sees a crash landing on the horizon for Jamison Homes and has encouraged other employees to pursue other career opportunities. Malea and other employees have tried to convince Cayleen to pursue another opportunity with more stability, but Cayleen refuses to leave. Cayleen has years of sweat, tears, growth, and opportunity with Jamison Homes; she cannot leave it all to Luke to deal with on his own. Her empathy toward her dad overshadows her own best interests. Little does she know it is a misuse of the gift of burden bearing God has given her.

"Hey." Cayleen finds Malea on an elliptical and takes the treadmill beside her. Cayleen jabs the controls on the machine and starts walking.

"Hey." Malea is breathy but not yet breathless. "Another rough night?" Malea smiles.

The past months have taken a toll on Cayleen. After separating from Hunter, Cayleen did not take the self-reflecting approach she took with Noah. Rather than taking time alone to analyze her feelings, wine was her friend.

"Not bad." Cayleen has had worse evenings and more difficult times getting to the gym for their workouts. Today is on par.

"What's going on at Jamison?"

Cayleen knows Malea asks out of genuine concern for Cayleen, nothing more. Malea's new position is in a different industry, and she has no personal gain from gathering information about her past employer.

"Nothing. No investors and no banks will even listen anymore, and creditors keep calling. We have so many liens on all our properties that it's a filing nightmare to keep all the liens organized. We haven't had a closing since I bought the house a few months ago." Cayleen tries to keep a positive outlook in the office, but it saps her energy. With Malea, she can let her guard down and be honest. "Did I tell you I cut my salary in half?"

Malea shakes her head.

"I asked the employees to look at their finances and see if they could take a pay cut and start working part-time or anything else." Cayleen smiles. "I researched bloodletting from Victorian times and included sugary sweets on the conference table when I brought it up." Cayleen attempts to chuckle.

"Did anyone ... take you up on it?" Malea has been working out longer than Cayleen and is showing more signs of breathlessness.

"Surprisingly, most people went to three-quarter time and pay; only two employees need to stay full-time to cover their family expenses. I understand. I just feel fortunate to be able to survive on half my income."

Malea raises her eyebrows. "Yeah, that is nice ... for the company ... not for you!" She takes a minute to catch her breath. "How are things personally? Gavin still in your thoughts?"

Cayleen was able to convince herself that Hunter was not the right match. She found her list of qualities she wanted in a man several months ago with the intent of revising it. Since Gavin meets all her desired qualities, and is a trusted professional friend, Cayleen has fantasized about being with Gavin again. When she talks with Gavin, there is nothing between them romantically on his part. She is so emotionally low, and professionally drained, that she cannot see past their friendship to find someone else to pique her interest.

"Yeah," Cayleen admits. Only one time has Cayleen been in such a low emotional state, fifteen years ago, and she turned to drugs. Cayleen doesn't know whether her sad state is from not being in a romantic relationship or the downward spiral of her professional dreams, but taking time alone does not help her become centered. Rather, the time alone facing her feelings makes her feel even worse.

"Run him out," Malea says breathlessly, smiling and looking at the controls on Cayleen's treadmill.

Cayleen smiles and turns up the speed.

An hour later, Cayleen feels the endorphins of exercise making her spirits rise. While walking up the stairs to her condo, she has a deep pressing on her heart about Hunter, a feeling of love and empathy for him. Her spirits sink in despair. Crying in the shower, she hears the voice: *It's okay. It's okay, Mommy.*

Immediately she stops crying and focuses on the shower wall. *How much did I drink last night? Whatever it was, it was too much. I need to slow down!*

While getting ready for work, Cayleen gets a text message from

Hunter: Mom passed away. Cayleen's promise to Dawnette repeats in her head, and Cayleen's emotions take over. She texts Hunter: "I'm sorry to hear about your mom. I love you."

Hunter replies: "I miss her, and I miss you."

Cayleen can feel his pain through his texts, and she calls him. Within days, Cayleen is organizing the funeral, going with Hunter to meet the pastor, making the video in remembrance, and renting the park venue for the reception Dawnette wanted in celebration rather than sadness. It feels so natural to Cayleen. It has always been what she does: taking care of Hunter. She stays.

After the funeral, the wake is at his house. One of the last people to leave is a good friend of Hunter's, Natalie. Cayleen never trusted Natalie. Once in high school, after a party, Natalie and Hunter shared a bed while Cayleen stayed on the floor. Cayleen figured Hunter fell asleep since he would fall asleep standing up when he was that drunk. In the morning, Cayleen tried to wake Hunter.

Natalie said, "Go home, Cayleen. We'll take care of him. Really, just go home."

Several days earlier, Natalie and Hunter went off alone for hours at a party. Cayleen asked Hunter about it when they returned. Hunter said Natalie had had a bad experience where another guy raped her, and Hunter was just talking with her about it. Natalie needed a friend. It seemed to Cayleen that Natalie had a lot of male friends, but Cayleen never suspected Hunter of cheating on her. After all, Cayleen was smart, beautiful, and friendly. Why would he ever do something so hurtful?

Natalie and Cayleen sit at the dining room table with Hunter, retelling stories and laughing.

When Hunter goes to the bathroom. Natalie turns to Cayleen and says, "Are you staying?"

"I really don't think he should be alone yet," Cayleen says, looking at the house full of flowers. Hunter's family had stayed at his house since Dawnette passed away; after her funeral would be his first completely alone.

"You know, you really hurt him the last time you left, Cayleen. You left him in pieces the rest of us had to pick up." Natalie looks sternly at Cayleen.

Cayleen feels the weight of shame in Natalie's words. Cayleen always leaves, and it's always Cayleen's fault. Cayleen makes a promise on the inside not to leave this time. "I'll stay as long as he'll have me."

Cayleen remembers her promise to Dawnette and is determined her mind will win this battle.

Hunter stumbles out of the bathroom and joins them in the kitchen.

Natalie turns to him and says, "Well, I should go home. I love you, Hunter." She walks around and gives him a hug.

Hunter hugs her. "I'll walk you out."

Hunter and Natalie walk out the front door.

A few minutes later, Hunter comes back inside.

Cayleen is cleaning up the kitchen and looks up at Hunter. "You should get some sleep."

"Are you staying?" Hunter is so emotionally weak that it is neither a question nor a statement. Just words.

"Yes, I'll be here. I have to go to work tomorrow, but I'll stay tonight. I can sleep on the couch or something. I don't want you to be alone tonight."

"You can sleep in the bedroom," Hunter mutters as he walks back toward his bed.

Once done with the dishes, Cayleen walks to the bedroom. Hunter is already in bed, covers cuddled around his head and eyes closed. She lifts the covers and gets into bed. He pulls her close and begins kissing her.

"Hunter, I don't want to have sex right now," Cayleen whispers. They have not slept together since they separated.

"Why?" Hunter asks.

"You're hurting over your mom's passing. I don't want you to confuse that hurt with emotions toward me. I want you to heal from the loss." Cayleen holds his arms, determined not to hurt him more by having a sexual relationship with someone so emotionally drained.

"Whatever." Hunter rolls over with a groan.

The next morning, Cayleen wakes alone in bed.

In the living room, Hunter is wrapped in a blanket and watching TV. Cayleen helps herself to a cup of coffee and sits next to him.

"Are you going to work today?" Cayleen asks.

"Tomorrow," Hunter replies, staring at the TV.

"Okay. Well, I should get home so I can get ready for work." Cayleen thinks about Jamison Homes; it is a funeral that has been going on for months. They only have enough cash flow to get through two more weeks of payroll. Luckily, Cayleen paid rent for their office space in advance; they still have an office to last through the month. Cayleen doesn't know what she is going to do after Jamison closes the doors for the last time. She needs to think about that later. She doesn't have the energy to worry about it yet.

"Okay, see ya." Hunter sips his coffee and stares at the TV, not looking at Cayleen as she leaves.

> Let them no longer fool themselves by trusting in empty
> riches, for emptiness will be their only reward.
> —Job 15:31

Cayleen looks at the small baby in her arms and smiles. Cheyanne is on her second child with Clay; their first is still nursing at two years old. They prefer living a simple life, living off of what they can make themselves and wanting to homeschool their children. Cheyanne teaches parent-child interactive music classes a few times a week while Clay does odd jobs for construction. They sold their house and moved in with Jessica, making a good chunk of money. However, after living with Jessica for a year, Cheyanne has indicated that money is running out.

"How are things with you guys?" Cayleen asks.

"Good," Cheyanne replies. "How's it getting ready to teach?"

Cayleen took up her childhood dream of teaching when Jamison Homes closed their doors. She had immediately been offered a math position teaching eighth grade in a lower-income area of town—the same middle school Jessica taught at when she started. Cayleen wasn't sure she appreciated that she would be teaching like Jessica. Sometime between watching Jessica from a distance in college and working for years with Luke, Cayleen had realized Jessica lied to her when she was growing up. Jessica often twisted the truth in favor of whatever she felt best at the moment. Cayleen did not want to be like her mother.

"Cool. It's exciting. This new math program lets the students explore to find different things, like the Pythagorean theorem. Instead of me telling them what it is and the students working problems like we did in school, they use projects and find the information themselves. And the best part is that, since they're just starting it this year, all the teachers are learning together. There are different in-service days, and we learn how to teach it together."

"Nice. When does school start?"

"Week after next! Thankfully, I have a little more time." Cayleen would be working fervently to get everything set for the students. She couldn't remember being so nervous when she started any of her years of school.

"How are things with Hunter?" Cheyanne asks.

"Hunter is doing okay. We got his stuff submitted to the county regarding Dawnette's estate. He's working, and I think that's a good distraction. I think he's still pretty down; he watches a lot of TV. He gets lost in his thoughts sometimes." Cayleen bites her tongue and thinks, *And he doesn't call me during the day.*

"I'm sure it's hard." Cheyanne's words are cut short as she turns to her oldest, who is getting into trouble.

Don't go back to worshiping worthless idols that cannot
help or rescue you—they are totally useless!
—1 Samuel 12:21

CHAPTER 15

"So, are we ever going to get married—or are we just going to live together forever?" Cayleen's question is an attempt at being light and humorous, but it is strained underneath. She moved in with Hunter in the fall, and they are approaching Valentine's Day. They never talk about anything, including their relationship, and it is finally getting to Cayleen. A lot of things have been getting to Cayleen in the past few weeks. *It's just that time of month for me,* Cayleen thinks. She is irritated that she has to go to Salt Lake in order to spend Valentine's Day with Hunter. There is a hunting expo in Salt Lake, and Cayleen agreed to go just so she could see him on Valentine's Day, even though she has never been hunting and has no plans to go hunting anytime soon.

"Uh. Well, I guess I figure we should get married someday," Hunter says.

After checking in to the hotel, Hunter insists on Cayleen opening his Valentine's Day card. Cayleen hesitates. "Valentine's Day isn't until tomorrow. I could just wait and open it then." Cayleen doesn't mind waiting for gifts and likes the anticipation. Besides, maybe she can sneak away and get him a card so he won't know she forgot to get him one.

"No, I'd like you to open it now," Hunter says. "Here, sit down." Hunter backs Cayleen toward the bed.

She sits. "Okay." Cayleen opens the card, which feels thick. Cayleen's heart sinks with shame for not having something to give

Hunter. She begins reading. On the final page, Hunter has written some words in French. "I can't read what it says in French." Cayleen's voice trails off as she looks up from the card to see Hunter kneeling on one knee in front of her, ring in hand.

"It says: I love you—will you marry me," Hunter asks, nervousness showing in his voice.

Cayleen is shocked. "Yes."

> Tainted wealth has no lasting value, but
> right living can save your life.
> —Proverbs 10:2

Two weeks later, Cayleen is staring at pregnancy stick. Her period has always been like clockwork. During the two-minute wait, she paces in the kitchen. She thinks of the prayer she prayed years ago when healing from her relationship with Noah: "Lord, please make me pregnant next time so I'll know it's right." The prayer seems so silly now.

Cayleen thinks of the Mardi Gras party they had planned for weeks, which happened last weekend. It turned into their engagement party with the way things worked out. It was fun, but Cayleen did drink alcohol. It was not enough to get sick, but she was worried.

Last week, she was starving after work. She stopped at Walmart, and trail mix sounded delicious. She bought a one-pound bag. By the time she was near the house, the bag was nearly empty. She couldn't believe she'd eaten the whole thing.

The timer on Cayleen's phone goes off. "It's been two minutes!"

Hunter meets her in the kitchen, and they look at the stick.

"What does pink equal sign mean?" Hunter peers at the plastic stick, careful not to get too close. He'd also made Cayleen wipe it down with an antibiotic wipe.

"It means we're pregnant," Cayleen says slowly. On the inside, she realizes she already knew it.

"Take another one—just to be sure." Hunter shoves another stick toward Cayleen.

"I don't have to go yet," Cayleen says, grabbing a glass of water and chugging. The past two weeks have been filled with excitement of wedding planning. Cayleen thinks back to their drive home from the hunting expo when they decided on a wedding venue. When Cayleen called the venue, they only had one weekend available for the summer. She immediately booked it and paid the hefty deposit.

"If I am pregnant, that means I'll be six months pregnant for our wedding." Cayleen looks worriedly at Hunter.

Hunter looks back at her. "Do you have to go yet?"

Cayleen jumps up and down a few times. "Oh! Yep, I'll go try." Cayleen grabs the stick and runs to the bathroom.

Several minutes later, Cayleen comes out of the bathroom and walks to the kitchen.

Hunter is watching TV in the living room. From his spot on the couch, he hollers, "Did you wipe it down?"

"Yeah, I'm doing that now." Cayleen doesn't understand how he can be so weird about it. There's a shield, and it's not like the entire thing is wet. She sets her timer for another two minutes. Suddenly she remembers the dress! *Oh, no! I found the perfect dress and now I'm going to be as big as a whale when I get married and won't be able to wear it!* She imagines the dress: strapless with a zipper down the back they were planning to take out and replace with some ribbon laced up across the back. She had tried on an eight, which was a little big. With the ribbon she wanted on the back, the saleswoman had recommended ordering a size six.

"Oh, no!" Cayleen says.

"What's wrong?"

The timer goes off.

"The dress!" Cayleen and Hunter walk toward the stick on the counter and peer down at the second pregnancy test.

"So, if it's pink and not blue, does that mean we're having a girl?" Hunter asks.

"No," Cayleen says softly, looking Hunter in the eyes. "But it definitely means we're pregnant. Should I take the third one just to make sure?"

"I thought that second one was to make sure." Hunter chuckles and turns toward the living room. "No, it'll be all right." Hunter sits on the couch, eyes turned toward the TV.

Several weeks later, Cayleen dials the number for her doctor, remembering her twelve-week checkup is two days away. She holds for the nurse. Cayleen only has seventeen minutes until her students get back from lunch. She thinks about how thankful she is that she can call this doctor. She and Hunter decided to get married so Cayleen and the baby could be on Hunter's insurance, which was much better than the insurance provided by the school. They had driven to a smaller mountain community and signed the paperwork—just the two of them. They still intend to have the full-blown celebration in the summer.

"Hello, Cayleen? How can I help you today?" the nurse asks.

"Yes, hi. I … um … noticed some spotting today. I come in for my twelve-week checkup on Friday. Is spotting normal?"

"Well, that kind of depends. How much was it?"

"Not very much." Cayleen doesn't really know how to gauge.

"How's everything else going?"

Cayleen thinks for a moment. "Things are going well … I think. It's been two weeks since I've had morning sickness, so that's been really nice."

The nurse says, "Why don't you give us a call if the spotting gets worse?"

"Okay." Cayleen ends the call, feeling helpless.

That night, a little after midnight, Cayleen wakes up. *Do I have to go to the bathroom? No, it hurts … oh, that's cramping … oh no!* Tears fill her eyes. She gets up from the bed, gets the large pads from the spare bathroom, and lays down on them in the spare bedroom, knowing what's coming next.

Cayleen thinks of when it happened before. At the age of

nineteen, she had miscarried twins. *It's probably why I so immediately fell into Noah's arms, after realizing how badly I wanted a baby.*

School! Cayleen's thoughts take an entirely different direction. It is now three o'clock, and she needs a sub for tomorrow. Slowly, carefully so as not to be messy, she makes her way to the living room. She emails her core leader for the eighth grade teachers and the principal, explaining she is having a miscarriage and probably will not be in for the next few days. She then completes the online sub request.

While walking back to the spare bedroom, Cayleen thinks back to the recent return of Hunter. Hunter had been on a trip to Alaska for work. He had called once that week, which was nice for Hunter. Hunter was supposed to be gone for ten days, but on his return, rather than telling her, he had gotten a ride from the airport and been quietly waiting in the spare room. He had been in the bed when she got home from school. It startled her so badly her insides jumped, seeing his feet first. When she realized it was Hunter, her anger overshadowed her excitement for him to be home. She couldn't wrap her head around why he would do that—he didn't even get up to greet her. He just let her find him on the bed, fully dressed, seeing his boots first as she started past the door.

Cayleen thinks about going to the master bedroom where Hunter is sleeping. *This nightmare will be here when he wakes up no matter when that is. Might as well let him sleep as long as he can,* she thinks.

Cayleen is quietly sobbing in pain when Hunter finds her in the spare room a little after four.

This is what the Lord says: "Stop at the crossroads and look around. Ask for the old, godly way, and walk in it. Travel its path, and you will find rest for your souls. But you reply, 'No, that's not the road we want!' … Listen, all the earth! I will bring disaster on my people. It is the fruit of their own schemes, because they refuse to listen to me. They have rejected my word."

—Jeremiah 6:16

"I can't believe this day is here," Cayleen says to Cheyanne as she helps Cayleen into her wedding gown. Hunter and Cayleen decided to follow through with the large summer celebration for their friends. "I sure look better in this dress than I thought I would." Cayleen looks at herself in the mirror. The pain of the miscarriage, both physical and emotional, had been intense. Cayleen had come to the conclusion that God had allowed them to experience that miscarriage so they would know they wanted children and appreciate them more.

Cayleen had in no way taken it as a sign from God that she and Hunter should not be together. Three days after Cayleen miscarried, she found Hunter's pornography on the computer. She had not taken that as a sign. Within a week of her miscarriage, Cayleen came home to an irate Hunter who had read her diaries. He had read one portion of when they were broken up and Cayleen had written about Gavin, and Hunter demanded she never write in a diary again and forced her to get them out of their home. Cayleen was too committed to her promise of never leaving Hunter. She didn't see any of it as a sign.

"It's a fifteen-year love story in the making, huh, sis?" Cheyanne says.

Cayleen knows Cheyanne's life with Clay is rocky. They purchased a home, and Clay still does not have a job. Cheyanne took a job as a teacher's aide. Cayleen can sense the independence in Cheyanne—the part of Cheyanne that is like Cayleen, which wants a plan and wants to see financial struggles end. Jessica and Cheyanne envy Cayleen's determination and independence. Cayleen appreciates Cheyanne's attempt at encouragement.

"It is." Cayleen smiles at her sister while Cheyanne ties something on the back of Cayleen's dress. "I can't wait until you see the video! We made a video of all of our pictures—from high school dances all the way to now."

Cheyanne smiles. "I'm excited too. The French theme really came together well." Cheyanne's eyes meet Cayleen's. "You did good, little sister." Cayleen took the French writing Hunter proposed in and made it a theme. She and Hunter didn't have a song, so they picked a French song to dance to and named the tables with French names. The venue was a French-named winery, and she had a French-style wedding cake.

Cayleen stops Cheyanne to embrace. "Thank you."

The door opens, and several of the other bridesmaids come bustling in the room. Hunter wanted to have five groomsmen and Cayleen had asked three of her best friends, Cheyanne, and Hunter's sister, Nichole, to be on her side.

"How are the butterflies?" Cayleen turns to Nichole. Cayleen had ordered butterflies online. The whole family viewed butterflies as a symbol of Dawnette. To honor Dawnette, Cayleen asked Nichole to release them during the ceremony.

"I think they're okay." Nichole looks at Cayleen. "I put them downstairs in a closet. They were kept cool in the pantry at your house, but they're starting to move around in there a bit." She giggles. "Thank you so much for thinking of Mom like that. It's really special."

"Your mom is special too, and I want her honor her ... to have her be a part of things." Cayleen embraces her new sister.

There is a knock at the door, and the photographer pops his head in. "Are you ready for a few candid shots before we start the formal pictures?"

The rest of the day is like a fairy tale for Cayleen: fun, lively, and a blur. Pictures with the wedding party, the ceremony, the reception, the food, dancing, cake, video, hugs, and visiting. Cayleen loves entertaining, and before she knows it, they are retiring to the balcony as the guests who aren't staying at the venue leave. The evening has been filled with friends and drinks, and Cayleen finds herself a pleasant shade of buzzed. Hunter is off with a friend, and she and Malea sit with James, Hunter's best man.

"Cayleen, I always thought you were the devil ... all these years and all the things you've done to Hunter." James takes a drink of his beer. "Now I guess we'll see."

Hunter and several other friends barge onto the balcony before Cayleen has a chance to respond.

Cayleen leaves Hunter with his friends on the balcony while Malea helps her out of her dress. Hunter doesn't wake Cayleen when he comes to bed hours later.

Your wickedness has deprived you of these wonderful blessings. Your sin has robbed you of all these good things.
—Jeremiah 5:25

Cayleen hops out of Hunter's truck and walks behind Hunter toward the group of people gathered in the park. They drove several hours to meet Hunter's dad and stepmom, Karen, for Karen's birthday party.

Cayleen sees Karen and gives her a big hug. "Thank you for inviting us! Happy birthday."

"Well, thank you guys for driving over for it!" Karen is full of smiles and warmth. Her short, athletic frame grabs Cayleen in a hug so quick it makes her ear-length brown hair bob back and forth. Karen is often direct, which Cayleen appreciates. After a few minutes of catching up, which includes who is currently pregnant and who has recently had a baby, Karen asks, "Are you all pregnant yet?"

The question catches Cayleen off guard, but something inside her clicks in truth. "No, not that we know of," Cayleen says.

For the rest of the party, Cayleen is distracted by the question and the unexpected truth inside her. Cayleen thinks about her cycle—and how much she has wanted and prayed to be pregnant. She thinks about the one time that month that Hunter had allowed her to have sex with him. She researches online baby websites and calendars and tries to be as educated as possible about it. *That time was way too early in my cycle to get pregnant.*

The nagging feeling continues during the drive home, and Cayleen tells Hunter about it.

"Do you want to get a test?" Hunter asks.

"I bought a three-pack, and there are two left. I have it at home. We can just take those when we get home." The possibility of being pregnant is exciting, but Cayleen is holding back. It has been four months since she miscarried—maybe her cycle is still adjusting. The feeling on the inside of her laughs at her: *You know you've always been like clockwork. Two days late or two weeks late, you know you're pregnant.*

Once home, Cayleen takes a test. Double pink lines. Pregnant. She has no excitement. She turns to Hunter and says, "They say that first thing in the morning is more accurate. I'll take the second test then."

Hunter grunts. "Whatever you think." He walks back to his station on the couch.

> For you have seen my troubles, and you
> care about the anguish of my soul.
> —Psalm 31:7b

Seven weeks later, Cayleen is at the doctor for her twelve-week appointment. Hunter made the eight-week appointment and heard the heartbeat. He is not at the twelve-week appointment. He says he will be at the sixteen-week appointment when they find out the sex of the baby.

"When am I going to stop worrying about this baby?" Cayleen asks. She had some spotting at eight weeks. She has not allowed herself to get excited about the baby, thinking that she may miscarry again. She doesn't want the heartache again. The last time she was pregnant, Cayleen had come up with names before she miscarried. She somehow knew it was a girl and had a name. Now, she won't allow herself to get excited enough to think of names yet.

The doctor laughs and turns to his female assistant. "Rendi, do you still worry about your kids?"

Rendi chuckles. "Yep—and they're in high school!"

Cayleen smiles, but she is not in good enough spirits to laugh.

"The chances of miscarriage drop dramatically at twelve and twenty-six weeks, right?"

The doctor, with the best bedside manner Cayleen has ever known, says "Yes, the chances of miscarriage drop at twelve weeks. At twenty-six weeks, there is a greater chance of a baby surviving if it is born prematurely due to the development of the baby. There's always a chance something is going to happen, whether the child is in your womb or outside playing."

The entire pregnancy, Cayleen cannot shake the gloominess from fear of losing her baby.

> Let all that I am praise the Lord; may I never
> forget the good things he does for me.
> —Psalm 103:2

"No Hunter this morning?" Jessica asks. Every week, regardless of what is going on in Cayleen's life, she meets Jessica and her grandmother for church and a meal. Hunter would sometimes come with her to eat, but only once had he come to church with her.

"No Hunter, Mom," Cayleen says seething. "He's horribly mad at me."

"What did you do?" Jessica asks.

"I didn't do anything!" Cayleen is emotional, and it's not just because she is pregnant.

"Hunter's a great guy. I really think you should pray about this and let it blow over." Jessica's answer to everything lately is prayer. Cayleen wonders if Jessica listens to what God is saying about the prayer or if Jessica prays to tell everyone else she prays. Cheyanne's marriage had taken a bad turn, and she had moved in with Jessica. After several months of separation, Cheyanne and Clay were seeking counseling from a pastor at a different church. Jessica had apparently experienced some sort of revival, but she was still going to the same Episcopalian church as Cayleen.

Cayleen thinks it is nice that Cheyanne and her family

sometimes join them for breakfast since they get up for church anyway. Cheyanne has not made as firm a commitment for their weekly visits, but they are at breakfast this morning.

Cheyanne turns from her oldest child, who is now eating her breakfast, and Clay has the youngest in his arms. She whispers, "Cayleen, what happened?"

"He went out to the bar with his friends last night. That's fine. I don't want to change someone. I don't want him to not have fun just because he's married to me."

Cheyanne nods and takes a bite of her bagel.

Cayleen says, "He didn't come to bed last night. I went and found him sleeping naked in the spare room—the front spare room farthest from the master bedroom."

"Yeah, so."

"I felt there was a girl in our house. I had a dream last night there was a girl in our house … that Hunter brought home a girl. When I was getting ready this morning, about the time I was done, Hunter stumbles into the master bedroom. I told him I had a dream a girl was here last night, and I kinda laughed at the absurdity of my dream. He told me there was a girl there in our house last night, but that she just had to use the bathroom."

Cheyanne raises her eyebrows. "Yeah, so, why is he mad at you?"

"Use the bathroom? A drunk girl needs to use the bathroom? Who actually uses a bathroom rather than the front yard when they're drunk? When people are drinking, no one cares where they go! Why would a girl be in my house?"

Cheyanne turns to her daughter for help.

Cayleen says, "I asked Hunter very calmly why she didn't go in the yard. He said he didn't know. I asked what happened. He said she used the bathroom and then she left … that their ride was waiting outside for her."

"So, what's the big deal?"

"The big deal is Hunter is mad at me for even asking about it. He's mad at me, like raging, and won't talk to me mad. Why is he mad at me? What gives him the right to be mad? I have every right to be mad at him. Regardless of what happened, even if it is as innocent as he says, I'm pregnant with his child in the house. He doesn't need to let any woman in without me knowing about it and being okay with it!"

"Yikes." Cheyanne turns her attention to Clay and takes the baby.

"Yeah, yikes. He chooses to go out and get drunk and not call me to pick him up from the bar like I asked him to." Cayleen shakes her head and turns to her breakfast.

If a man is discovered committing adultery, both he and the woman must die. In this way, you will purge Israel of such evil.
—Deuteronomy 22:22

CHAPTER 16

"I've decided I don't want to do this anymore." Cayleen looks at Cheyanne with fear in her eyes, brimming with tears.

"Well, baby sister, I'm sorry, but it's a little late for that." Cheyanne holds on to Cayleen's arm. Cayleen is in the hospital bathroom, trying out the hot tub to relax.

Cayleen has been in labor since two o'clock in the morning. She told Hunter to get ready to go to the hospital at ten. At her doctor's appointment the day before, she had a weird feeling on the inside.

"Heartbeat is strong … things are going well. The little guy hasn't turned back, has he?" The doctor hadn't had anything out of the ordinary. The baby boy had been breech for the majority of Cayleen's pregnancy. During the first false alarm of labor, at thirty-seven weeks when they had been admitted into the hospital, Cayleen had the baby turned. She did not want to have to be cut open with a C-section. If the baby was breech, Cayleen would have to have a C-section.

Cheyanne had been talking her through it—stroking her hair, holding her hand, and speaking encouraging words. Hunter sat on the couch and watched from a distance. Two doctors had stood, one on each side of Cayleen's belly, pushing the baby out of her pelvis and rib cage to turn the baby around. Silent tears of pain had fallen from her eyes, not clouding her intense stare at the ceiling tiles. Each time the doctors pressed down into her sides, the baby came up, pushing against her skin so tightly that they could see him through her skin.

Once the baby was out of her pelvis and rib cage cavity, the two doctors would press on the baby. One doctor would push on one side, and the other would push on the other side in an effort to spin the baby under Cayleen's skin. On the third try, with a disturbing popping sound, he finally went in the right direction. Cayleen had never felt such pain.

"No, thankfully, I haven't felt much of anything. I think he's pretty comfortable!" Cayleen said. "I have this funny feeling that when I come in next week, something will be wrong."

The doctor looks at Cayleen. "Like really bad wrong—that you won't find a heartbeat. Is that a feeling all moms have?" Cayleen attempted a light tone and made an effort toward the end of the pregnancy to be excited for the new baby.

The doctor had looked at her directly in the eyes with a look Cayleen hadn't seen since he gave her Pitocin to miscarry more quickly than naturally over a year before. "If you have any labor pains at all, go to the hospital. Sometimes moms know more about what's going on than doctors do." There was a pause while he turned away from her and then back to make eye contact again. "I'll see you soon."

The next day, today, they came to the hospital. Cheyanne has been with them since noon; Clay has their kids, and since Cayleen had been in the room with Cheyanne when her kids were born, she wants to be there for Cayleen. Cheyanne is the only one Cayleen wants aside from Hunter when the baby comes.

Jessica and Cheyanne are in the bathroom with Cayleen. Hunter is still watching TV in the other room.

"Oh, I hate seeing my baby in pain!" Jessica cries. "I'm going to go home." Cayleen and Cheyanne share a glance that says it's best for all three of them. Jessica looks at Cheyanne. "Let me know if anything happens."

"I will, Mom." Cheyanne rubs Cayleen's back.

"I know I just got in here, but I don't think I want to be in the water anymore," Cayleen looks at Cheyanne apologetically.

Cheyanne helps Cayleen back to the bed. Cayleen has been on

Pitocin all day. Her water broke around seven—three hours ago. The contractions have intensified since then, but Cayleen's body is still not allowing itself to be ready for the baby to come. The doctor increased the Pitocin past the hospital recommendations an hour ago. Since then, the contractions have been nearly unbearable.

At midnight, a nurse comes to check on Cayleen.

"Can you tell me how long this is going to last?" Cayleen breathily asks.

"Sweetie, that's up to you—could be a couple hours or could be a couple days."

Once the nurse walks out, Cheyanne gently touches Cayleen's arm. "You doing okay?"

"I just wish I had a deadline. I can bear this pain, but I just need to know how long I need to do it."

"I'm tellin' ya—epidurals are the way to go! I loved that drug, and I'd do it again if I could." Cheyanne's spirits are encouraging, which is amazing since they've been in that little room for at least twelve hours. "You are not in a competition and don't need to be Super Woman. This is supposed to be an amazing experience that is going to change your life. You may as well be as comfortable as you can. You made it longer than me with my first, and then with my second, I walked in asking for it."

Cayleen smiles, quiet for a few minutes. A contraction hits, and her entire body tenses.

Cheyanne says, "Breathe and relax. Let your body do what it was meant to do. The contractions help your body open up and allow the baby to come out. Let the contraction do what it is supposed to do. Try to relax."

Cayleen looks at Cheyanne and exhales. "I can't relax during that! I think I'll get an epidural."

Five hours later, after twenty-seven hours of labor, Logan Evan Blake comes into the world. The doctor hands Cayleen the baby, putting him on her chest. Cayleen is overjoyed at the emotion, crying tears of joy. At the sound of Cayleen's voice, Logan turns his head. A deep feeling of unconditional love—unlike anything she has ever felt—presses on Cayleen's heart. She knows her life will never be the same. And it is good.

It will be like a woman suffering the pains of labor.
When her child is born, her anguish gives way to joy
because she has brought a new baby into the world.
—John 16:21

"How long are you going to be gone?" Cayleen is holding the three-week-old Logan.

"Three weeks." Hunter is packing his bags. "It's work, babe. I gotta go."

"I know, and I'm grateful for your job. We talked about you trying to work your way into a supervisory position, and I know this is what that takes." Cayleen tries to be empathetic. Having a new baby has been an adjustment. Aside from the multiple feedings at night, which Cayleen does since she is nursing and doesn't want to bother Hunter with being up at night since he works all day, Cayleen didn't realize how much work it is just to stay at home with a baby. It seems to have gotten better, but initially, the baby went through ten or fifteen diapers a day and often a new diaper came with new clothes. Diaper changes, laundry, feedings, baths—it took two weeks for Cayleen to learn how to get the baby ready and out the door. Their first outing aside from doctor's appointments was to church.

One week into Hunter's work trip, Cayleen realizes she has less work with Hunter being gone. She doesn't have to cook dinner for them, and it seems like she is walking on eggshells when he's around. She doesn't want to be a bother or have the baby be a bother to Hunter. Hunter hasn't expressed much interest in Logan; he'll hold the baby for a while, but if Logan starts to cry, he hands the baby back, turning to the TV.

Since leaving on his trip, Hunter went as long as three days without contacting Cayleen. Cayleen texts pictures daily and calls, but when it went three days without him getting back with her, she told him she was hurt. Hunter said he lost track of time and just didn't get back with her. He said he didn't forget about them, but Cayleen couldn't be sure. She knows his work allows him to stay in a hotel every night. *He's not even staying on the jobsite.* With the new baby, Cayleen doesn't have much time to wonder why he doesn't call or text daily.

Several weeks later, Nichole comes to visit her first nephew. "Cayleen, you and Hunter made one fine baby here! He's so cute! I love him so much," Nichole says while playing with Logan on the couch. "How are you adjusting to life as a mama?"

Cayleen smiles at Logan. "It's nothing like I was expecting. Everyone told me it was life changing, but I had no idea."

"And how are things with my brother? Did you guys get everything worked out?"

"I've not been called back to teach next year, so it looks like I'll be staying home with Logan for now. That will be nice, tight financially, but nice not to have to give him up for day care right away."

"I loved that I got to stay home with my boys. Then when they went to school, I just started being the teacher at preschool." Nichole plays with the baby again and then turns back to Cayleen. "But that's not what I was talking about. Did you guys, you know, get things worked out between you and Hunter now that the baby's here? You're past your time that you can't have sex, right? You guys get everything figured out?" Nichole smiles mischievously, her blue eyes twinkling. Her honey brown hair falls in a teasing way.

Cayleen shifts uncomfortably on the couch. "Well, not really."

"You haven't yet?" Nichole asks.

"No." Cayleen looks at the couch cushion below her.

"How long has it been?"

"Ten weeks."

"Ya'll need to get that figured out. And now!" Nichole giggles, her acquired Texas accent showing itself. "Things aren't going to get any easier. Babies grow up and start walking around in the middle of the night." She flashes another mischievous grin.

Cayleen smiles softly and nods. She thinks of the times she's initiated and Hunter has turned her down. She thinks about how few times he's ever initiated with her in their married life. "Hunter hasn't really been up for it that much." Cayleen confides a portion of what she's thinking to Nichole.

"He probably just didn't want to because you were pregnant, and now he's scared he'll hurt you. Maybe seeing that whole birthing experience was a little much for him." Nichole giggles again. "You gotta show him your stuff is still the same. 'Cause it is, ya know. If you wait too long, you both will be nervous. Just do it!"

After Nichole's encouragement, Cayleen gains courage to initiate with Hunter … again. Cayleen wishes Hunter would initiate. Without him making the first moves, Cayleen feels she is not wanted, not desirable.

Cayleen continues confiding in Jessica and Cheyanne during a weekly Bible study. Not wanting to disclose all her marital problems and still wanting to honor her husband, Cayleen is vague with details. "It doesn't seem like anything I do matters—no matter how hard I try. Hunter gets home from work, sits on the couch, and opens the computer. He doesn't talk about things. When I ask about his day, he snaps at me. I take the baby in the kitchen so we don't bother him and make dinner. When dinner's ready, he may or may not eat at the table with Logan and me, and then he goes back to his spot and opens his computer. I clean up from dinner, play with the baby for a few minutes, do a bath, and put Logan down. Hunter doesn't play with the baby or interact with us."

Cheyanne looks over toward Cayleen with sympathy. She and Clay had recently reunited and Cheyanne had become pregnant within two months. Cayleen wasn't exactly sure what had changed in their relationship except that they went to church now. Clay had called her once to apologize for the hateful words he has spoken against Cayleen's Christianity while they lived with Cayleen, which

Cayleen had accepted. At a birthday party several weeks after his apology, Cayleen overheard him saying how her grandmother had paid his tax debt in the tens of thousands of dollars—and he wouldn't have to repay her.

Cheyanne says, "Well, sister, sometimes you just gotta love 'em through it. Maybe he's depressed or struggling with something at work."

Love him through it? He's turned me down for sex more in the past six months than he has sex with me. He forgets about me when he's on work trips and might text me once in a weekend. I feel unwanted.

"Remember you made the decision to get married, Cay," Jessica says. "Marriage is work. Have you read *The 5 Love Languages?* Maybe you should try that."

After thinking about it, and praying about it, Cayleen reads the book. She decides to do all five languages at least once a week for six weeks. Though frustrated after seeing no results, Cayleen trudges on after the six weeks are over, not knowing what to do.

Lisa calls.

"Hey there! How are you all doing?"

"We're good. How's Logan doing?" Lisa's bubbly voice is contagious.

"Logan's good. How are the kids?" Cayleen enjoys adult conversation. She's so socially deprived that she's taught Logan how to use sign language so she has some interaction during the day.

"We're all doing well," Lisa says. "Hey, is everything okay with you and Hunter?"

"About the same as normal, why?"

"James and Hunter went to lunch yesterday, and Hunter told James he doesn't feel like you love him anymore."

Cayleen thinks back to yesterday. "How is that? Hunter didn't have his work truck, and Ryan came to pick him up. Logan and I walked him out, blowing kisses as they drove away. How can he not be feeling loved?"

"I'm not sure …"

"Lisa, have you ever read *The 5 Love Languages*?"

"No."

"Well there's this book, and it says we all feel love different ways. There's five ways people feel love. I've done a little experiment over the past few months. I've done the five love languages at least once a week—leaving notes in his lunches I pack, blowing kisses goodbye, buying him small gifts at the store. Nothing has changed, Lisa. I don't know what to do!"

Lisa is silent.

"You know what happened last week? He brought home a credit card bill and told me we needed to pay it. It's $1,200! He told me they didn't send a statement of what he spent it on. I asked him to look it up online, and he said he couldn't."

"What!" Lisa says. "What are you gonna do?"

"By the grace of God, a friend I used to work with at Jamison Homes called and said she's taking maternity leave from her family's business and would like me to fill in." Cayleen had been praying and watching Joel Osteen and doing Bible studies. She was trying as hard as she could to do what her family said and love Hunter through it. She was not able to make a daily prayer time with her Bible, but she tried for something daily.

"Oh, that's nice! What will you do with Logan?"

"Luckily, they have a childcare there at work."

"Don't tell Hunter I told you about this.".

"I won't." Cayleen wasn't sure how she would resolve this without disclosing the source, but she knew she would find a way. "I looked online about the lack of sex thing, and it says he's cheating on me."

"No way is Hunter cheating on you. He loves you—you're the only one for him." There was a large crash on Lisa's end of the phone. "Oh, no. The kids just broke something. I gotta go. See ya."

"Bye." Cayleen hangs up the phone and looks at the ceiling. "I need your help now," she says out loud to God.

Several hours later, Cayleen put Logan down, sits on the couch, and turns to Hunter. "We need to talk."

Hunter looks uncomfortable. "Okay."

"You know that book I've been reading? *The 5 Love Languages?* I'm not sure if you've noticed, but I've been doing the five love languages on you for two months. Notes in your lunch, small things from the store, cleaning up after you, sitting next to you on the couch, trying to tell you how proud I am you provide for us as a family."

"You have?" Hunter says.

"Yes. It's frustrating that you haven't noticed. And you haven't initiated sex since I've been doing these things. Are you not attracted to me?"

"No! You're incredibly hot, Cayleen. I don't know. I just don't want to initiate sex with you."

"It seems like we don't really have anything in common. We don't like any of the same things."

"Yeah, I guess I see your point," Hunter says.

Then silence.

"So where does that leave us?" Cayleen says.

More silence.

"Well, I guess I don't know." Hunter shrugs.

Silence.

Cayleen sighs. "Good talk, then, good talk." She stands and goes to bed. Alone.

> During these persecutions, little help will arrive
> and many who join them will not be sincere.
> —Daniel 11:34

CHAPTER 17

"Daddy's home!" Cayleen carries Logan toward the door to wave hello to Hunter.

Hunter unloads his keys and gives a small, tired smile to Cayleen and Logan. Silently, he turns to items on the table.

Cayleen carries Logan back to the kitchen and continues making dinner. Logan is content on the floor with a few Tupperware pieces he's using for toys.

Hunter enters the kitchen, something Cayleen is not used to, and she smiles. "Burritos sound okay?"

Hunter grunts in what Cayleen believes to be support. "I put my name in the hat today for a trip to Africa."

Cayleen is startled. "With the new position you just took, I thought you would be home more …"

Only weeks before, Hunter had taken a promotion to work out of the office, making similar pay. Cayleen had been looking forward to less time alone and more of them being able to work on their relationship. An uneasy feeling stirs inside her.

"Yeah, that's the plan. But I have to earn it with this trip. It's twenty-eight days, and then I'd not have to go out of town like this again. Just a weekend trip here and there to see my crews in the region."

Cayleen pinpoints the feeling. The impression is something terrible is going to happen. With the uneasy feeling, she feels a calming peace even more deeply that everything will work out in its own way. She feels like Logan might not be raised with his father. This second feeling, without words to match the emotion, make her unsure if Hunter will make it back. At the same time, the calming peace makes her doubt the impressions inside her. "I don't feel right about the trip."

"Babe, I gotta go. It's part of my job now. It's not certain yet, but I wanted you to know it's a possibility."

Cayleen doesn't know what to say. It's the trip or his job—and their family can't survive without his job. Cayleen stays home with Logan for the most part, aside from a few group fitness classes she teaches every week at the gym, which won't pay the bills. The maternity leave she is filling in for starts in a few weeks, but it is only for six weeks.

Cayleen turns back to dinner. "When will you know if you're the one going?"

"Tomorrow."

Cayleen gets the news over the phone. Within days, Hunter is scheduled to leave for nearly a month. In the whirlwind of getting a phone that will work overseas and packing and caring for the baby, Cayleen stifles the small voice telling her bad news is about to surface with Hunter's trip.

Hunter arrives in Africa, and they are able to Skype with some success for the night he's at the hotel. Hunter describes the accommodations as very poor. The streets have no pavement; he's seen nothing like it. Cayleen can sense his fear for his security even through the virtual connection.

A day after Hunter departs for the small island his oil and gas company is working on, he emails saying he has no cell service or strong enough internet to Skype. Cayleen takes pictures of Logan throughout the day. Every night, she reduces the size of the picture to small enough to get through with minimal internet. She emails about their days with about ten pictures of what they have done. The time difference is ten or twelve hours, and she looks forward to his short two-to-three-sentence email in the mornings. Once Cayleen receives an email, she fires out an email to the family that are all praying for him, giving the prayerful intercessors the positive spin on Hunter's circumstances. Several times during Hunter's stay in Africa, she doesn't hear from him for several days. Three times, it goes more than two days without hearing from Hunter. She emails Hunter after two days and says she will contact his boss if one more day goes by to see if Hunter is okay. He always seems to email back in time.

Cayleen is driving to the gym to teach a group exercise class when her phone rings. The caller ID comes up with unrecognizable numbers. She answers, "This is Cayleen."

"Babe. Oh, babe. I just needed to hear your voice." Hunter is on the other end, sounding frazzled.

"Hunter! It's good to hear your voice," Cayleen exclaims. It's been weeks since they've talked. His journey is set to end in two days, and he should be home within the week.

"I'm okay. I'm not sure what you've heard yet about what's happened on the island, but I'm okay. I'm calling from the satellite phone, so I can't talk long …"

"Oh … okay … What happened?" Cayleen is having a difficult time processing what he's saying.

Hunter chokes up. "Oh, Cay, this kid … I'm not sure if he lost his leg. I'm not sure if he made it. But I'm okay and wanted you to know. I'm going to try to get off this island. I've got to go now. They don't know I'm using the satellite phone. I love you."

"I love you too," Cayleen says before Hunter ends the call.

The next day, Cayleen gets a Skype call from Hunter. Between the bad connection and the baby, Cayleen learns that a native had gotten his foot caught in a piece of equipment. Hunter had been the first responder. They were not able to get his foot out of the equipment, and the man was pulled in, losing his leg. In that culture, having a mutilation or handicap is worse than being dead, and the man would not let the onsite doctor amputate his leg. Instead, Hunter and many others took eight hours to tear apart the machine that held his leg. Finally, just before Hunter called

Cayleen, the man had been loaded into the plane, his leg still in the piece of equipment. Hunter thinks the man was dead by the time he was loaded on the plane.

Two days later, Cayleen and Logan greet Hunter at the airport with a handmade sign. Cayleen had gone throughout the house pasting signs of welcome to Hunter. Hunter is tired and wants to sleep. Before he goes to sleep off the jet lag, Cayleen beckons him to the kitchen to get a bite to eat.

"I ran into a guy at the airport."

"Yeah?" Cayleen looks up from her preparations.

"He said things like this happen and can ruin a guy." Hunter sounds like he agrees with the stranger.

"What?" Cayleen's asks.

"This guy is from Florida. He said he had a similar experience seeing a guy die on the job. He said it ruined his life. His wife and he divorced, and he went in a different direction in his career because he couldn't handle doing the same thing anymore." Hunter shook his head and began to slowly eat the food Cayleen had set in front of him.

"Well, don't let that happen!" Cayleen exclaims. "I told you that your HR department called. They said you could file for medical leave if you need to, but I told them you'd probably want to go back to work. You should meet with their doctor though. Just to talk about things."

"Yeah, that's what the guy from Florida said. Talk to somebody about it so it doesn't ruin your life."

With the help of a stranger from Florida, Cayleen successfully convinces Hunter to see a counselor. Upon his return, he is agitated.

"That guy's not going to do anything for me. It's exactly as I told you in our Skype call while I was in Africa. Nothing more. A guy's dead, and I couldn't help him. There's nothing to talk about. Nothing to do."

Share each other's burdens,
and in this way obey the law of Christ.
—Galatians 6:2

"How's the new job going?" Cheyanne asks at Sunday breakfast.

"Good!" Cayleen is torn between the desire to make money and stay at home with Logan and straddles feelings of not being good enough on a daily basis. When trying to put in extra effort at work, Cayleen feels like she's not a good enough mother. When trying to be a good mother, she feels like she is not performing well enough at work.

Cheyanne has made the decision to stay at home full-time and home-school their children, a decision Jessica publicly and enthusiastically supports. Their opinions are so strong toward mothers staying at home with their children.

Cayleen adds, "They've hired me permanently full-time."

"Oh ... what are you going to do with Logan?"

"We met with the woman from your church who stays at home home-schooling her two high school-aged children and needs a bit of extra money. Thank you for the suggestion! Logan will go with their family."

"Oh, good. I'm glad that's working out for ya!" Cheyanne says.

"Things aren't really improving with Hunter," Cayleen whispers. Hunter had not come to breakfast.

"Well, I'm prayin' for ya, sister." Cheyanne pats her leg and turns to one of her children.

Cayleen attends to Logan so the words don't pass her lips. *Yeah, I'm praying, listening to Joel Osteen, reading the Bible, and nothing's happening! I can't handle the silence. The nothing. No interaction. Something has to give.*

Cheyanne turns back to Cayleen. "He's not still weird from the bad experience he had in Africa, is he?"

"It's been three months ... I don't know. He acts the same way he did before he left. Logan and I are lucky to get a phone call when he's traveling in his region for work over the weekend. He's silent all the time. He doesn't play with Logan; he just sits there in his chair with the computer in his lap and the TV on. I make dinner, and he eats in the kitchen or living room. He hardly ever sits and eats at the table with Logan and me."

That night, Cayleen puts the baby down and approaches Hunter. "Do you feel it?"

"What?" Hunter looks up from his computer.

"The silence. You can almost slice it with a knife; it's like the air is thick," Cayleen says. The silence makes her shoulders feel heavy. She feels apprehensive when Hunter comes home from work, not knowing what mood he'll be in or whether he'll talk with her. She feels like, if she opens her mouth and says anything, he will yell at her or stalk off and give her the silent treatment like he has done in the bedroom for years.

Hunter continues his blank stare. The darkness in his eyes doesn't tell Cayleen if he is registering what she's saying or if he will jump up and stalk out, raging mad.

Cayleen is unable to walk on eggshells any longer. "We need to do something. We have nothing in common—we agreed about that. We should go to counseling."

"Okay," Hunter says. "I can't miss work, so you'll have to make the appointment for a night or weekend."

"And arrange day care for Logan?" Cayleen says. "Why don't you make it? I do everything around here—you can make a counseling appointment. Then I have a better chance of you going." Cayleen continues folding laundry.

"Fine." Hunter opens the computer and is silent.

Keep on loving each other as brothers and sisters.
—Hebrews 13:1

CHAPTER 18

Two weeks later, they are driving home in Hunter's truck. Cayleen had asked Jessica to watch Logan while they attended the counseling appointment Hunter had made. Hunter found a counselor who worked on a Saturday, but he didn't take insurance. It ended up being double the cost of what insurance would have charged. On their tight budget, it was not a pleasant surprise.

Cayleen had mentioned that she thought Hunter might be suffering from depression.

The counselor immediately explained that he didn't deal with depression.

They drive in silence for ten minutes.

Cayleen says, "Well, I think we could probably agree that he was a really bad counselor, right?"

Hunter nods. "Yep."

"Where should we go from here?"

"I don't know. What do you think?" Hunter says.

Cayleen says, "I don't want to fake it and sleep in the same room tonight. I'll sleep in the guest bedroom. I think we should talk about having some space between us so we can figure things out."

"Space? What does that mean?"

"I don't know. I just feel confined when we're together. It's like we can't be ourselves. I think we need to be ourselves and then try to see what we have together."

Cayleen sleeps in the spare room since its closer to Logan's room—and since it is her unspoken responsibility to care for their son. The next morning, Cayleen wakes with the baby and makes coffee like usual.

Hunter showers in the bathroom adjoining the master bedroom. He comes out and gets a cup of coffee, sitting silently at the table. "I think we need to talk. Let me know when you want to talk."

"Now." Cayleen grabs her coffee and gets up from where she has been sitting on the floor with Logan. She sits directly across from Hunter at the dining room table.

"I think you should move out," Hunter says. "You can handle it. You have family you could go to, and you have rental properties. You could kick out a tenant."

Cayleen is shaking. The chandelier above Hunter's head seems like it is growing.

"Logan can stay, but you need to go. You can't sleep here anymore," Hunter continues.

Cayleen says, "So what does that look like? I stay with my mom, who lives fifteen minutes away, and need to be here to bathe him and put him to bed and then be here in time to wake up with him?"

"Yeah, that will work," Hunter replies.

The chandelier is now swinging rhythmically.

"Logan will go with me." Cayleen feels the power growing in her. The mama bear is coming out.

"Okay." Hunter says. "You will need to remove yourself from my bank accounts."

Shock paralyzes Cayleen. The entire world is now moving for her—even though she still sits in the chair across from Hunter at their dining room table. She looks at her coffee cup and feels the imminent change that is occurring. She wonders if Hunter feels the weight of the words and actions he's forcing into place. She wonders if he realizes it. Permanent change. "Is this a temporary move until we work things out—or is this permanent? Because with me removing myself from the bank accounts feels permanent."

"It's just temporary, Cay," Hunter replies. "Like we talked about last night. A couple weeks until we have some space."

"Okay, well, let me figure out a few things." Cayleen gets up from her chair, careful to avoid the wildly swinging chandelier Hunter still hasn't noticed. Looking at her son playing on the floor, Cayleen's heart begins to break. A realization throbs through her body—things will never be the same.

One large suitcase and eight hours later, Cayleen returns to pick up Logan. It is the longest Hunter has ever watched Logan alone. Cayleen's heart aches to see him again and hold him in her arms. Jessica was amenable to Cayleen and Logan coming to stay with her temporarily. Cayleen took hours to clean the bedroom, living room, and kitchen spaces, and Cheyanne and Jessica told Cayleen some of the details she should be thinking about.

Hunter needs to be in Logan's life. If that is the case, they should have an agreed-upon time that Logan goes with Hunter. The rest of the advice they had was a blur to Cayleen.

Sitting on the floor and playing with Logan, Cayleen says, "Mom and Cheyanne mentioned we should agree on set times for Logan to be with each of us."

Hunter grunts from his spot on the couch.

"What about one weekend night with you? You wouldn't have to worry about day care or anything."

"Okay. You still want to take him to church with you?"

"Yes, that is important to me."

"Okay. I'll take him Friday nights and drop him off to you on Saturday."

"Okay." Cayleen gathers Logan, and shaking on the inside from the unknown future ahead of her, leaves the home she had tried so hard to make their own.

Suppose a man marries a woman but she does not please him. Having discovered something wrong with her, he writes a document of divorce, hands it to her,

and sends her away from his house. When she leaves
his house, she is free to marry another man.
—Deuteronomy 24:1–2

The first Saturday, Cayleen picks up Logan from Hunter. She was not able to remove herself from the bank accounts; each of them had to open new accounts. Going to the bank takes her toward Hunter's house. Cayleen offers to pick up their son.

Cayleen realized the day before why Hunter wanted her off of the bank accounts. He had received a bonus to the tune of nearly ten thousand dollars. He hadn't told her about it before their separation. Cayleen had looked at the accounts and told him the money had been deposited. He acted surprised.

On Saturday morning at seven, Hunter had texted to ask when she was coming to pick up Logan. Hunter had kept Logan from after work Friday until ten on Saturday morning when Cayleen finished at the bank.

The second Saturday morning of their separation, Hunter drives Logan to Jessica's house and asks to talk privately with Cayleen. Logan and Hunter and Cayleen climb into Hunter's truck to talk.

"We're not talking. We're not working through things here," Cayleen repeats the same words she's said many times before.

"Well, I think I should tell you, Cay, that I have been withholding sex from you."

Cayleen says, "Why would you do that? Were you mad at me?"

Hunter says, "Yeah! Do you remember that party we had at our house when you didn't kiss me in front of your friends?"

"Uh, no, Hunter. I don't remember that." *I honestly can't remember when we even had friends over.*

"We had a bunch of our friends over for a party—a themed party," Hunter says. "I tried to kiss you in the kitchen, and you pushed me away."

"Our engagement party? No, I don't remember you trying to kiss me. I doubt I even knew you were trying to kiss me. I was drinking that night, Hunter. Do you think that's okay? You withheld sex from me from before we were married and married me anyway? You started our marriage off with a grudge! You have to tell me if you're mad at me—or I will never know! This isn't going to work if you're not telling me things."

"I'm telling you now!"

Cayleen opens the truck door. "Years later? Whatever. I'm going inside."

Hunter is silent as Cayleen jumps out and closes the door. He drives away as Cayleen approaches the house, flooded with emotion. She was right. He had been mad at her for their entire marriage. He had been punishing her. She thought he had possibly married her to get back at her for breaking up with him in the past. Since Cayleen had made Hunter miserable by breaking up with him, Hunter somehow felt he should make Cayleen pay by making her miserable in their marriage. Cayleen had not imagined he had truly been withholding intimacy from her on purpose.

Once inside, Cayleen sits on the couch next to Jessica as Logan plays on the floor. "Hunter said he's been withholding sex from me our entire marriage. He was mad at me for something I did at our engagement party." Cayleen is numb.

Jessica says, "Cayleen, you made a commitment in the eyes of God. There's no going back on that. You can't blame Hunter for this. You need to be a family—all living in one house. You need to work this out and just keep your mouth shut." Jessica gets up and leaves the room.

With a smile on her face for Logan's sake, she scoops up Logan and places him on her lap. Her heart aches when he is not with her. She misses him so much. Now that she has him in her arms, it helps the ache, but the hurt and sorrow about not being in their own home mix with confusion about her marriage. As Logan taps the toys in his hands, tears cascade down Cayleen's cheeks.

But for those who are married, I have a command that comes
not from me, but from the Lord. A wife must not leave her
husband. But if she does leave him, let her remain single or else
be reconciled to him. And the husband must not leave his wife.
—1 Corinthians 7:10–11

"Do you need help with anything?" Jessica asks.

"I've got it. Thank you," Cayleen calls over her shoulder, arms
full of their stuff as she walks toward her small nine-year-old car.
It has been three weeks since moving in with Jessica. Cayleen is
very familiar with how little time she can spend in the same space
as Jessica and wastes no time. She researched apartments where she
and Logan could live and even suggested to Hunter that Logan stay
at their family home so Hunter and Cayleen can have another place
to stay when they're not with Logan. Hunter didn't go for that; he
was not leaving his house. Luckily, the lease on Cayleen's furnished
two-bedroom condo came up for renewal, and the tenants agreed
to move out.

With Logan at Hunter's house for the night, Cayleen plans
to have the condo fully ready to live in by tomorrow. She finishes
cleaning the bathroom and bedroom she and Logan have been
staying in. "Okay, well, I think that's it. See you on Sunday at
breakfast!" Cayleen calls from the hallway.

Jessica is in tears and meets her at the door. "Can I give you
a hug?" Jessica grips her and holds her firmly. "I just can't believe
this is happening. You know you should be moving back to be with
your husband." Jessica looks at Cayleen. "You're breaking up your
family! You're just like your dad. You've always been like him. Now
you're doing to your family what he did to me." Jessica stomps away,
shaking her head, and yells, "Goodbye."

Cayleen takes a deep breath and walks out the door. Sunshine
meets her on the chilly March morning. *Lord, give me the strength.
You know I would not have left my marriage if Hunter had not kicked*

me out of the house. You were in this. I feel it. Please, God, show me the way.

I can do everything through Christ, who gives me strength.
—Philippians 4:13

CHAPTER 19

On Sunday, Cayleen and Logan meet Jessica and Jessica's mother at the breakfast spot. They go to the early church service at the Episcopal church. Logan is the only child there and goes to the nursery to play.

It is unsettling to Cayleen that Logan is the only child at their church service. *I really want him to be raised with friends in the church, to help him make Godly decisions when he asks others rather than asking what I think.* During the week, she researched churches with larger children's ministries. She feels like trying two of the big churches in town and getting their service information. She has a strong feeling inside that there has to be more.

After the service, Jessica goes to the nursery with Cayleen to pick up Logan. They rejoin Cayleen's grandmother at a table.

Cayleen's grandmother is talking with another woman. As Cayleen takes Logan to get a snack from the assortment of treats in the buffet line, Jessica says, "Oh, yes, Cayleen is amazing working full-time. She's doing so well with Logan. It's a real treat that I get to watch him every Friday."

Cayleen groans on the inside. Jessica tears her apart in private, but when they're in public or around family, Jessica sings Cayleen's praises. Cayleen's come to the conclusion that Jessica truly hates Cayleen—but the rest of the world loves her—and Jessica doesn't want to look bad.

Jessica looks over at Cayleen and Logan when they arrive. "What are you doing for the rest of the day?"

Cayleen gets Logan's snack ready. "We're going to go to Calvary."

Jessica says, "Two church services in one day? What are you trying to do there?"

Cayleen says, "I want Logan to have consistency of coming here, but I'm looking for a church with more of a children's ministry. I want Logan to have some friends from church. And did you see, last week, there were three kids in regular church—and they didn't even put on a children's church?"

Jessica nods. "That's just like me when you girls were little. That's why we went to Monument rather than here when you were growing up."

Cayleen thinks back to when she was growing up. She always thought they had gone to Monument because it was within minutes of their house and because Jessica did not want to spend another hour in church each week with her own mother and grandmother in addition to their lunchtime together. Cayleen remembers being in one Christmas pageant and one bell-ringing festival, but nothing more from her time at Monument ... except for walking in late to nearly every church service.

"You know, we went to Calvary a few times when you were growing up," Jessica says. "It was a good church from what I remember. And Peter and Dianne go there. I don't remember why we didn't go there more often."

Cayleen couldn't figure that out either—except that it was even farther from their house than the Episcopal church. "We'll see. I'll keep Logan with me during the service to see if it fits with me. If it does, then we'll try again. If not, I'd like to try Community."

"Huh, I've heard that Community is a bit pretentious. Let us know what you think," Jessica says.

Cayleen has had similar thoughts about both churches. With services in the hundreds or maybe even more, Cayleen is apprehensive about them being pretentious. Cayleen has never been one to do what is popular, yet something is telling her that she needs to change. She needs more Christian friends for a support. The feeling on the inside tells her she needs to go to one of those churches. There are no real words to the feeling or impression she's getting on the inside—just the feeling that she needs to show up and try it.

Less than an hour later, Cayleen finds herself in the second church service of the day. Logan is quietly playing beside her. During the announcements, they make a reference to Community, saying, "We're not like that church." Not being one for comparisons or competition, Cayleen is not yet feeling a connection. The announcements go on to explain how their ministry in Africa is performing. Cayleen focuses on redirecting Logan, allowing her mind to wander. Later, with Logan in her lap, nearing his naptime, the sermon describes Jesus as a hippie complete with long hair and robes. Cayleen winces as the audience laughs. The speaker goes on to joke about our heavenly Father. Cayleen purses her lips, ready to try Community next week.

On the way out of church, Cayleen runs into a friend. He is friendly and takes her around the children's ministry. Cayleen's heart yearns for Logan to have such a ministry—a nursery, then at older ages, making crafts of biblical stories.

A week later, Cayleen and Logan sit in their second service of the day at Community. Cayleen's ears perk up at the announcement about the church's ministry: bringing the twenty thousand children under the age of eighteen in the area to Christ. The sermon is about the valleys of life and how to keep faith and confidence in God when struggling through difficult times. The pastor talks about how God uses the valleys to build character and allow us to show our faith in God. Not one time during the service did Cayleen hear any form of comparison, competition, or call to popularity. She left the church not feeling quite at home—but wanting to come back for more.

The following week, the sermon spoke to her heart again: face your fears by knowing God is with you. She and Logan tour the children's church. Passing security guards around each corner and pleasantly smiling at the families passing by, they approach the two-year-old room. Logan is not yet two, but he will be soon enough. Cayleen is pleased to see a system making sure the person who drops off the child is the one to pick up the child, complete with armband and sign-in papers. She sees *VeggieTales* on the TV in one corner, books in another, and toys throughout the room.

"Do you want to try out this room next week, bubba?" Cayleen bends down to look Logan in the eye.

"Mmm, not yet," Logan replies with a sippy cup in his mouth.

Cayleen smiles, thinking about him dancing to the praise music at the beginning of the service. "Well, you let me know when you are ready to go to your room for church. They do lots of fun things in here. They play with toys, watch *VeggieTales*, and read books. But you can stay with me in my room if you want."

Logan nods and reaches for his mama.

> Direct your children onto the right path, and
> when they are older they will not leave it.
> —Proverbs 22:6

CHAPTER 20

Cayleen walks into the counselor's office.

"Go ahead and have a seat," the counselor says while his back is to Cayleen. He is walking toward the large desk and picture window at the other side of the room.

"Uh, where?" Cayleen sees two couches and two chairs.

Scott Martin laughs slightly. "It doesn't matter to me—wherever you are most comfortable."

"You usually sit there?" Cayleen points to a chair near the center of the room.

"Yes, but if you're more comfortable …"

Cayleen takes a seat on one of the couches, near the armrest. *That was much more difficult than it needed to be. I guess it has been a while since I've been to counseling.*

"So, tell me why you're here," Scott begins.

"Well, as I said on the phone, my husband and I are separated."

"Okay, tell me about that."

Cayleen tells Scott about the first counselor they saw, Hunter asking her to leave their home, and him taking her off the bank accounts.

"Tell me about where it started. I'm glad you shared with me about the separation itself, but why did you decide to go to this poor counselor? You said the counselor was poor because he wouldn't deal with depression. Why did you think Hunter was suffering from depression?"

"Hunter has always been distant with everyone—even in high school. He just won't talk to me. He won't do things with me. Hunter sits on the couch all day and watches TV in the dark or plays on his computer. In addition to that, he's not been having sex with me. Maybe once a month or less." *I was going to say since we had the baby, but it was before that because it was like pulling teeth to have sex to get pregnant.*

"He would turn you down?" Scott gently asks.

"Yes. And then it got to the point where I wouldn't ask that often. I don't think I'm unattractive." Cayleen thinks about her five-foot-nine, 140-pound frame. She has been teaching at the gym for their entire marriage and keeps herself in good physical condition.

"No, you're not unattractive." Scott is writing. "Was money an issue?" Scott looks at Cayleen.

"Not at first. Then, a little over a year ago, Hunter came home with thousands of dollars in credit card purchases that he didn't show me what they were. He told me I had to figure out how to pay them. All I could figure out he bought was a gun-loading kit, but that was only $500. Then he went to Africa and saw a guy get really badly hurt." Cayleen's eyes meet Scott's. "I'm sure it was a terrible experience!" Cayleen looks at her nails. "It's just that before that happened, he forgot about us."

"You? Being who?"

"Me and Logan."

"What happened that you think he forgot about you?"

"I would take pictures of the baby and me and email them to Hunter every night with a short snip of what we did that day. I would have to threaten to call his boss to get him to email me back … but that wasn't new either. He did that right after the baby was born. He went to North Dakota for work and didn't call or text for three days. He said he was too busy. He said he thought about us but just didn't call or text. Now that I think about it, Hunter did that before the baby was born too. Maybe that's just the way he is."

After a few moments of silence, Scott says, "What do you see my role being in this? How would you like me to help? You seem like a well-adjusted, healthy woman."

"Could you do marriage counseling for us?"

"Yes, I could do that."

She smiles.

He says, "Do you think Hunter will come?"

"I guess that's up to him." Cayleen grabs her purse, stands, and follows Scott to the door. "Scott, you've seen marriages in trouble more than I have. Do you see any hope for our marriage?"

Scott says, "Honestly, Cayleen, asking you to remove yourself from the bank accounts is a pretty big red flag."

"I appreciate your honesty." Cayleen walks out the door.

Give honor to marriage, and remain faithful to one
another in marriage. God will surely judge people who
are immoral and those who commit adultery.
—Hebrews 13:4

That week, during one of their nightly calls to Hunter that Cayleen makes Logan do, Cayleen asks Hunter to talk once Logan is sleeping. Hunter agrees. Once Cayleen is sure Logan is asleep, she calls.

"Hey, Cay. What's up?"

"Hunter, it's been six weeks since Logan and I moved out."

"Yeah, so."

"You said this would be temporary."

"Yeah, so."

"We haven't even talked except once at my mom's house about you and me and—sheesh—Logan and I moved in here three weeks ago. We're not talking. We're not doing anything. We're not getting anywhere. I can't stand this in-between stage."

"What do you want to do?"

"We have to do one thing or another. We either have to try to work on us or be done. I can't stay in limbo, not knowing were our relationship stands."

"What are you saying?" Hunter asks.

"I'm saying either we file for divorce or go to counseling."

"Fine. What counselor do you want to go to?"

"I've been to a guy by the name of Scott Martin. He's a Christian counselor. He does horse therapy in some cases. I've only been to him once, but I think you'll like him. And insurance pays for most of it."

"Okay. When do we go."

"I haven't made an appointment yet. I'll make one and text you the information."

All who do evil hate the light and refuse to go near it for fear their sins will be exposed. But those who do what is right come to the light so others can see that they are doing what God wants.
—John 3:20–21

CHAPTER 21

Six long weeks later, Cayleen sits alone on her couch. After listening to many motivational sermons from Joel Osteen, Cayleen made the financial commitment to purchase materials from their ministry. After receiving the Living Translation of the Bible several weeks ago, Cayleen is—for the first time ever—reading her Bible daily with enthusiasm. Cayleen spends time daily with her Bible and devotional materials. In addition, the founding pastor at Community makes consistent reference to having "coffee with God." Cayleen loves coffee.

Now with her coffee cup half full, having read the daily portion assigned in the study guide she's following to read the Bible within a year, Cayleen's thoughts turn to where she and Hunter have gotten themselves. The Bible says to seek many advisors, and Mom and Cheyanne say I should stay with Hunter. Even Scott asks why I don't move back in with Hunter.

"I don't trust him!" Cayleen says quietly to the empty room, speaking out loud to God. She thinks back to the conversations in the counselor's office. Hunter refuses to come by the apartment, which is on his way home, to have dinner and see Cayleen and Logan during the week. Hunter doesn't call Logan. Cayleen makes the call to him every night to encourage his relationship with Logan.

Cayleen's thoughts shift to the future. She and Hunter have booked a trip to Las Vegas in two days for Cayleen's birthday. When they were booking the trip, Cayleen felt some hesitation, but she had a stronger feeling about trying her hardest to make the relationship work. She feels strongly that this is the last chance for their relationship; this trip will make or break their relationship recovery.

Yesterday, Sunday, Cayleen felt compelled to tell Hunter she wasn't sure what he was expecting out of the trip to Las Vegas. Without trust, Cayleen wasn't sure she could open herself up for intimacy with Hunter. Cayleen had struggled and prayed about whether to talk with Hunter about it. Finally, she decided it would be better to go with similar expectations since they would share a room and a bed. She felt the alternative of having that uncomfortable conversation hundreds of miles away in a hotel room—where they could not get away from each other—would be worse.

The conversation did not go well. Cayleen asked Hunter to go to Jessica's house so they could talk without Logan hearing. Hunter had taken the information that Cayleen didn't trust him and didn't want to share intimacy with him and demanded her wedding ring back.

Hunter explained that, if she didn't want to sleep with him, they were no longer married. He threw his wedding ring at her, stomped to the driveway, and drove away.

Upon walking into Jessica's house, Jessica encouraged Cayleen to repair the relationship. Later in the afternoon, Cayleen texted Hunter. Cayleen was still willing to go to give their relationship a shot. Hunter was too.

"The trip's already paid for," Cayleen mutters and sips her coffee. She lets her thoughts gather and go blank, waiting to hear and let her thoughts be directed by God. A realization starts in her heart and radiates toward her head. *He's broken every promise he's made me in counseling.* The knowledge starts gathering.

She forms a list of the two things she asked for in counseling. Scott had been shocked Cayleen only wanted two things. First, she wanted Hunter to allow her to express herself without overreacting. Hunter overreacted by throwing his ring at her and demanding hers back.

Second, Cayleen asked Hunter to allow her ownership of her own feelings. Often, Hunter gets mad at Cayleen when Cayleen is mad. He doesn't know or ask why Cayleen is mad. He senses

Cayleen's anger and gets mad at Cayleen. Last week, Cayleen had her hair done to get ready for their trip to Las Vegas. Hunter had taken Logan to his house rather than dropping Logan off at her house—as they had agreed ahead of time. Cayleen had to drive half an hour to pick up Logan and drive back to her apartment, another half an hour, putting them home after Logan's bedtime. Cayleen was mad when she arrived at Hunter's house because Hunter had not done as they agreed. Rather than ask for an explanation of why Cayleen was mad, Hunter sensed Cayleen's anger and reciprocated anger.

> In the same way, husbands ought to love their wives
> as they love their own bodies. For a man who loves
> his wife actually shows love for himself.
> —Ephesians 5:28

In her quiet time with God, a realization comes to Cayleen. She opens her eyes. *Hunter is not acting as a Christian husband, putting her first, as when dealing with someone you love. Hunter acts out of hate, forgiveness, and bitterness. He's never forgiven me. Will he ever?*

She feels an impression inside her chest: *This isn't about Hunter forgiving you, Cayleen. It's bigger than that. I'm bigger than that.*

"What do I do now?" Cayleen is worried about going to Las Vegas. *Go. You won't be able to let your marriage go unless you go.* She realizes the impression is right and gives her a feeling of peace and calm. Counseling is over for her and Hunter. Cayleen won't go back. Hunter doesn't keep the promises he makes in counseling, making it a waste of time and money. The alternative is divorce, which is a hard pill for Cayleen to swallow. If she doesn't go to Las Vegas for one last try at a relationship without the stresses of everyday life and Logan, she won't feel like she has given it her all. If their relationship can't survive what's meant to be a fun vacation, then it can't survive. Period. Divorce is only the alternative.

And you will know the truth, and the truth will set you free.
—John 8:32

On the third and final full day in Las Vegas—amid the delicious food, fruity cocktails, fun shows, and dancing—it becomes apparent that she and Hunter are not compatible. Cayleen is enjoying herself. Hunter is enjoying himself. Yet the feeling inside Cayleen is that there's nothing left. *This is over.*

When she is alone in the bathroom, she thinks, *God, I think this relationship is truly over and you want me to move on. If that's true, please give me a confirmation to make me know that is what you want for me.*

Seek His will in all you do,
He will show You which path to take.
—Proverbs 3:6

After getting ready, she and Hunter walk the short distance to the Wynn. Cayleen convinces Hunter to stop at the roulette table, the only table where Cayleen really knows the odds. Cayleen bets the $15 minimum bet on her number, thirteen. A spin of the wheel and a roll of the ball. Rolling. Rolling. Bouncing. Slowing down and dropping in the slot for … thirteen. The payout is $525 on the minimum bet, which Cayleen collects. Cayleen has never won on anything but red or black before—and never anything near $525.

"Thank you, God. I receive that confirmation," Cayleen mutters toward the ceiling.

Dear friends, don't be surprised at the fiery trials you are
going through, as if something strange were happening to you.
Instead, be very glad—for these trials make you partners with
Christ in his suffering, so that you will have the wonderful
joy of seeing his glory when it is revealed to all the world.
—1 Peter 4:12–13

Driving from the airport to pick up Logan from Jessica, Cayleen says, "How do you want to do this?"

"Do what?" Hunter doesn't take his eyes off the road.

Cayleen says, "Well … I don't think things went well. I had fun in Vegas, but it was just confirmation for me that we shouldn't be together."

"What do you mean?" Hunter asks. "I had a great time and thought you were having a great time. We did everything you wanted."

Cayleen says, "I had a good time. I still think we should not be together. Before we left, you broke every promise you made me. Vegas didn't make everything better. It wasn't exactly a fairy-tale trip, was it?"

"No."

"So, would you like me to fill out the paperwork? How do you want to divide things?"

"Wow, Cay, that seems kinda harsh," Hunter says.

"I'm sorry. I just don't see why we beat around the bush anymore. We tried counseling, we tried going to Vegas, we tried everything." Cayleen is tired. Not from their trip, but from the roller coaster they've been on in their relationship—not knowing what direction they're going in, not knowing what to hope for.

"So, are you going to get an attorney now?" Hunter's asks.

Cayleen says, "No, Hunter. I don't want to hire attorneys. Are you going to hire an attorney?"

"No."

"Then I can fill out the paperwork and get it to you." Cayleen's thoughts center around what her boss had told her several weeks before: "If you go to a consult with an attorney, that attorney cannot represent the opposing party." Because of that, Cayleen had organized three consults. She had attended one, had one scheduled for the following week, and had another scheduled for the next week. She would not use the attorney from the consult she had gone to. It didn't fit with Cayleen, and the attorney had represented Luke's most recent ex-wife. Maybe she would cancel the third consult; she knew she wouldn't use that attorney. Catherine Baker had a reputation for being a harsh attorney. Malea said she went to a consult with Catherine when she was facing divorce. Catherine had come across as wanting to destroy Malea's ex-husband financially, as a parent, and in any way possible. Malea didn't want that—she just wanted what was fair. *Could Hunter handle being treated like that? It might break him.*

"So, are you going to take half my retirement?" Hunter asks.

"No. Are you going after my properties or my money from my grandma?" Cayleen thinks about the properties she acquired before their marriage and the $5,000 bank account that her grandma put in her name when she was born. Cayleen had done her best not to ever touch that money. As such, it is significantly more now.

"No."

"The way I see it … you have your two houses, and I have my houses. You have your retirement, and I have my money from my family. You get your truck, and I get my car. The property we have comes due for a $50,000 balloon payment this year. Since I can pay for that, I can keep the property. Does that work for you?"

"Yeah, what about the money in Logan's account?"

Regret washes over Cayleen, causing her to squirm in her seat. She'd kept it secret when they were living together. Anytime Hunter did not have a credit card bill in excess of $,1000 to make her pay, she put money into Logan's bank account. It currently had $6,000, a fact she now regrets telling Hunter after their separation the same day they agreed to book the trip to Las Vegas. "What about the money in Logan's account?"

"I want half," Hunter says. "I'm entitled to half of that."

Cayleen says, "What do you mean? I saved that money. If you had known I was putting it aside, you would have spent it! It's for Logan, not for you or me."

Hunter says, "Fine." He pulls the truck into Jessica's driveway and puts it in park. "Let me know when you get the paperwork ready for me to look at."

Cayleen opens her door. "Okay. I'll try to get to it this week." Since she has an appointment with an attorney this week, it wouldn't hurt to have the attorney review it before giving it to Hunter. Cayleen jumps out and looks at Hunter, but he does not look back. Cayleen grabs her overnight bag and shuts the door.

When Hunter drives away, Cayleen goes inside Jessica's house to see their son.

> He trains my hands for battle; he strengthens
> my arm to draw a bronze bow.
> —Psalm 18:34

CHAPTER 22

Two weeks later, Cayleen waits in Catherine Baker's waiting room. She had met with Abby Wall after returning from Las Vegas. The meeting had gone well; if needed, Cayleen knew she would use Abby. Malea and Luke had used Abby. Abby's stance was that Cayleen and Hunter would have to get along for the rest of their lives—or at least until Logan was eighteen. Abby viewed the divorce as a formality to get things in line and stressed that the work really comes when Hunter and Cayleen are left to raise Logan once the courts are no longer involved.

Abby reviewed the paperwork, and Hunter agreed to sign it a week later. While signing the paperwork at Cayleen's office, Hunter had given her back her wedding ring. He had also asked if they could meet for lunch the following day.

Over lunch, Hunter had gone from one end of the spectrum to the other, making Cayleen uneasy. Hunter began lunch by saying he was suffering from mental illness, citing Cayleen's perception of him having depression. Hunter told Cayleen he needed her to walk through his dark path with him. She was all he had left.

Cayleen held firm and stayed calm throughout lunch. She explained that they would no longer be a family as they had been. She could not walk his journey, but she told him that he did need to get help for Logan to be raised by an emotionally healthy father.

Once Hunter realized Cayleen would not be moving back in

with him, he took it to the opposite extreme. His words echo in Cayleen's mind even a week later: "I will find a new wife and family without you, Cayleen."

Hunter's words stung Cayleen to the core. She knew he wanted a reaction and refused to give him one. Cayleen's answer had been polite, encouraging him and agreeing that he would. Hunter ended up walking out of lunch.

As Cayleen walked to her car from lunch, a very bad feeling formed in her chest. She had called Catherine Baker's office in an effort to make sure Hunter didn't use Ms. Baker. Luckily, the popular attorney had a cancellation and was able to fit her in a week later. Now, she has been sitting in the waiting area for fifteen minutes.

"Ms. Blake?" A short, thin, older woman calls from an office. She has a firm stride and urgency in her steps. Her face shows wrinkles, firm and rigid in her expression. Anger seems to exude from every inch of her body.

Cayleen stands with a warm smile and extends her hand. "Yes."

"Ms. Blake, I won't be able to meet with you today. As sometimes happens with consultation visits, we are not able to thoroughly check our records before you come in." Ms. Baker was speaking very rapidly. Cayleen detects a smugness in her tone that matches what Malea has told her about the woman. "I am representing the opposing party in this case."

Cayleen feels her ears ring, and her chest begins to tighten. The world seems to spin. Keeping her composure, straightening her shoulders, bringing back her outstretched hand, and pushing her lips into a line, Cayleen asks, "And when am I to be notified that Mr. Blake has representation?"

Ms. Baker looks at the receptionist sternly. Cayleen is glad she doesn't have to work for Ms. Baker and feels sorry for the receptionist. A small, soft voice says, "Yesterday."

"It appears the notice went in the mail yesterday." Ms. Baker walks toward the door, holds it open for Cayleen, and smiles. It is the first time Cayleen has seen her smile. The smile on her face is so unnatural that Cayleen wonders if her face is going to crack. "I hope this is the only time we have to see each other."

Cayleen makes no effort to smile. "That's not what I hear." Cayleen hears Ms. Baker wants to spend as much time in court as possible so she can charge fees for every hour of preparation and court time. Cayleen strides toward the elevator, Ms. Baker harshly firing questions at her back. Cayleen is too upset to slow down and listen.

Once outside the elevator, Cayleen dials Jessica's number, needing empathy and support.

"Hunter hired Catherine Baker, Mom!"

"Well, I told both of you, if it were to get that far, that she's the best lawyer in town."

"What?" Cayleen says. "You never told me to hire Ms. Baker."

Jessica says, "I most certainly did! You were on the deck. It was right after your fight with Hunter—before you went to Las Vegas."

Cayleen thinks back. It is all a blur. The fight with Hunter was clear, the harsh words he said to her, but Cayleen couldn't remember Jessica's words. Cayleen feels quiet, defeated. "Oh, I don't remember you telling me that. You know how I found out? I had an appointment with her. She made me wait fifteen minutes in her lobby before she came out and told me she was representing the opposing party. Why would you tell Hunter to hire her?"

Jessica says, "You are just like your father, Cayleen, leaving Hunter the way you did. Now you're involving me in this mess. Why did you even file for divorce, Cayleen? Hunter told me you are the one filing the paperwork. You are why this is all happening! This isn't God's will, Cayleen! God's will is for parents to be together and married. Think about your son!"

Cayleen realizes she must detach from her own emotions in order to deal with her mother's emotions. She blinks a few times. "Okay, Mom. Well, I was calling to try to involve you in my life. You've told me before I don't involve you in my life and that hurts you. I'm trying to let you know what's going on with me. I was really hurt today and thought of calling you—"

"You? You were really hurt! Well! Do you even know who all you're hurting with this divorce? I'm hurt, Cayleen! You're hurting me! And Logan and—"

"Mom, I don't think it's a good idea for us to talk right now," Cayleen says. "I think maybe we should cool down a bit. I'll see you at church on Sunday—if not before."

Jessica hangs up.

> Better to be patient than powerful, better to
> have self-control than to conquer a city.
> —Proverbs 16:32

Several days later, Cayleen sits at her desk in hopeful anticipation of a meeting with her boss. She has been working full days while Logan is with the nanny and then taking her computer home to process payroll in the evenings while Logan sleeps. She stays late the night Hunter has Logan every week and comes in early the following day.

Cayleen has asked her boss for help in the form of an assistant or office staff on several occasions.

"Tell me what I can do for you right now. I have a few minutes."

That response is not what Cayleen is hoping for. She wants an assistant—someone she can teach to do tasks and then pass the tasks off to, freeing up Cayleen's time for other pressing items. Cayleen feels blessed to work for a company that is growing, but she feels like she is not able to process new employees and the pay for the company of more than eighty people.

Cayleen's Outlook reminder pops onto her screen. Time to go to the meeting.

In preparation for the meeting, Cayleen compiled a list of duties she would like to delegate. She wears three hats: payroll, human resources, and most recently the vague task of Canadian administration. The company has received investors from Canada, and Cayleen is the person they chose to begin operations there. Several months ago, when the opportunity was presented to her, Cayleen felt privileged to be chosen. They had also promised to take payroll off her plate, but there was no sign of accomplishing that. Cayleen struggles to keep her head above water. Looking back, Cayleen regrets agreeing to go exempt at the same time and should have kept her hourly pay plus overtime.

Bethany, the woman Cayleen worked with at Jamison Homes, is present. Bethany's mom, Liz, is Cayleen's boss. The other two women in the meeting have been with the company longer than Cayleen.

Liz says, "Cayleen is struggling right now and is not able to accomplish her job duties."

Cayleen's heart sinks, and her mind clings to what Liz said. *I'm not able to accomplish my job duties! I am at this office more hours than anyone in this room. I work nights. I work weekends. And I'm not able to accomplish what's expected of me?* Cayleen loosens her grip on her list of duties she has prepared, dumbfounded, and keeps her mouth shut.

Without skipping a beat, Liz says, "We're growing, but that does not justify hiring another office person. What I need each of you to do is determine what you can do to help Cayleen."

Cayleen thinks of the four new people Liz has hired for office staff. Cayleen's chest heats with embarrassment and anger.

"Cayleen, what tasks did you prepare to get help with?" Liz asks.

"Well, I'm not sure any of you have time to help out with these things." Cayleen looks at her list. "I really need someone to file my human resources paperwork for me." Cayleen looks in Liz's direction and then toward Bethany; both were present months ago when the conversation took place. "I think you said I would no longer have to process payroll if I was also doing Canadian administration, right? Can someone take that?"

Liz sighs and nods. "Oh, yeah. That is right." Liz looks at

Bethany and one of the other women in the room. "Can you guys take that?"

Bethany sighs heavily. "We could probably take that and rotate." She looks toward the other woman. "Being in accounting, you may need to know how to process payroll."

Liz says, "Okay, Cayleen. That's taken care of. What else you got?"

Cayleen feels like she has failed by even asking for help. "I'd like some help with the human resources paperwork and new-hire processing."

"Vanessa's been helping out with that already, right?" Liz says.

Cayleen has been asking Vanessa, the fifth woman in the room, for help in filing. However, Vanessa's workload is too much in addition to the paperwork processing. Vanessa does the filing on her weekends.

"Vanessa has been helping out with that," Cayleen says.

"Okay! Sounds like we got it all worked out then. You got anything else?" Liz asks.

"No. Thank you." Cayleen gets up and walks back to her office—with fifteen minutes less time to do her work for the day.

> Remember, O God, all that I have done for
> these people, and bless me for it.
> —Nehemiah 5:19

CHAPTER 23

S everal months later, Cayleen reads another one of Ms. Baker's nasty letters. *This is unbelievable. Hunter would never say this about me.* Cayleen picks up her phone.

"Yeah?" Hunter answers.

"Hi, Hunter," Cayleen says. "I just got a letter from Ms. Baker. It's saying some pretty bad stuff about me. Have you seen this?"

Hunter says, "Uh, no. I haven't seen anything yet. But she usually mails things to me."

"My attorney just emails everything over. This letter, amongst other things, says you're requesting a parenting evaluation and my deposition. Is that what you want? You really want to spend all that money on those things? I thought we talked about a parenting evaluation and decided against it."

Hunter says, "You know, Cay, a parenting evaluation is warranted here. We don't know what the experts say about what a two-year-old should handle. And when we talked about it before, you emailed me a document from Arizona. We don't even live in Arizona. What relevance does that have to our son?"

"What relevance does it have to our son for a person to come in and spend an hour with you and an hour with me and tell us what types of parents we are? How is that person supposed to know Logan after that short amount of time? It's not about Logan! That would be about the general population of two-year-olds." Cayleen takes a breath. "And the deposition?"

"Cay, that's a fact-finding mission. I don't think you've been completely honest with me, and that will give us an opportunity to flush out some facts before the trial."

Cayleen thought about the two-day trial Hunter's attorney had requested. To get on the calendar for the judge and all attorneys, they had to schedule court for over a year after they filed for divorce. Cayleen sighs quietly and rolls her eyes. "So, I would guess the other things in the letter about how I'm a bad mom are also from you."

"Ms. Baker does a pretty good job of representing my position. Like I said, I haven't seen this letter you're talking about, so I don't know specifics—"

Cayleen says, "Doesn't that bother you that she's just sending things—and you don't know what she's sending? My attorney emails me everything before she sends it and makes sure it's okay. Don't you think it's illegal or something for her to just keep sending things?"

Hunter says, "Uh … well, I don't know."

Cayleen says, "I'm not sure how much you're paying Ms. Baker, but do you ever think about how much this is costing you? Every letter she sends—and I get at least one every two weeks sometimes one a week—the parenting evaluation, and the deposition with both of our attorneys present. It seems like a lot of money, Hunter."

"I need to look out for my own best interest Cayleen. I can't trust you."

"What? Why can't you trust me? Obviously, we're going through a divorce, but why not?"

Hunter says, "You checked the box on the divorce paperwork for maintenance. You want me to pay you alimony? You agreed not to!"

"I checked every box on the paperwork, Hunter." Cayleen is ready to get off the phone. "This conversation is going nowhere. I'll have my attorney respond if she thinks we need to. I'll have— er—you can call Logan tonight if you want." Cayleen had taken the advice of her attorney and not instigated the phone calls between father and son. If Hunter wants a relationship with Logan, Hunter needs to make the effort.

Hunter says, "What about temporary orders? We go to trial next week if we don't get them settled." The court system requires Hunter and Cayleen to have temporary orders before final orders, but Cayleen is still not sure why. They went to mediation without their attorneys and had gotten to somewhat of a resolution during the session, but the paperwork has not been written up yet.

"I think we should have our attorneys work those details out too. Goodbye, Hunter." Cayleen hangs up after hearing Hunter's short reply.

Minutes later, Liz walks into Cayleen's office. The walls are thin, and their desks face the same wall. "Is everything all right?"

Cayleen cannot tell if Liz is being empathetic or just wants gossip details, but she gives Liz the benefit of the doubt. "Yeah, temporary orders are next week." Cayleen smiles, finished with her explanation.

Liz says, "Are things better without having to process payroll and having Vanessa's help?"

"Vanessa is a great help. I think she's pretty swamped and doesn't have everything filed, but when she has time, she does a great job." Cayleen pauses, breaking eye contact, and thinks of the time the week before when she skipped the office debriefing meeting because she was so stressed she was in tears and couldn't show her face. Bethany had come into her office to get her for the meeting; after seeing her, she said she'd be taking payroll as soon as she finished the project she was working on. "I'm still processing payroll."

Liz adjusts the waistline of her jeans. "Oh, yeah. Bethany has been working on a big project for me. I'll get with her about taking that off your plate. Let me know if you need anything." Liz walks back to her own office.

Cayleen's thoughts center on the meetings she's witnessed for Bethany's project: conference calls, lunches, laughing in Liz's office, something about new software they're testing to be able to streamline payroll and documentation systems. *If they want to streamline payroll, why aren't they processing it—or asking me about it?*

Cayleen thinks of the time when she was filling in for Bethany during her maternity leave, right before she was offered a permanent positon.

Bethany says, "Sheesh, Cayleen. You're doing everything in thirty hours that I was doing in forty. You're making me look bad." Though her tone was playful, her eyes flashed with anger.

Cayleen is still not sure how to take Bethany's comment. *Stop thinking about things, Cay, and get to work!* Cayleen pushes the button to turn on her Christian radio and picks up a paper from her desk.

> So if you are suffering in a manner that pleases God,
> keep on doing what is right, and trust your lives to the
> God who created you, for he will never fail you.
> —1 Peter 4:19

A week later, Hunter arrives at Cayleen's office. The temporary orders paperwork has been signed, but Hunter owes Cayleen additional child support dated from the date of their separation. Cayleen has been putting all monies Hunter pays her into Logan's separate savings account and living off her own salary. She doesn't want to depend on Hunter's money. It's not that she doesn't want the money or need the money or have anything to prove. Cayleen feels in her heart that things will change someday, but she doesn't know how. To prepare for that time, she needs to not depend on Hunter's contributions.

Hunter opens the door, and Cayleen knows he is mad. Her unknown burden-bearing gift allows her to feel his feelings before other signs emerge. He begins yelling at her in the lobby of their small office. Cayleen doesn't even know what he's saying, but she urges him outside so they do not make a scene.

Hunter is ranting.

Cayleen can't follow his words. "Where is this coming from? Why are you yelling at me?"

"You cheated on me, Cayleen! With Gavin! People saw you. I was in Alaska for work, and you cheated on me."

"Hunter, I did not cheat on you with Gavin. Gavin and I had a date, but I told you about that—and it was before we got together the first time ... well, before we got together before your mom died. Gavin and I have been friends since." *Alaska was years ago, and we're getting divorced! Why does it matter now?*

Hunter says, "You went to some sort of conference. You were in a hot tub with a bunch of people and cheated on me!"

Cayleen instantly sees in her mind's eye one of the woman in the hot tub that night so many years earlier having drinks with Hunter at a bar. The much older woman is laughing, telling stories, and trying to seduce him. Cayleen didn't realize this was another one of her gifts from God; she thought it was an overactive imagination.

"Oh, I know what you're talking about. Gavin and I did go to a conference together. Gavin walked me to my room, and other people were still in the hot tub. They saw us leave together. Gavin and I didn't sleep together that night." Cayleen sees that her words are finally getting through. "How did you hear about that? That was, what, five years ago?"

"I ran into someone at a work lunch who was talking about it," Hunter says.

The image of Hunter at the Sports Page, one of the most popular bars in town for socializing singles, is still clear in Cayleen's mind. She sees Hunter talking to the older woman and the older woman trying to get on Hunter's good side by telling him the juicy details. Though her vision doesn't extend that far, Cayleen imagines from Hunter's reaction that it didn't go as the woman had planned.

Cayleen thinks about Hunter's words. *If what I've seen in my mind is wrong, how did a lunch conversation turn to talking about Gavin and me having an affair?* She can't imagine it happening in a professional setting. Cayleen lets it go and ends the discussion with Hunter as calmly as possible.

Once Hunter leaves, Cayleen calls Jessica. The weather is nice, so Cayleen makes the personal call outside the tight quarters of their office, wandering around the small parking lot.

"I've never liked Gavin," Jessica says.

"Why is that? He's been a great friend, he encouraged me to make investments, and his sisters are the reason I have a job right now."

Cayleen says, "Did I tell you Hunter is going to do a parenting evaluation?"

"Uh, Hunter told me that. He asked me what I thought about it. I told him, if it's what his attorney is recommending, he should do whatever she says. She's the expert."

"When are you talking with Hunter?" Cayleen asks. "His attorney is out for money—writing nasty letters that my attorney doesn't even bother responding to just so she can bill him for it."

Jessica yells, "You made all this happen, Cayleen! Hunter wanted you to move back into the house. A parenting evaluation will tell you the best thing for your son. Hunter admits he doesn't know what the best thing is for Logan, and as a matter of fact, do you? How do you know what's best for your son? Taking him away from his father is not best for him!"

"I'm not taking him away from Hunter, Mom! Hunter can't handle Logan more than one night at a time. And with temporary orders, he'll get every other weekend. We'll see how that goes. I'm Logan's mom—I feel how he's doing."

"You feel it? Huh! You never let him spend the night at my house! You're keeping Logan from Hunter, and you're keeping him away from me!"

"Mom, I've told you, if you want Logan for an overnight, just tell me what night. I need to plan for it. I can't just do whatever and change everything at the last minute." Logan doesn't do well with changing plans. Once he gets his hopes set on doing something, if it does not happen, Logan doesn't handle it well. Jessica has flighty ways, which she calls being *flexible*. If they make plans for Jessica to take Logan and she changes them, Cayleen will be stuck with an upset, screaming toddler.

"And you *are* keeping Logan from Hunter by not staying *married* to Hunter! You are hurting everyone with what you've done, Cayleen. You're doing exactly what your father did."

Cayleen has kept her composure though Hunter's burst of anger, but she is unable to keep herself calm any longer. The sting of her mother's hatred is too much to hide. "How am I just like Dad?"

Jessica flips from anger to hysterical tears. "You left—and you're never looking back. You're ripping apart a family. I can't be a part of this conversation anymore." Jessica hangs up.

Though Cayleen's journey with God has grown in a deeper knowledge of him, she is not aware of the spiritual network around her. Cayleen is not familiar with spirits or people acting in ways that express the intent of the spirit rather than their own power. Specifically, Cayleen is not familiar with a shrike spirit, which epitomizes her mother.

Cayleen is silent, pacing the parking lot, kicking herself for not grabbing her car keys before coming outside. If she could get into her car, she could have privacy and maybe some Christian radio to lift her spirit. She takes a deep breath. Another. One more. Finally, she is able to walk back inside the office, fully composed.

For we are not fighting against flesh-and-blood enemies,
but against evil rulers and authorities of the unseen
world, against mighty powers in this dark world,
and against evil spirits in the heavenly places.
—Ephesians 6:12

CHAPTER 24

Cayleen's phone gives the silly tone she has set to alert her when she gets a text message. Cayleen is driving nearly to the nanny's house to pick up Logan. The sound of the tone sparks Cayleen's thoughts back to her day, when her new office roommate heard her text message sound. "You gotta have some fun, right?" Cayleen thinks about her new office roommate, Sandy, and smiles.

Bethany and the other accounting positon had been processing payroll for two months, since Bethany went to Cayleen and stated the need to hire an additional employee to process payroll. Cayleen had been happy to help find someone. Cayleen was only trying to work toward the team goal of success for the company.

Cayleen, under her human resources hat, had contacted Sandy for the interview and had sat in on the interviews. Though not the decision-maker, Cayleen was glad to be included in the decision-making process. Sandy seemed like she was going to be a good fit.

The first time Sandy walked into Cayleen's office, she mentioned that she listens to the Christian radio station all the time and asked Cayleen to keep it on. Cayleen smiled. *Sandy will make a good fit.*

At the nanny's house, Cayleen checks her phone. The message is from Jessica: "I just got back to town and would love to help you with your VA project. I'm in cell service now. Give me a call so we can coordinate."

She already told me she is back in town, Cayleen thinks. *VA Project?*

The only veteran that Jessica would be texting is … Hunter. This must be for Hunter. Cayleen's chest burns with anger. She calls Jessica.

"Well, hello, darling daughter," Jessica says.

Cayleen strains to keep calm. "Mom, what was the text you sent me a few minutes ago?"

"What text? I didn't text you. You mean when I got back into town earlier? That was lunchtime. I've been with Grandma—"

"Mom, you just sent me a text about a VA project. I'm pretty sure you meant that text for Hunter, didn't you?"

"Oh." Jessica laughs uncomfortably. "I sent that to you, huh? Yeah, Hunter did ask for my help on a project for the VA. I have lots of friends who are veterans. I really appreciate the service Hunter and the other veterans did for our country. Of course I agreed to help Hunter—"

"Mom, you agreed to stop interacting with Hunter except when it came to Logan. Does this VA project have to do with Logan?"

"Logan is a citizen of the United States of America, and benefits from the freedom our veterans provide for us—"

"Mom, does the VA project involve Logan?"

"Well, I guess from *your* perspective, it doesn't involve Logan directly."

"Mom, I've asked you to stop doing this. Have you thought about how it makes me feel for you to go behind my back and talk to Hunter about things?"

"Hunter is busy!" Jessica says. "He's got work—and Logan and this terrible divorce you're putting him through. Hunter doesn't have a mom. He needs my help."

Cayleen laughs silently through her nose in disbelief. "You know, Mom, Hunter has enough time to coach fifth-grade football four times a week and then go to the games on Saturdays."

Cayleen has taken Logan during the practices that fall on Hunter's parenting time, and Hunter has allowed Cayleen to pick up Logan early on the days he has football games. It is becoming clear to Cayleen that Hunter prefers his image of himself as a father than developing a relationship with his son. Being a football coach is great for getting the single moms to see him. What a great thing to be able to say to his friends. Cayleen imagines his conversation: "My ex is ripping me away from our son, but I miss him so much. I gotta be around kids, so I coach football."

"Who coaches football to kids who aren't even theirs? Unless they're teachers to the kids? Regardless, Mom, what do you expect me to do when you keep doing the exact opposite of what I'm asking?"

Jessica smiles. "The Bible says we always have to forgive. Forgive and forget, Cayleen. Live every day like it's a new day. That's what I do. That's what God says to do."

Cayleen feels dirty, like Hunter and Jessica are hiding more than a project. Cayleen thinks of the married men Jessica dated previously in her life, calling them *freebies* since they weren't able to make Jessica commit. For a fleeting moment, Cayleen wonders if Hunter and Jessica are sleeping together. *No, they can't be. Jessica is twenty-five years older than Hunter and has gained a lot of weight in the past fifteen years.* Cayleen's stomach is sick. "I gotta go, Mom."

"I love you, darling! Bye!" Jessica says.

"Bye," Cayleen whispers, rolls her eyes, and pushes the end button on her phone. She opens the car door and takes a deep breath. On the short walk to the nanny's door, she takes purposeful breaths and rolls and relaxes her shoulders to let go of the situation before she reaches her son. Cayleen has vowed to try her hardest not to be like Jessica and tell Logan any of the bad things about his other family members. He needs to make up his own mind. If Cayleen does as Jessica did and tells Logan how to think, one day he will make up his own mind, just like Cayleen did. Involving Logan in her struggles with the family members he loves will confuse him and could turn him against her in the future. *Besides, it's building my character.* Cayleen chuckles under her breath, thinking about a sermon she heard earlier in the week. Shaking her head at the daunting task of character building ahead of her, Cayleen grabs the screen door. She knocks on the door and plasters a smile across her face. It may be fake, but she's willing to risk faking a smile and pretending everything is okay in order for her son not to worry.

> If another believer sins, rebuke that person; then
> if there is repentance, forgive. Even if that person
> wrongs you seven times a day and each time turns
> again and asks for forgiveness, you must forgive.
> —Luke 17:3–4

Cayleen looks nervously at the computer screen on her desk at work, waiting for the attachment to download and open. Her attorney has just forwarded the parenting evaluations—one hired by Hunter and one hired by Cayleen. The deadline for submitting the parenting evaluations was too close to trial for Cayleen to wait for Hunter's to come back. After hearing her attorney say it could go either way, Cayleen errored on the side of caution and paid for her own parenting evaluation to be performed.

Hunter's attorney had hired an evaluator from out of town to come in and do the evaluation. Cayleen's parenting evaluator had an office in the same building as Scott Martin. Both had asked for the same information—sources to call, signoffs from any previous counselors, one meeting with each parent individually, and one meeting with each parent with Logan for about an hour. Cayleen had explained her previous experiences, always presenting the encouraging, positive side of things. When asked if she had seen counselors before, she said, "Yes, for various life experiences," but she never went into details. The parenting evaluator Hunter hired left Cayleen feeling physically drained after meeting with him. She felt good about her presentation of herself with both evaluators.

Cayleen reads the medical doctors' diagnoses. There is a clip from Scott Martin stating he wasn't sure why they didn't come back to counseling since everything seemed to be going well. Scott doesn't understand why they didn't get back together. Cayleen rolls her eyes.

Further down, Cayleen sees the diagnosis from Hunter's medical doctor. Hunter was meeting with her weekly for treatment for his post-traumatic stress disorder, which was brought on by the experience he witnessed in Africa. He is doing well, better than most patients with treatment, and she does not expect him to require treatment much into the future. Clean bill of health mentally.

Cayleen doesn't have medical diagnoses, but there are some comments about her personality test scores being so high that she is in the category that may exhibit narcissistic tendencies. Cayleen doesn't know what narcissistic means and googles it on another window. Narcissism—extreme selfishness.

"Seriously?" Cayleen whispers to the empty room. Sandy is at lunch.

Cayleen reads on. She gets to the interview with Jessica. The first line stops her from reading further. It is listed as a direct quote from Jessica. "Hunter is the most compassionate man on the planet."

Cayleen's heart pounds in her chest. It beats so hard, she can hear it in her ears, and it throbs in her head. She is tempted to call Jessica immediately, but she takes a deep breath. *I'll read them both, and then I'll call her. Maybe he got it wrong, and she didn't say anything like that.*

Cayleen nears the close of the evaluation Hunter paid for. The evaluator recommends fifty-fifty parenting time with a five and two schedule. Cayleen doesn't even know what that means and is too scattered to understand the examples listed in the report. She makes a mental note to ask her attorney.

Reading the parenting evaluation she paid for, Cayleen is somewhat disheartened. Though it does not make her look nearly as bad, Cayleen finds much of the same information in the first few pages. She gets to the doctor evaluations and has to read it twice. Hunter's VA doctor treating him for PTSD states in this report that he is seeing her weekly and that she expects that to continue at least until the divorce is final. The doctor also states that Hunter may suffer from manic depressive disorder rather than PTSD, but the symptoms are similar and it is difficult to tell.

Cayleen thinks back to high school and the times Hunter was unresponsive to her, ignoring her and not calling her. She thinks about the time right after Logan was born when Hunter forgot to call or text for three days. *That was a year before he went to Africa! Maybe he does suffer from manic depressive disorder. Why are the recommendations in the report I had prepared and the one Hunter paid for so different?* Cayleen looks to see if there is a date of contact for his medical doctor. She looks to Hunter's report. Hunter's report is one week later. Cayleen rolls her eyes and reads on.

Scott Martin has the next words that are shockingly different: "It was pretty obvious infidelity was the elephant in the room that was never talked about."

Obvious infidelity. Obvious infidelity. The words keep repeating in Cayleen's head. She reads on with them echoing between her ears, numbness in her heart. The instances Hunter was out of town and conveniently forgot to call Cayleen start coming back. Cayleen feels stupid for not seeing it before and blaming his behavior on depression. The weekends away, which he always said were for work. The girl who came home from the bar with him. The credit card bills.

Cayleen wants to stop thinking about it and decides to keep reading. Jessica had told Cayleen's evaluator that she already gave an evaluation and refused to speak to him. Jessica told Cayleen's evaluator he should use Hunter's evaluation for her testimony. *Oh, that's nice, Mom.*

Cayleen nears the end and finds the parenting time. Numb from the sting of negative words she's read about herself and the echo of "obvious infidelity" still ringing in her heart, she has no emotion to give to the shock of seeing that her evaluator has also recommended fifty-fifty parenting time over the course of two years.

"Hunter doesn't want Logan for half the time! He can't handle that!" Cayleen says to her computer. Sandy, who is back from lunch, looks over her shoulder.

Cayleen smiles, grabs her phone and keys, and walks outside. Her heart pounds as she touches the screen to call Jessica.

"Hello?" Jessica says.

"Hi, Mom. I got the parenting evaluations today."

"Oh?"

"Yeah, and I'm not sure if this is all true. Did you really state that Hunter is the most compassionate man on the planet?" Cayleen allows the very uncomfortable pause and waits for Jessica's response.

"I'm not sure of my exact words. I do think Hunter is an amazing person—very compassionate and a great father—and I definitely could have said he was the most compassionate man on the planet."

Cayleen stops. Her world shatters. For a moment, she feels as if the trees are falling. The earth beneath her feet disappears. Her vision has cracks like glass going though, throbbing and cracking. Everything is falling apart. The fact that the trees are still standing and the parking lot still exists and the ground is still under her feet— it's all an illusion. She longs to fall to her knees in the middle of the parking lot—on the curb she's been pacing on—and be swallowed into the earth. She wants to fall apart too. "You didn't say anything nice about me. You said I am book smart, but that's it. You made me sound so impersonal."

Jessica says, "It's not my fault—that's the way you are, Cayleen! You are impersonal. You are just like I said! You are just like your dad, Cayleen, dragging me through all this all over again. I feel the same as I did twenty-five years ago when you put me through this before."

"*I* didn't do that to you, Mom. Dad did."

Jessica's hysterical voice is still yelling on the other end of the phone. Cayleen can't register any of the words. "I didn't call to have a screaming match, Mom. I thought I was reading a lie. Now I know it wasn't a lie. It is what you said. I don't think there's any more to talk about."

Jessica is still screaming on the other end, but Cayleen is too numb to comprehend what Jessica is saying.

"Goodbye." Cayleen hangs up. Frozen, Cayleen takes a deep breath. Keys. Cayleen grabs the keys from her pocket and stumbles toward her car. She sits in the driver's seat and turns on Christian radio. She can't hear anything; even if the stereo was on full blast,

Cayleen couldn't hear anything. Cayleen puts her head back on the headrest and closes her eyes.

Cayleen takes a deep breath and focuses on her breathing, head back, eyes closed. The song finally registers with Cayleen, and she is able to hear the words. The voice is singing about crying out to God to keep her head above water. Cayleen thinks back to the sermon the week before about crying out to God. The pastor was comical at the time, stating that we can even throw temper tantrums and jump up and down to get God's attention. His point had been to cry out to God when we need him.

"Well, God, there's been no time more than now I've wanted to yell at you and get your attention. So here goes." Cayleen is aware of how close her office building is. She grabs a spare jacket from the backseat, pushes it against her mouth, and yells, "God, I need you. Not tomorrow, not next year, now! I need you to hear me! I need help here! I try to get closer to you, and it seems like my world is falling apart!" Cayleen pauses, allowing the jacket to drop to her lap, and pounds the steering wheel with her fists. After sufficient pain in her hands and fearing the steering wheel to her ten-year-old car might not take much more, she stuffs the jacket back in her own face. "I need some help here! I've been asking and asking for you to take away romantic distractions so it's clear to me who you've chosen. Well, I need someone in my life. Now!" Cayleen allows the jacket to fall once more, her voice and body calmer now. "I need a friend who will help me through this, God. I feel so alone. I need someone to talk to."

Cayleen sits in her car and listens to Christian radio. After a few minutes, she sighs, grabs her phone, and walks back inside.

And the Holy Spirit helps us in our weakness ... the
Holy Spirit prays for us ... And we know that God causes
everything to work together for the good of those who love
God ... If God is for us, who can ever be against us?
—Romans 8:26, 28, 31

Six days later, Cayleen walks up the steps to the town event center. She is going to a charity event. She got tickets from work for free, and no one else was able to attend. Cayleen called everyone she knew to try to get them to go with her, but no one could go. It was during Hunter's time with Logan. Cayleen had been texting one of her friends when it came to her: Cinderella went to the ball alone.

Nervous, Cayleen opens the door and hands one of the ladies her ticket. She sees a woman who looks familiar. *Do I know her from Jamison Homes?* Cayleen approaches with a smile. "What do I do with this stuff?" Cayleen gestures to the glass and plate she's been given.

The other woman smiles and grabs the two from Cayleen. "You just do this." She puts the two together so the glass slides on the plate.

Cayleen says, "Oh, wow. Look at that. That's great. Thank you. I'm Cayleen, by the way. You look very familiar."

"I'm Elise," she says with a gentle smile. "I don't think I know you. Have you been to this event before?"

"No, I haven't."

"It's great. You should go on inside." The woman urges her toward the doors that lead to the event.

Cayleen thinks the event is great and sees people from Jamison Homes who she hasn't seen in years. Enjoying herself, Cayleen runs into Elise again. Not wanting to be rude or intrude, Cayleen walks past with a kind smile.

Elise steps in front of Cayleen, blocking her path. "Cayleen, right?"

Cayleen smiles and nods.

"This is my husband, Jack, and my brother, Eric. Why don't you hang out with us for a while?"

Two hours later, Cayleen has met Eric's other brother who happens to be married to a high school friend of Cayleen. Their kids go to the same day care. During the divorce proceedings, the nanny had said she needed to quit giving care to Logan, which was understandable to Cayleen, but difficult nonetheless.

As the event comes to a close, Eric asks for Cayleen's number. Though she hasn't done it in years, Cayleen gives Eric her number.

There is a path before each person that
seems right, but it ends in death.
—Proverbs 16:25

CHAPTER 25

In addition to the excitement of a new romantic relationship, Cayleen is excited that they are hiring her replacement at work. Several months earlier, Liz told Cayleen that the board of directors wanted to focus on training. Liz presented it to Cayleen as an opportunity to focus on training and hire a replacement to do human resources. After the company had been established in Canada, Cayleen had spoken with Liz and other staff. Cayleen encouraged the company to handle Canada as the other states were handled, by the people that are specialized in those areas—fleet, payroll, human resources, and accounting. It didn't make sense to Cayleen for Canada to have one person do all those roles. Cayleen had been so busy with her other roles that she had begun pushing off Canadian tasks to the person who handled the task for the US company. It had worked out well.

Liz is excited for Cayleen's replacement to start. It is her sister-in-law. In order to hire her, she was offered more money than Cayleen since she was making more money at her previous company. She had also requested a month's notice at her former employer. It worked out for the company since the company was moving to a larger office building. They didn't really have a place for anyone to sit in the old building.

Cayleen stands to greet her new replacement. After her interview, Cayleen had honestly told Liz her one concern with Jeannie was her ability to get things done on their company's time frame. Cayleen asked what happens when Jeannie has too many tasks to do in a day. How does she handle it? Usually candidates prioritize and get the job done by staying late or delegating tasks.

Jeannie said, "I would prioritize, but there are only so many hours in the day. Work stays at work—you can't take it home with you."

Cayleen expressed concern to Liz about the answer, but Liz said she knows Jeannie well enough to know Jeannie would be able to get their job done.

Cayleen shakes hands with Jeannie, and the two get situated in Cayleen's office. Jeannie will shadow Cayleen for a week or so before Jeannie takes over. Liz asked Cayleen to prepare a guide for Jeannie, and Cayleen worked on it for several days, outlining various tasks handled under her human resources role complete with websites, passwords, and step-by-step instructions. Cayleen begins with the new-hire process. Ten minutes into the session, Cayleen is explaining rather slowly, Jeannie asks Cayleen to hold on a minute.

Jeannie walk into Liz's office. Just like in the old office, Liz made sure Cayleen's office was right next to Liz's. Cayleen feels the only reason Liz was adamant about having Cayleen so close is to hear Cayleen's conversations. It seems paranoid, but it matches Liz's management style. Liz put a window from her own office overlooking the cubicles to watch people. Why didn't she take the corner office Cayleen had or one of the larger offices the accounting and contracts administrators had that were also near an exit?

"I need an assistant," Jeannie says.

"Okay," Liz says.

Cayleen hears the click of the door shut. With the door closed, it is hard to hear exactly what the voices are saying. Cayleen can tell if they're talking about who to hire. Cayleen stuffs the anger welling inside her. Jeannie asks for—and gets—an assistant on her first day after Cayleen has been asking for an assistant for years.

"Jesus," Cayleen says in an attempt to release the emotion.

Several minutes later, Jeannie walks back into Cayleen's office.

Cayleen resumes the training she has planned, walking slowly through the tasks. Cayleen points out where Jeannie can find the various explanations of the tasks.

"Okay, I think that's good." Jeannie stands up.

Cayleen was planning on Jeannie staying to go over more information. They'd only done one of the items on her two-page bulleted list. "Okay." Cayleen doesn't know what else to say.

"I'll let you know if I have questions." Jeannie starts toward the door.

"Do you want this copy of the training document I made?" Cayleen holds the document in the air.

Jeannie walks back and nonchalantly grabs it out of Cayleen's hand. "Yeah, thanks."

Jeannie walks out. By Friday, Jeannie has an assistant.

Let all that I am wait quietly before God,
for my hope is in Him.
—Psalm 62:5

Cayleen walks out of the courthouse with her attorney, Abby Wall. The two full days in court have left Cayleen drained and unable to take everything in. Abby stops walking at the end of the block and turns to look at Cayleen.

"All in all, it went pretty well, I think."

Cayleen nods.

Abby says, "I'm still shocked she didn't give you any questions!"

Cayleen smiles. To end the proceedings, Cayleen was on the stand. Ms. Baker stood and told the court she had no questions for Cayleen. Not one.

"Apparently the deposition told Ms. Baker everything she needed to hear," Cayleen says softly.

"You did great at deposition. You did great today after your mom's testimony," Abby says.

Jessica's testimony was devastating to Cayleen. Cayleen took the stand after her mom and was in tears within minutes.

Jessica told the court about a conversation that she and Cayleen had when Cayleen was hurting and upset. Jessica had told Cayleen that she didn't know how she was supposed to react. Jessica asked Cayleen what Cayleen wanted her to say.

Jessica repeated to the court what Cayleen had said: "Baby, I'm sorry." Jessica followed up that she couldn't say that because she didn't call her kids *baby*.

When Cayleen took the stand, the first thing Abby did was clear the air on that conversation. Asking Cayleen her side of the story, Cayleen included the last part: "I don't know what to say, Mom. I'd like some sympathy."

Cayleen says, "Maybe, baby. I'm sorry you're going through this right now. I'm sorry this is happening to you." She was in tears the first time the conversation occurred and while retelling the conversation in court.

Jessica's response: "I can't say those things."

Cayleen had been devastated, feeling completely abandoned and alone.

Jessica told the court that Cayleen did not allow Jessica to see Logan and that Jessica and Cayleen had no relationship. Jessica repeated what she told the parenting evaluators about how great Hunter is and that Cayleen was book smart but not emotional.

Cayleen took the stand and told the court how, less than a week before, Cayleen had been digging up an irrigation pipe at Jessica's house with Logan close by.

Abby pointed out in Jessica's own testimony that Cayleen and Logan go to church and breakfast weekly with Jessica. However, in Jessica's mind, weekly breakfast and church do not qualify as a visit with Logan or make a relationship with Cayleen.

Over the two days of court, Hunter called Jessica to testify—and Cheyanne, their accountant, the nanny, and the parenting evaluator.

The parenting evaluator was the first to testify. During his testimony, Ms. Baker had heatedly demanded if Cayleen had told him about her childhood rape. Abby had looked at Cayleen, as had the parenting evaluator, who had just been testifying how well Hunter had done at recovering from a traumatic experience. Abby could not object since the rape was true; the evaluator was also stunned that Cayleen had not mentioned the rape to him.

Hunter had also paid for Cayleen's properties to be appraised. Cayleen had done an informal property assessment using online real estate tools for free and submitted those to the court. Cayleen's method had turned out to be in Hunter's favor, and he had rescinded the appraisals at the last minute in front of the court. Quite humorously, Abby had offered to call the appraiser as a witness for Cayleen, which was allowed by the court. Once Ms. Baker saw they could not get the appraisals thrown out, Hunter's position changed again.

At the end of things, Cayleen thought Hunter looked like a really bad character—wanting financially as much as possible and giving up parenting time with Logan—but Cayleen didn't know how divorce final orders proceedings went. She definitely didn't know how the judge would rule.

"I think things went well," Abby says. "You never know about these things, but with the judge saying it may take a long time before he has time to issue orders? That's a good thing, Cay, what we want is for things to stay the same. If he doesn't issue orders, the temporary orders stay in effect."

Cayleen takes a deep breath and nods. She is drained.

"Is Eric coming to pick you up?" Abby asks.

"He's parked over there." Cayleen nods in the direction of the parking lot. Eric had been there to pick her up for lunches and drop her off every day, which had been a relief to Cayleen.

"Okay. I'll let you know when we get orders. And remember— no news is good news." Abby turns toward her car.

Cayleen walks toward Eric's truck and gets in the passenger door. Relief washes over her as she sits in the passenger seat. Excitement at the thought of it all being over. The roller coaster she's been on since Hunter told her to get out of his house. She closes her eyes, sighs, and sinks into the seat.

"How'd things go?" Eric asks.

Eric has been a good friend. Cayleen has made a lot of concessions for their relationship. Eric is attractive, and he has dark skin, dark hair, and dark eyes. Eric has not had many relationships and shows some immaturity, but nothing detrimental to their relationship at the moment. Eric had quit his job and had no investments. The irresponsibility of quitting his job without having another one lined up somewhat bothered Cayleen. She overlooked it for his ability to be a friend to her and mesh so well with Logan. Eric had no ties, but he longed to stay in Spring Forks near his family. Eric's closeness with his family strikes Cayleen as odd, but Cayleen's family is far from normal. *Maybe that's how things are supposed to be.*

Cayleen takes a deep breath, feeling freedom in breathing. "I don't know." She smiles and looks at Eric. "Abby said she thinks things went well, so that's good, I guess." Cayleen shares a smile with Eric. "I'm just glad it's over."

He will keep you strong to the end.
—1 Corinthians 1:8

"I don't get it, Cheyanne," Cayleen whispers. They are at Logan's soccer game. Soccer for three-year-olds is entertaining. The coaches try to keep them on the small rectangle they have designated as a soccer field for that age group. "I have no idea who that is—and neither does Logan. If Eric and Hunter were to both be here at the game, I would introduce them. I don't understand why he's not even introducing me. That's weird."

"It's immature," Cheyanne mumbles. They speak so Cheyanne's kids don't hear. "Kinda like when he and James came to the game a couple weeks ago on their motorcycles."

"Yeah, but that was because Logan told Hunter Eric would be

here." Cayleen giggles. "And then Eric had to go out of town for work." Cayleen shouts encouragement to the kids on the field. They are huddling around the soccer ball, trying not to use their hands. "Good kicks, good kicks!"

Cayleen lowers her voice and says, "Cheyanne, it's frustrating! He shows up sometimes to the games. He brings his girlfriend, but he won't introduce me—and he refused to help pay for Logan to do soccer because I didn't give him an option to say Logan couldn't play soccer."

"I hear ya, sister. Are you still having Mom drama?"

Cayleen had blocked Jessica from her phone after her testimony in court. Since then, she has had internal conflicts because the Bible says children are to honor their parents. "I called the church and the counselor even told me to cut her out. I went to a work conference a few weeks ago, and a woman said she had to cut her mom out of her life because it was not healthy for her. But I can't do it. I talked to Mom about it and asked her what she recommended."

Cheyanne smiles. "What did Mom say?"

"Forgive and forget—live every day as if it's a new day." Cayleen's feels defeated just repeating the conversation.

"That's tough, Cay. I'm sorry." Cheyanne turns to one of her children who needs her immediate attention—conversation over.

> And remember your journey ... when I, the Lord, did everything I could to teach you about my faithfulness.
> —Micah 6:5b

CHAPTER 26

Cayleen runs to the kitchen to grab her ringing phone. Abby Wall comes up as her saved contact. Cayleen's stomach lurches, but she tries to steady her voice. "This is Cayleen."

"Hi, Cayleen. This is Monica. Abby has not had a chance to review the final orders yet, but we did get them in our office. I'll email them to you right now so you can have them. Abby should follow up with you next week after she gets a chance to read them."

"Okay. Thank you." Cayleen is nervous … and excited. She ends the phone conversation and presses the buttons to get to her email. After refreshing her emails twenty times, the email from Monica comes through.

Cayleen begins scanning the attachment. Her and Hunter's names. Descriptions of properties—Hunter gets his house, Cayleen gets her properties—just as they wanted it. Cayleen reads on.

Because Hunter had losses and foreclosed on one of his properties, and Cayleen keeps her properties, Cayleen has to write Hunter a check for $8,000. Cayleen drops to her knees on the hard tile kitchen floor. She doesn't register pain. She reads on.

Cayleen will pay for day care and health care expenses. Cayleen will determine school choices, and Hunter will determine extracurricular activities. They will share parenting time fifty-fifty with a full implementation in six months. *Six months? That's no time for Logan to adjust!* Cayleen reads on.

Hunter will get one more overnight starting next week. *Next week?* Cayleen sinks even further toward the floor. Hunter will get access to the bank account in Logan's name, and Hunter and Cayleen will decide jointly how to use the funds.

"What? That was my child support! I used that for the down payment on this house." Cayleen says.

"What about our new house, Mama?" Logan comes running into the kitchen to join Cayleen. "Are we having a picnic?"

Cayleen washes the emotion from her face with a bright smile, puts her phone aside, and takes her son into her lap. "What would you like to do, bubba?"

"I like picnics! But I like my TV show, Mama." Logan is only allowed to watch a very limited amount of TV at Cayleen's house. When he is given the opportunity to watch TV, he takes it. "Can you watch TV with me? We can have a picnic in there."

Cayleen smiles at her son's inviting nature, proud of his ability to speak so well at three. "Sounds good, son. I'll grab a drink and be right in. Do you want something?"

Logan was already excitedly running toward the TV. "No, I got my drink in here."

Cayleen pours herself a glass of wine and looks toward the ceiling. "God, I'm not sure what's going on here, but I'd really appreciate you showing me."

Arise, Jerusalem! Let your light shine for all to see. For the glory of the Lord rises to shine on you …For the Lord your God will be your everlasting light, and your God will be your glory … At the right time, I, the Lord, will make it happen.
—Isaiah 60:1, 19b, 22b

It takes Abby ten days to call Cayleen. Cayleen is at the office when Abby calls her cell phone. Cayleen rises from her chair, closes her office door, and says, "This is Cayleen."

"Cayleen, its Abby."

"Hi, Abby."

"Cay, I have no idea what happened with the final orders. I really thought we had that one. I guess it must have been your mom's testimony. That's the only thing that we had going against us. But your testimony really refuted that completely. I'm really confused as to what happened. We can fight anything in there you want … if you want."

"Thank you for your words, Abby. I don't want to fight anything. This really is a God thing. The final orders are against me because I'm not obeying God. Until I got the final orders, I had still had Jessica in my life." Cayleen pauses. "I've talked to Hunter about Logan's bank account. I used that money for the down payment on our new house." Cayleen remembers Abby advising against buying a new house. Cayleen's heart had told her to buy it; she and Logan could not remain in her second-floor condo with a small balcony much longer. "Hunter has threatened to sue me if I don't put the money back."

"I'm not sure he can do that, but it would be just as much money to fight it, I suppose."

Cayleen takes a deep breath. She has already had clarity on how to handle the funds; it's as if she was shown these things rather than having to think of them on her own. Painful as it may be for her to take the money out of her accounts, she says, "It's okay. I'll use other funds and put it back."

"Well, Cay. I'm sorry things went this way. Let me know if you need any other representation in the future. We'll keep the file for you, but we generally close things off after getting final orders."

"Sounds good. Thank you Abby." Cayleen signs off, puts her phone on her desk, and lets her thoughts drift to the other things God has revealed to her to change.

Cayleen's relationship with Eric was not pure biblically. Cayleen had always thought that if God had wanted to save sex for marriage, he would not have allowed her to be raped to lose her virginity. Recently, God revealed to Cayleen that he is not mad at her for her interpretation. However, he has shown her it is incorrect. Even with her relationship with Eric, sex confuses things and connects their relationship in ways that it would not have been without physical intimacy. They had a bond between them that would not have been there had they not had sex. It was a false bond, a false sense of closeness, a false trust. It made Cayleen feel bound to Eric, like she owes him something and can't shake free of the debt. Cayleen did not have knowledge of soul ties, but God was showing her the effects of them.

In bed last Saturday morning, Cayleen had asked God to reveal to her if Eric was the one he intended her to be with. The previous day, Eric had done exactly what she had asked him not to. He was trying to be helpful, but Cayleen had specifically talked with him earlier in the week and asked him not to. As a result, Cayleen had asked Eric not to contact her for a few days. She wanted the weekend to think about whether she wanted to make the choice to be with Eric or if their sexual relationship had caused her to feel emotions toward Eric that biased her decision-making ability. Rather than respect what Cayleen had asked, Eric texted her on Friday afternoon and asked Cayleen to call him. Not immediately recognizing the passive-aggressive move, Cayleen called him that night.

Then she opened her eyes to see the swimsuit and spare clothes he used to leave at her house were gone. A realization hit her without her having to think about it. Eric got mad enough to yell at her in front of Logan the week before. Eric blew off her family engagement because he wanted to sleep until noon. Eric had done things exactly opposite of what Cayleen asked. Eric had moved his stuff out. *Eric doesn't want to be with me—he just doesn't want to be the one to break up with me. He wants to be the victim and allow everyone to feel sorry for him.*

Cayleen had texted Eric to let go of the relationship; her words were kind and direct. Knowing how the previous text had been taken and not respected, she immediately blocked him from her phone and all social media. Cayleen felt a sense of freedom—like a weight lifting off her shoulders. She had received an email from Eric on Sunday and a few handwritten notes on her door during the week. She was happy and confident in blocking him so he couldn't keep convincing her through sympathy and guilt to be with him.

Cayleen sits in her office, listening to Christian radio and trying to focus on work. She has an email from Hunter with a picture of Hunter with Logan in a backpack carrier on Hunter's back. *Ugh—like I want to see that!* The email is in response to her asking why Logan came home from Hunter's house and said, "Daddy and I went walking around Mommy's house."

Hunter explains that the day care told him there were great hiking trails around Cayleen's house. *My house is half an hour from your house, Hunter, and there's great trails within five minutes of your house. You're still creepin' me out.*

Cayleen's office line rings, and her thoughts are pulled back to work. "This is Cayleen."

"Hi, Cayleen. This is Justin. I got a phone call from you about returning to work?"

"Oh, yes. We're doing a class, and you are registered to attend."

Justin says, "Uh, well, that's kinda funny. I told my supervisor that I'm going to school this semester to finish my degree."

"Oh, so you're not returning to work?"

"No. I really don't want to let anyone down, but I thought I made it clear to my supervisor that I wouldn't be returning."

Cayleen thinks the entire situation is comical. She was told to call Justin because Jeannie wanted to make sure he wouldn't file for unemployment—and they had a hard-quit date if he was not returning to work. With a smile, she says, "No worries, Justin. You're not letting anyone down. Best of luck in your education."

We stopped relying on ourselves and learned to rely only on
God … and He will rescue us again. We have placed our
confidence in Him and He will continue to rescue us.
—2 Corinthians 1: 9–10

CHAPTER 27

Cayleen and Logan are sitting on their couch and watching TV. After looking on her phone, she sees the florist is closed; there is nothing available to get flowers to Jeannie's husband. Liz sent Cayleen a text message nearly an hour before saying Jeannie's husband probably wouldn't make it through the night. Liz is in Florida and asked Cayleen to get them flowers. Cayleen had been searching online and calling florist shops to see if anyone could get flowers there at six o'clock on a Saturday night. No luck.

"Come on, bubba. We're going on an adventure." Cayleen makes her voice sound light and enthusiastic. The only option she can think of is the grocery store and delivering the flowers herself, which means Logan will be along for the ride.

Logan is less than enthusiastic about leaving his cartoons. "Where we going, Mama?"

"We're going to do something nice for someone I work with. Her husband is sick, and we're going to give him flowers. Will you help me pick something out?" Cayleen asks, opening the door to get into the car.

"One of your work friends is sick?"

"My work friend's husband is sick. Not my work friend." Cayleen thinks of the way Jeannie treats Cayleen and how opposite it is from a friend, but for the sake of it all fitting into the head of a three-year-old, she agrees.

She buckles Logan into his car seat, and he asks, "Flowers? For a boy?"

Cayleen smiles. "Yes, bubba. Flowers for a boy." She kisses him on the head and gets into her own seat. As the children's music fills the car on their way to the store, Cayleen's mind thinks of the actions Jeannie has done toward Cayleen since starting six months earlier. Several months ago, Cayleen, as trainer for the drug-policy program, questioned the hair follicle testing Jeannie and Liz were implementing. Cayleen had heard horror stories about women with bald spots for months after hair follicle testing. In return, Jeannie had told her in an email to both Cayleen and Liz that Cayleen was not adhering to company policy and that she may need to have a closed-door conversation with Jeannie to make sure Cayleen knew what it meant to be a team player.

Cayleen smiles at the irony of the thought—piling her son in the car at six o'clock on a Saturday night for another employee's sick spouse to deliver them flowers—and she's not a team player. Cayleen thinks to the most recent time Jeannie walked into Cayleen's office and reprimanded her for not doing something correctly for payroll.

Cayleen was proud of her own response. She smiled and said, "Jeannie, it's a good thing I'm not doing payroll anymore. I'm glad your department is able to catch those mistakes!"

Jeannie had not been happy with that response and had made more remarks about how she didn't know how anyone could mess up as badly as Cayleen had. Cayleen had smiled silently until Jeannie had her fill and left Cayleen's office.

Cayleen smiles, at peace with the situation and knowing that Jeannie always has to have the last word. Cayleen's frustration with work drove her to interview with other companies. Cayleen thought the treatment from Jeannie must be God's sign of Cayleen needing to switch jobs.

Then, during the interview process, God allowed Cayleen to realize how much the company trusts her. Two years in a row, the direction the board wanted to take with the company was placed on Cayleen's shoulders. Cayleen had realized God had her there for a reason. She asked for God's peace with how Jeannie and Liz treat her, and he had granted Cayleen peace.

After minimal arguing over which bouquet to purchase, Cayleen and Logan arrive at the hospital. Cayleen stops Logan at the info counter, which is not manned. Cayleen takes a picture of Logan standing next to the bouquet with a silly smile and texts it to Liz.

When they approach the room, Cayleen doesn't know what to expect. She knocks on the partially open door.

"Come in." The man's voice is much louder than Cayleen would expect for someone who is not going to make it through the night.

Cayleen enters, Logan walking behind her legs, mostly hidden from view. "Hi there. Are you Brian?" The man in the bed nods. "I'm Cayleen. I work with Jeannie. These flowers are for you from the company." Cayleen gives a warm smile to the two gentlemen in the room. One is standing close to the door, and the other is sitting in the hospital bed. Cayleen marvels at how good his color is for someone so close to death. "And this is my son Logan." Logan hides behind her legs and gives her the stare as if she's broken all the rules by revealing his presence.

"Thank you," says the man in the bed. Cayleen thinks his voice sounds strong too.

"I'll just put them over here ... if that works?" Cayleen walks toward the window, Logan still shyly hiding behind her legs.

"That's fine. Thank you," says the man in the bed.

Turning to face the room, Cayleen gives a warm smile and moves back toward the door. "Well, we should be going." Cayleen smiles looks to the men, and grabs her son's hand.

Once in the safety of the solitary hallway, Logan says, "That was a fun adventure, Mama."

Cayleen smiles and allows her eyes to grow larger with enthusiasm. "It sure was, wasn't it? Now, how about you get to push the buttons for the elevator?"

> Don't be concerned for your own good
> but for the good of others.
> —1 Corinthians 10:24

Cayleen sits in the church meeting room as the pastor finishes the closing remarks on his discussion of boundaries. With Hunter getting more parenting time, Cayleen has taken the opportunity to attend classes at church during the week. Cayleen feels the boundaries message has spoken directly to her heart about her relationship with Jessica.

Once the pastor is finished, she turns to a woman she's recently met in the classes. Melissa's powerful prayer life gives Cayleen a sense of mentoring on her spiritual journey. Melissa is slightly shorter than Cayleen and has shoulder-length blonde hair. One of Melissa's ministries is through the use of horses, and her ability to work with horses fits her usual jeans and dressy casual shirts. Melissa is a hard worker in her spiritual life and in her life on her family's farm. The two women stand behind their chairs, and Cayleen senses someone approaching from her right.

"Hey, Justin!" Cayleen reaches up to hug her former coworker. Justin has shaved his head and is growing a small beard. Cayleen remembers the conversation she heard when she visited the field about Justin's beard being a perfect man beard. It may have been the funniest conversation she heard in a long time, but after looking at him, she agrees.

When Justin was in the office, Jeannie had asked, "Who is that? Am I drooling?"

Justin is stunning, but he also has a feel of familiarity for Cayleen. She's known him since she hired him nearly two years ago in human resources.

"What a coincidence! I didn't realize you were going to school here? You go to Community?"

Justin is finishing his degree in mathematics and then is planning on teaching. Cayleen feels a longing in her heart to return to teaching. She brushes it off, an unattainable dream given the pay cut she would suffer. Cayleen is amazed that Justin is doing the same program she did before Logan was born.

In what seems like no time, they talk about colleges, education, and not returning to work. They both go to Community—Cayleen to the early service and Justin to the later service.

Cayleen realizes they have been talking for fifteen minutes. She hasn't called Logan, which she does every night he's with Hunter, and tries to politely excuse herself.

After taking a step away, Cayleen turns back around, wanting to make sure she's not being rude by excusing herself. "It was nice catching up with you, Justin." She smiles and makes eye contact.

Justin smiles. "You too, Cayleen."

> For You bless the godly, O Lord, You surround
> them with your shield of love.
> —Psalm 5:12

CHAPTER 28

Jeannie sheepishly walks into Cayleen's office, fidgeting with her hands. "Do you know people at church? Like ministers? Sandy said you go to church and would know."

Cayleen is slightly confused but honored to have been asked. Cayleen nods. "Yes."

"Well, Brian has some questions and is wondering about getting baptized before he goes. We've had a couple ministers in there from the hospital, but he's sent everyone away so far." Brian had made it through the rough patch he was having a few months before when Cayleen delivered flowers. Cayleen had heard rumors that Brian had been given one to four weeks to live. Cayleen didn't know what to believe since he had been dying since Jeannie started nearly a year ago.

"Yeah. I'll call someone right away," Cayleen says.

Jeannie's gaze shifts several times. "Yeah, if someone could come by today, that would be good. It's getting pretty close." Jeannie wanders out of Cayleen's office.

Cayleen picks up the phone and calls the church. The first time, she leaves a voice mail. She picks up her cell phone and texts Melissa to see if Melissa has any advice. Setting the phone back down, she doesn't feel right. She listens to that inner feeling and calls the church again. She explains the situation to the receptionist and asks to speak to someone who might be able to visit someone in the hospital today.

Within minutes, Cayleen has been reassured by one of the pastors that he will visit Brian that day. As soon as Cayleen sets the phone down again, Melissa texts back: "You get a hold of anyone, sister?"

Cayleen smiles at the timing of Melissa's text. She replies, "Yes, thank you for checking. Hugs."

Two days later, Sandy walks into Cayleen's office. "Did Jeannie tell you?" Sandy's voice is low; she has always seemed paranoid that everyone is listening to her talk.

"Tell me what?" Cayleen asks with a smile.

"She and Brian are getting baptized this afternoon. I guess Brian liked that guy you sent them."

Cayleen smiles at the wonderful news of saving lives. "God is good."

"He certainly is. Did I tell you about when they were laughing about that guy laying hands on Brian?" Sandy shifts her weight and looks toward the door.

"No, I didn't hear about that."

"After that bad spell a few months ago, they called a guy and prayed over Brian. Laid hands on him and everything. He got better, as you know." Sandy raises an eyebrow. "I heard them laughing about it in Jeannie's office a few weeks ago. The doctors told them he had been mistreated or diagnosed or something, and it wasn't a big deal anymore. They were laughing about having crazy people praying over him. Next thing you know, he's worse than ever—and the diagnosis is less than a month to live."

Cayleen feels the truth and power in Sandy's story, and she feels recognition in her heart. It radiates throughout her body in the form of goose bumps. She shakes off a shiver. *He was healed, but their unbelief brought the illness back.*

Sandy looks nervously toward the door. "Anyway, I gotta get back to work. I just wanted to thank you for doing that for them. I know how Jeannie treats you …".

Cayleen smiles with true peace in her heart due to mornings of praying it off and giving her problems to God. "God's got me here for a reason."

Sandy steals a quick glance toward Cayleen before walking to her office. "Maybe Brian's it."

> Let your good deeds shine out for all to see, so that
> everyone will praise your heavenly Father.
> —Matthew 5:16

Cayleen sits on the futon in Logan's downstairs playroom. She saw an opening for math teachers in the district the night before and has been longing to start the application process—just to see what it's like. She couldn't help but register for an account last night when she saw it. But then it was Logan's bath time, and bedtime came soon after. Cayleen makes a conscious effort not to be on her phone when around Logan unless he is otherwise preoccupied. With breakfast finished on Saturday morning, Cayleen looks at Logan playing with toys and decides she has time to look on her phone to see what it takes to fill out the application.

While reading the fourteen steps to the application process, Cayleen's phone screen changes to show Hunter calling. Cayleen asks Logan to come over and talk to his daddy, answers the phone, and pushes the speaker button.

"Say hi to your daddy," Cayleen says.

"Hi, Daddy," Logan says, distracted by the toy in his hands.

"Hi, bubba. How's your day?" Hunter says.

Cayleen recognizes Hunter as tired or depressed. *Maybe he's hungover.* She smiles to herself. *He didn't call last night—maybe he was out at the bar. It's his parenting time now anyway.* He just happened to call earlier in the week and tell her he couldn't take Logan this weekend … again. Weekends seem hard for Hunter to take Logan lately. He had taken Logan for the first two months for the specified parenting time, but since then, there was nearly always a call for something coming up and Cayleen needing to take Logan.

"Good." Logan's answers are short. He is preoccupied with his toys.

"Mind if I just talk to Mommy for a minute?"

"No." Logan goes back to his play area, excited not to have to be on the phone any longer.

Cayleen takes the phone off of speaker and holds it to her head. "Hi there."

"Hi."

"So … what's up?" Cayleen isn't friends with Hunter and doesn't know what this conversation could be about. Hunter rarely takes Logan more than one overnight a week. Cayleen considers it a blessing. She loves having Logan around—even though not being able to plan anything because Hunter doesn't give her more than twenty-four hours' notice is annoying. The fun she has when she's with Logan and comfort knowing he is safe in her care make up for any annoyance Hunter could ever give her.

"I'm trying to keep you in the loop about things going on in my life … as Logan's mom." As you know, work's not going so well. They've laid off a lot of people lately."

For months, Hunter has been saying he's going to get laid off. He'll call and say he was going to get laid off in two days. When he wasn't laid off, he still couldn't take Logan for that parenting time. With all the ups and downs, Cayleen doesn't care anymore.

I'd just quit and move on if my life was in such turmoil. Or stop talking about it and bringing it on yourself. She keeps her thoughts to herself. "Yeah."

"Well, they've given me the opportunity to take layoff with a severance package or take twelve weeks of paid time off for medical leave."

"What is the medical leave for?"

"PTSD. This company is why I suffer from that. The incident in Africa is why I have PTSD … and the dreams and nightmares …"

"Oh, okay. I thought you were over that. Isn't that what the doctors said during our divorce proceedings?" Cayleen's tone is as pleasant and soft as she can make it. If she upsets Hunter, he may lash out and do something to Logan or take more time with him.

The time Hunter does spend with Logan has been rocky lately. Logan refuses to talk to Cayleen, the day care provider, or anyone else about what happens when he's at Daddy's house. After Logan has spent one night or more with Hunter, Logan does not play with others and socialize like he usually does, and he acts mopey in Cayleen's opinion. The behavior pattern has been prevalent for three months—she's measured it. It takes three days for Logan to recover from spending one night with Hunter.

Hunter says, "PTSD is not something that you get over! It's something I will suffer from my whole life."

Cayleen says, "Hunter, I'm sorry. I didn't realize that."

Hunter's tone softens to the low, depressed tone Cayleen heard earlier. "I've been struggling for months. I was fine when the doctors reported for our divorce trial, but then last October—two months later—the nightmares came back. Now it's been seven months of this."

Cayleen says, "Wow. Yeah, that would be tough." Cayleen wonders how he could be emotionally fine during their two-day divorce trial when he suffered from PTSD before and then after the court proceedings. Even Cayleen was emotionally upset by the ordeal—how could Hunter be just fine?

"Sometimes I just don't know how I'm going to go on … how I'll make it through."

Cayleen's ears ring as she hears more red flags. Just weeks ago, Hunter offered her all of Logan's furniture if he were to move out of his house—almost like he was tidying up his affairs. A few months ago, Hunter designated her as the executor of his will. She remembers when she thought Logan would grow up without his father. "You'll make it, Hunter. What would be best for you right now? And what would be best for Logan right now?" Cayleen fears the suicidal words and having their son alone with Hunter after he's said them.

Hunter says, "That's kind of why I'm calling you. I'm not really sure. I'm taking medical leave for PTSD and going to look for other work while I'm off … I'm not sure if I'll be working here in town or if I'm going to have to work out of town. Right now, I've got some options to pursue in Washington and North Carolina." Hunter's voice speeds up.

"Okay, why don't I plan to have Logan for a while, and when things settle down for you, you can take him again." Cayleen moves upstairs, away from Logan, to continue the conversation. "I'd like you to think about what is best for Logan and what happens when he's at your house. When I was living there, sometimes you would get into a space within yourself where you would sit and not interact with either of us. I love to have Logan with me. Think about what's best for you … and how difficult is it to put on a happy face and pretend when Logan is around if that's what you have to do? We could plan to do things together—like maybe swimming next weekend—so you can still see Logan."

"Yeah, I'll be out of town next weekend for a fishing trip for a week with some of the guys."

"Okay, so how about we plan for Logan to see you at his birthday the following week—and then we'll go from there?" Logan's birthday party had been a peace offering from Cayleen to Hunter and Cayleen's attempt at seeing Logan on his birthday. Months ago, Cayleen knew that Logan's birthday would fall on Hunter's time with Logan, and she had planned an extensive birthday party for them all to share. Hunter had been on board. Now, with the parenting time Hunter gives up on a weekly basis, it looks like Cayleen is going to have Logan on his birthday anyway—to her pleasant surprise.

"Okay."

"Is there anything else you wanted to talk about?"

"No, I think that's it. I'll call Logan later." Cayleen wonders when *later* means to Hunter. She remembers the times he told her the same thing and would go days without speaking to her.

"Okay, goodbye."

"Bye." Cayleen ends the conversation and makes her way back downstairs.

Her thoughts turn to the funeral she attended earlier in the week. Knowing Brian was going to heaven made it so much easier for Cayleen to be excited for him. Brian had suffered for more than a year with physical pain and ailments before he went to heaven.

Cayleen looks toward Logan and lets her thoughts wander about Hunter. Hunter has been baptized in a Christian church. If he were to commit suicide, Logan would be left without a choice of how to think about his father, and Cayleen would have to speak nothing but good things about Hunter. As Cayleen has experienced with Jessica, kids want to love their parents. Similarly, Logan wants to love Hunter. *If Hunter doesn't live long enough to show Logan his true character and allow Logan to make the choice of whether or not he likes his father when Logan's a grown man able to distinguish for himself the character of other people ...* Cayleen gets mad, and tears sting her eyes.

Cayleen sits up straight, rolling her shoulders back as if to brush off the feelings. She blinks away the tears and focuses on her son. With an upbeat voice, she asks, "Can I play with you?"

"Sure, Mama!" Logan is excited she's playing with him again.

The human heart is the most deceitful of all things, and
desperately wicked. Who really knows how bad it is?
—Jeremiah 17:9

CHAPTER 29

Melissa stops Cayleen after their weekly prayer group to talk. They've been meeting since before Logan's birthday every other week, at Melissa's lead. The experience of meeting with other women to pray has greatly benefited Cayleen's spiritual experience. Melissa has made comments recently that she doesn't want the ladies to be dependent on her for spiritual fulfilment. Cayleen has tried to explain that the synergy of having the women meet together is the experience the women gather together to obtain—not necessarily Melissa's leading. After explaining this to Melissa, Melissa opens the door. "How are things?"

Cayleen has a wash of recent events flood her mind. She picks through them, telling her friend honestly where she doesn't have to hide. "Good. God is at work in my life."

Melissa smiles.

"Last week, Hunter asked for the second overnight with Logan in the past two months. I realized God was leading me to have time with him that night, which I did. I ended up writing a letter and asking Hunter to forgive me for anything I may have done during our marriage or divorce. Just blanket forgiveness ... it's not like I cheated on him like he did me throughout our entire marriage, held a grudge against him for years, or hired a nasty attorney to make him feel bad about himself. In fact, I did just the opposite and protected him from my attorney even when ..." Cayleen stops herself from getting wrapped up in past events. She sighs. "So, I wrote him this a short letter asking forgiveness for anything I may have done." Cayleen smiles. "Then at nine thirty that night, Logan calls and wants me to pick him up, which is what happened the last time too. Did I tell you about that?"

Melissa shakes her head. "No."

"The other time Hunter took Logan, Logan came home and told me that he wanted to call me to pick him up and said, 'Daddy wouldn't let me call you.' So, yay for Hunter in letting him call me to pick up Logan. I delivered the letter to Hunter when I picked up Logan that night."

"What did he say?"

"Nothing. I told him it was a letter I had planned to mail him asking him to forgive me for anything I ever did wrong to him. I think he said, 'Oh, okay, thank you,' but that's it." Cayleen scrunches her eyebrows. "He has never asked me to forgive him, but this isn't about Hunter. This is about me. And I really feel that opens up the connection between God and me."

"Yes, sister," Melissa says. "Asking others to forgive us for any sins is admitting our sins as we're told to do in 1 John 1:9. We also need to forgive others for their sins, regardless of whether or not they ask for it."

Cayleen smiles. At first, Melissa's directness was off-putting, but after a while, Cayleen has come to appreciate that she can count on Melissa for pointing out any areas Cayleen needs to address. "Yes, sister. You're right. I've had a hard time forgiving him, but I think I'm getting there."

"Pray about it. Give it to God. He'll take it. It's not a burden you need to weigh yourself down with." Melissa smiles. "Matthew 6:14—if you forgive other people when they sin against you, your Father will forgive you."

"Thank you," Cayleen says.

"How's everything else going?"

Cayleen feels compelled to tell Melissa about the ongoing

feelings she's had toward teaching. "You know, something is going on—but I'm not sure what just yet."

Melissa says, "Why do you say that?"

"When you first told me you were in education, my heart felt that pull back to teaching. Then do you remember Justin who I ran into at our class last winter?"

Melissa nods.

Cayleen says, "He came by the office last week, filling out some paperwork for his brother who still works for us. He started talking about teaching and what he's doing to prepare for school starting." Cayleen pauses to gather her thoughts. "It's what I feel I want to do, but I am not sure how. Financially, it would be a huge cut—"

Melissa says, "With God, all things are possible. Don't let something like finances block you from doing God's work. If it's his call for your life, he will make it happen."

Cayleen smiles. "Thank you. Justin is teaching high school. Oh, man. It would be so easy—and so fun!"

"Pray about it. Give it to God. He'll make it happen." Melissa and Cayleen start toward the door. "How's little Logan doing?"

"He's good. He's with my mom."

Melissa stops walking and stares at Cayleen.

Cayleen says, "My relationship with Jessica has improved over the past months. I really think it's because of how my relationship with God has grown." Cayleen pauses, and they continue walking. "I've been stuck, basically in Isaiah and Jeremiah."

Melissa moans. "Yeah, the heavy stuff." Her eyes are light, and she smiles warmly.

Cayleen smiles and nods. "Yes, but when I'm reading them this time, I realize how much God's allowing me to practice boundaries. That really isn't all that fun!" She smiles. "I really need it in my life. I realize how much I've caved in so many areas, going with what other people tell me or what they're doing rather than waiting for God to tell me in my heart what I should do."

The women stop just inside the doors.

Melissa says, "Listening to the still, small voice."

"Yeah," Cayleen says. "It makes me wonder how many of the difficult experiences I've had in my life would not have happened if I had been quiet and patient and still before making a decision."

Melissa's body straightens. "You can't live your life wondering what would have happened. You have to look forward to what you can still do. Look at your beautiful child, your baby Logan, who you have. That's a blessing from God! Children are a blessing from God!"

Cayleen nods.

Melissa says, "You may be coming out of a dark night of the soul or a dark valley, but your journey through the darkness builds character. It shows us who we truly can be, the person God already knows is inside us."

Cayleen thinks about the idea of a dark night of the soul and her emerging from it. She recently learned the dark night of the soul is the dark journey we go through as believers. The only way through it is clinging to God, the shepherd who will never leave us as stated in Psalm 23. Only by faith and trust in God can we emerge from the darkness. With our human eyes, we see no way out.

"I sure hope I'm coming out of it!" Cayleen smiles. In the parking lot, Cayleen says, "Speaking of boundaries, did I tell you I think Jessica is talking to Hunter?"

"*Your* mother!" Melissa gasps. "No, you didn't tell me."

"Just a hunch I have … a feeling inside," Cayleen says.

"Listen to the hunch, sister. Pray about it. It may be more than a hunch. God will tell you."

Cayleen leans in to hug Melissa. "Thank you. How are your boys doing? Did they get over that cold they had last week?"

Melissa embraces her friend. "Yes, they did! Healthy, rambunctious boys again! See you soon!"

> Look, I am sending you out as sheep among wolves.
> So be as shrewd as snakes and harmless as doves.
> —Matthew 10:16

CHAPTER 30

Cayleen takes a deep breath, anticipating the fight that's coming with her four-year-old, and unbuckles her seat belt. Her mind has been somewhat distracted at the pressing voice she heard early that morning, waking her from her sleep. "Tim," was all she heard, waking as the voice spoke.

She was not afraid. She knew no one was in her house, and hearing the voice made her happy and excited. "What about Tim?" she had asked. Though she did not hear the voice again, she felt the answer inside her: "Pray for …"

In the middle of the night, she thought of every Tim she knew. None of them were very close to her, but she prayed for them. She wondered if everyone was okay, praying protection and lifting them up to God's will. Now parked in the church parking lot, she hopes she has done as God asked of her.

She consciously makes her tone several tones higher as she opens the back door and unbuckles Logan. "Are you ready to start in your new room today?"

Cayleen's raised eyebrows and smile are met with a firm, questioning stare. The two join hands and walk across the parking lot toward the church. She and Logan have been working for nearly four months, since Logan turned four, to get Logan to go into the new four-year-old room at church. Logan has been in the four-year-old room several times, but he loves his teachers in the three-year-old room. Cayleen thanks God that Logan loves church so much and chooses to pick her battles. They agreed to start in the four-year-old room once he started his new school for pre-kindergarten. Logan completed the first week at school the previous Friday.

Hunter took Logan sporadically for overnights during the summer. He didn't see Logan for four weeks at one time, and then he told Cayleen he wanted to get back to fifty-fifty parenting time. Luckily for Cayleen, she didn't have to fight the inconsistencies in Logan's life with Hunter. Hunter's schedule took him out of town enough that he only took Logan for six overnights over the entire summer.

Hunter had been hinting about getting back to fifty-fifty parenting after Logan started school. He hadn't pressed it the first week, even though Hunter chose to show up more in that week than the previous three months—attending back to school night and a karate practice, but he did have undisclosed other plans during the family barbeque. Cayleen guessed his seven o'clock appointment was one of his girlfriends. Hunter was still on medical leave from work and couldn't use work as an excuse for the evening appointments. Cayleen wasn't sure if he was actually going to the medical doctors for treatment during his medical leave, but she was pretty certain they didn't have evening appointments with clients.

Hunter had mentioned to Cayleen that he would be returning to work soon. Cayleen thought about how similar it was to Hunter having the entire summer off—off of parenting and off of work. In the same conversations, Hunter hinted he may have to return to work in California. The idea of California rang true in Cayleen's heart, but she wasn't sure why. It echoed her feeling of Logan not having Hunter in his life. Cayleen wasn't sure if that feeling was God trying to tell her something or her own selfishness in not wanting to ride the Hunter roller coaster any longer.

One day, Hunter is happy and excited. The next, he's sulking and down. One day, he claims he's depressed and wants to talk to me and not Logan because he doesn't want Logan to hear him that way, the next he's asking for fifty-fifty parenting time. Cayleen is less than thrilled about the next curveball Hunter has in store for them.

Luckily, after nearly three years, God has taught her not to worry. *There's nothing I can do about it, and worrying doesn't help anything. Pastor preached a few weeks ago about worrying being a sin. God's in control.* Cayleen thinks about the sermon a few months ago that told her Logan is her son—and he is God's son too. Her heart smiles at the thought: God wants Logan to be happy as much as I do.

With Logan still not answering Cayleen's question, they approach the double doors and walk into the children's section of the church.

"Here's your offering." Cayleen hands thirteen cents to Logan to give to his teachers at the appropriate time.

Initially, Cayleen didn't like the idea of Logan giving money to Logan to give as offering then the teachers would give candy. Then Cayleen realized that, as we give our tithes to God, he gives us what we need or want. In order for the children to see God's love, we must mimic it on a very primitive level. It took Logan a few weeks to give his offering to the teachers. Cayleen worked with them, even sneaking to give him the type of candy he wanted for giving an offering.

Still holding hands, Logan playfully steers toward the fun pictures on the walls that depict Bible stories. At the double doors with a post in the center, Logan pushes Cayleen through a separate door so they are stuck at the post, their joined hands pushing against the post. Logan laughs, and Cayleen presses their hands farther, pretending to try to walk farther without getting farther, making Logan laugh harder.

Cayleen starts laughing as they join to go through the same door, hands till held. "Silly, silly!" Cayleen giggles.

They slow at the base of a large flight of stairs; upstairs is the four-year-old room, and downstairs is the three-year-old room.

"You ready for your four-year old room?"

Without hesitation, Logan charges toward the stairs. "Yep, I'm a four-year old now." Marching up the stairs, his bravery gets him to the top, but he hesitates at the corner.

Cayleen is still holding his hand. "Come on, son. You can do it." Cayleen offers a smile and a soft tug on his hand.

Logan walks slowly toward the door to the four-year-old room. Once there, Cayleen sees the young girl working at the front and starts her friendly greetings, explaining Logan's hesitation with the transition between age groups.

Cayleen stops short when she looks into the room and sees a man's gorgeous, familiar eyes. *Who is that? Could it really be?* She doesn't fully comprehend who she is looking at, but the message from God that his presence represents is so very clear to her. Her heart stops; she feels like she is frozen for a long time.

"Hey, there. How are you?" Her voice is solid, normal—not revealing her true feelings. "Logan, this is Mama's friend, Mr. Justin."

Justin rises from his seat and approaches them. "Or do you want to be called Mr. Gregory?"

"Mr. Gregory works." Justin smiles and looks toward Logan. "Hey, buddy."

Cayleen's eyebrows raise. "You're teaching high school and Sunday school—and are you still doing the second job?"

Justin laughs lightly. "Yeah."

"That's a lot! Your first year teaching alone is a lot. You're a blessing! Thank you for doing this!" Cayleen turns her attention to Logan and assures him as they walk inside. Several minutes later, she leaves him working on a project, sufficiently distracted.

While walking to "her room," as she and Logan call the adult sanctuary area, Cayleen absorbs the full impact of Justin being Logan's Sunday school teacher. The feeling she felt inside her chest when she saw Justin unexpectedly was crystal clear to Cayleen. *Amen, God. I'll look into teaching.*

Cayleen listens as the church prays for the parents of students. She remembers how they prayed for students last week. It hits her.

We haven't prayed for the teachers. *Him—not Tim. You want me to pray for him!* Cayleen feels the giggling in her spirit at her silly recognition, knowing God is pleased that she has tried so hard to please him, not quite understanding what he's asking. Cayleen smiles, feeling the love and warmth only God can provide.

After service, Cayleen goes to retrieve Logan, knowing it may take several minutes for Logan to adjust to the transition of leaving the room he is now accustomed to. She walks over to Logan and tells him they need to go soon.

Justin is standing at one end of the room.

"Would that be okay if I pray for you?" Cayleen asks. "Either now or during my normal daily prayer time?"

Justin says, "Yeah. Now's great. Thank you!"

Cayleen turns toward Logan and reaches out to hold his hand. "Do you want to pray with us?"

Logan shakes, but stays he close, watching everything his mother does. Logan is used to Cayleen praying over him and not other people.

Cayleen is relieved on the inside, silently praying to God to give her the words of what to pray. "Is there anything in particular you'd like me to pray over you?"

"Uh, yeah. I guess to know what to say to the kids. I've been really lucky that other teachers have helped me out with a lot of the materials and stuff, so I guess just more of that?"

Cayleen purposefully breathes through the awkwardness she feels, knowing that not very many people just walk up to someone else and ask to pray over them—even in church. "I'm kind of a hands-on person. Would you mind if I placed my hand on you?" Cayleen places her hand on Justin's shoulder, pure in intentions for her prayers to be more powerful through touch than speaking alone.

Cayleen takes a deep breath, closing her eyes to break away from the worldly constraint of judgment. She closes her eyes to the worry of what other people think seeing her praying over Justin and breathes in the peace of the Holy Spirit. "Lord Jesus, thank you for your son, Justin. Thank you for the blessing he is to so many lives. You have given him wisdom in so many ways. Now, Lord, I ask for you to bestow upon him wisdom in his teaching. Guide him in talking to the students that come into his life. Let him know how to meet the needs of each student, whether that is a math lesson or a life lesson. Grant him resources—wisdom to find the resources and use the resources at his disposal. Lord Jesus, he is following your will. Grant him blessing and wisdom beyond what we can know to ask for. Thank you, God, for all you do for your people. Amen."

Cayleen opens her eyes to realize how sensual her touch on Justin's shoulder feels—and how very attractive Justin is. Cayleen had never seen Justin as attractive until that moment, feeling his shoulder beneath her hand, placed in all purity on the outside curve of the top of his arm. Suddenly, she feels an arm around her waist, pulling her close, and her face is pressed into his white shirt, her mouth near the bottom V of the collar. Her heart races, the feel of his body against hers makes such a good fit. She feels his muscles under his shirt. She has no choice. His strength overpowers her own—not that she would fight it anyway. Her body tingles like it does before she gets goose bumps, but the goose bumps never come. From head to toe, she feels something amazing. Cayleen had no teaching of spirit-to-spirit connections or how they make a person feel, but God is showing her what he can do.

"Thank you," Justin says.

Cayleen feels the warmth of his breath on her head. *Oh, that's not pure anymore.* Cayleen enjoys the radiating inside her body.

Justin releases her, their embrace not lasting longer than a normal hug.

"Blessings to you." Cayleen leans back on her normal church greeting. She hopes to portray her normal self, but inside, she is reeling with emotion and excitement. *A hug that felt so good it had to be wrong? I don't think I've ever felt that way about a hug!* Cayleen gathers Logan and his belongings and walks toward the door.

Then you will again see the difference between the righteous and the wicked, between those who serve God and those who do not.
—Malachi 3:18

CHAPTER 31

Three weeks later, Cayleen drops Logan off nearly effortlessly at the four-year-old room. Justin was only the teacher for the first two weeks; since then, Cayleen hadn't seen him. Cayleen had applied for her teaching license, and she interpreted Justin's appearance in her life to indicate God's leading.

Walking to the sanctuary, Cayleen begins to pray. *God, please don't let Eric approach me again. Make it so I don't have to talk to him. If I do have to talk to him, please give me the words to say.*

Two Sundays before, a man had approached her during the greeting time of the service.

"God gave me eyes to see you today, and he told me to introduce myself to you. So here I am. My name is Eric."

Cayleen had politely introduced herself and shook his hand. The way he used God's influence in why he was speaking to her and the fact that he had the same name as her ex-boyfriend told her he wasn't someone she wanted to date—regardless of his good looks.

The next Sunday, Cayleen had a work commitment to attend immediately after church and had rushed out of service, successfully dodging him. The next day, walking into a room to meet her new work candidate, she saw a man looking intensely at her. She thought of her logoed shirt and figured he was the new employee. She walked over and reached out her hand. "Hi, there. I'm Cayleen."

The man shook her hand, looked into her eyes, and said, "Don't you remember me?"

Bells rang in Cayleen's head. Warning bells. "Oh, yeah, from church." Cayleen looked at the name plate. "Eric." In the moment, Cayleen had played off the awkwardness of the situation, but she had been praying about it ever since.

Entering the sanctuary, Cayleen sits next to Cheryl. Cheryl is singing the worship music with the congregation and leans toward Cayleen. "I have something I want to give you after service if you can stick around for a minute."

Cayleen smiles and nods in acknowledgement. Inside, she's wondering how she will avoid Eric. She prays silently before she begins singing, "God, help, please."

Cayleen sings praises to God, lifting her hands in the air. A year ago, she wasn't comfortable raising her hands. Since raising her hands and showing publicly her following of her heavenly Father rather than worrying about the judgment she may face from people here on earth, she realizes she has also received more of his blessing in the form of ease in praying and sense of knowing. Several weeks ago, his voice had woken her in the night.

This morning, during her daily prayer time, Cayleen had allowed her eyes to relax while looking at the brown carpet in her dimly lit living room. Slowly, she saw a bronze rope; the color was one Cayleen had never seen before. The color was so vibrant that it nearly glowed. The rope was a tangled pile of knots. Slowly, the rope was lifting and untangling itself. One piece at a time, the rope untangled itself until it was left with a clean, straight line of rope.

Raising both hands, singing loudly, or praying quietly beneath the voices of the other singers around her, Cayleen asks for clarity of the vision God gave her that morning. Cayleen thinks back on her journey with God.

Church has always been a part of Cayleen's week. When she was with Hunter, she started reading the Bible not daily but regularly doing a study. Then she found Joel Osteen's ministries and started watching his program in addition to church and Bible study. When Hunter kicked her out of the house, Cayleen ordered more biblical resources and clung to God. Cayleen started going to Community Church and began a daily prayer time with God. Cayleen started listening only to Christian music. Cayleen called out to God for a helper, and God gave her Eric. Cayleen asked God to remove Eric if he wasn't the person God intended Cayleen to be with, and God removed Eric from her life. Cayleen began raising her hands to publicly worship God in church. Cayleen started recognizing more of the still, small voice inside her during her prayer time. Cayleen started attending classes and prayer groups at Community. Cayleen took a vow of purity until she was married, recognizing the Bible as a guideline God has presented to us to protect ourselves from pain—not to keep us from experiencing pleasure. Cayleen fasted from alcohol for six weeks, which was an entrance into boundaries with Jessica. Had Cayleen been drinking during that time, Cayleen might not have been strong enough to enforce her boundaries. Cayleen obeyed the commands she felt God was asking her to do and experiences her first vision.

The rope is my life. God is straightening my path.

"Thank you, Jesus." The peace accompanying her vision allows Cayleen not to worry about what may happen after service or as the ropes untangle.

Once service is over, Cheryl generously gives Cayleen a framed scripture quote, which Cayleen plans to hang as soon as she gets home. Smiling and excited, Cayleen turns to Melissa, who has approached her. Looking past Melissa, Cayleen sees Justin approaching them and turns her chest toward him, welcoming conversation.

"Hi, there. What are you doing at the early service?"

"I have a lot to do today, so I came to early service."

Their small talk continues easily.

As Eric passes them, Cayleen waves slightly, not pausing the conversation with Justin. Suddenly, Cayleen realizes how long they've been talking and feels guilty for not getting Logan yet. Justin continues their conversation as they walk to the children's area.

As the two part at the base of the stairs, Cayleen walks toward the four-year-old room and Justin strikes up a conversation with another friend in passing. Cayleen realizes the blessing Justin has been. She had been praying all week for God to keep her from having to face Eric. God sent Justin. Climbing the stairs, Cayleen is awestruck at the way God has been able to use Justin for his plan in Cayleen's life.

Alone in the stairway, she whispers, "Thank you, Jesus. Please give me discernment to determine the difference in the beauty of the messenger and the message."

Clarity hits Cayleen. She realizes she has been distracted by and attracted to the messengers in her life, though they were only intended to present a message.

Two hours later, in typical Sunday fashion, Cayleen and Logan have settled on the carpet in front of the TV, having a picnic lunch with a cartoon playing. Toys and a board game are strewn nearby, in case they need to be played with during lulls in Logan's attention span.

Cayleen's phone rings, an upbeat hymn as the ringtone. *It is Hunter, and it's not like him to call during the day.* Cayleen pushes the button to answer, puts the phone on speaker, and places it in front of Logan. Cayleen walks toward the kitchen to get a drink while Logan talks to his dad.

"Thank you, Jesus!" she says quietly and reenters the living room area.

"Is Mommy there, Logan?" Hunter asks.

"I'm here," Cayleen says.

"Can I talk to you a minute—off speaker?"

Cayleen grabs the phone.

Logan fully dedicates his attention to the TV.

Cayleen walks toward the kitchen, knowing Logan usually doesn't pay attention when she's talking on the phone, but she wants to be sure he doesn't hear their conversation.

"Hi, there," Cayleen says, phone to her ear.

"Can Logan hear me?"

"No."

"Well, I'm not sure where to start here. I'm going to be out of town for a while. I'm going hunting with Uncle Clint." Jessica had already spoiled the surprise and told Cayleen that Hunter would be out of town.

"Okay." Cayleen isn't sure how this pertains to her. They don't have scheduled visits between Hunter and Logan. Hunter just calls and says he wants Logan for a night, and Cayleen goes along with it.

Hunter's voice breaks, and Cayleen thinks he may be crying. For the first time, her sympathy is not there. "I'm not sure what is going on in my life. I've been having suicidal tendencies lately. I'm not sure what I'm going to do."

Cayleen thinks of the $250,000 life insurance policy she has maintained on Hunter since they found out she was pregnant with Logan. "Well, suicide isn't the answer. You have a son."

"I know! And he's the only reason I'm alive right now."

Cayleen wonders if Logan needs to think he's the only reason for his father being alive. *That would be a lot for a kid to handle.* "Okay, so what's going on?"

Hunter says, "I've lost my job! I've got a contract to sell my house. I have to be out in two weeks. The house I had a contract on fell through. Everything is spinning out of control."

Cayleen looks at her fingernails, unable to extend any more empathy to Hunter.

When Hunter went back to work after his medical leave, he was laid off. Cayleen knew a few too many things about human resources to fall for him being fired when returning for a medical leave of PTSD, which Hunter claims was caused by an experience that occurred while working for his employer. She knew he was offered the job in California and turned it down. Jessica had already told Cayleen that Hunter had been laid off.

Cayleen had heard about the contract falling through on Hunter's house from Logan. One morning while Cayleen was getting ready for work, Logan was playing in the bathroom beside her. He said, "Daddy doesn't have enough money to buy a house."

Cayleen still wonders why a four-year-old needs to know about house problems. From the quick research Cayleen had done online regarding the sale of the home she and Logan had once shared with Hunter, he was making more than $60,000 on the sale of the home.

Empathy gone, Cayleen now hears alarms sounding in her head for Logan. *What if Hunter were to do something—and Logan were to find his dad?*

Pacing the kitchen, Cayleen says, "You'll be able to work things out, Hunter. What is going on with hunting? When do you think you might be back?"

Hunter sighs audibly, and Cayleen thinks she can hear drumming of his hands on the steering wheel and the rhythmic sound of a turn signal.

"I'm not sure. I'm getting to Clint's house now. I should have cell phone service tonight. I'll call Logan then."

"Okay," Cayleen says.

"Bye," Hunter says.

"Bye." Cayleen pushes the button to end the conversation and looks at her phone. She looks at the ceiling. "Lord, I don't know what to do about this. Please help."

"Who you talkin' to, Mom?" Logan had walked into the kitchen when Cayleen hadn't been looking. She mentally goes through her side of the conversation with Hunter and tries to think of what Logan could have heard. *Not much.*

"God. I was talking to God, son." Cayleen walks toward Logan and brushes his hair with her hand.

Logan scrunches his nose. "On the phone?"

"No." Cayleen laughs. "I was talking to your daddy on the phone, and then I got off the phone with your daddy and prayed a prayer to God." Cayleen pauses and grabs her drink. "Let's go watch TV. Do you want a drink?"

"No. I've got my water." Logan starts toward the living room.

"Hey!" Cayleen says.

Logan turns toward her.

"I love you." Cayleen smiles and walks to him.

"I love you too, Mom." Logan smiles and walks to the living room.

Just after dinner, Cayleen's phone rings again. It's Hunter. Cayleen answers and puts the phone on speaker near Logan.

"Hi, Daddy."

"Hey there, bubba. What are you doing?" Hunter seems better to Cayleen.

"Watching TV."

There is a pause while Hunter waits to see if Logan will answer more. "Daddy ended up not going hunting, so Daddy won't be out of town."

Cayleen is shocked. *Just five hours ago, he was going to be hunting for days.* Cayleen rolls her eyes. "I have a work trip planned on Friday night, but I'll be back on Saturday. My mom is planning to watch Logan while I'm out of town."

"I'll be in town. I'll watch Logan," Hunter says.

Cayleen says, "We'll talk about it later." *Just hours ago, he was going to kill himself—and now he's going to wait to off himself until he takes his son for an overnight?* Cayleen thinks again about Logan finding his father dead on the floor. She leaves the room, unable to contain her anger when hearing Hunter's voice.

The next morning, during her prayer time, Cayleen texts Hunter:

> Hunter, you have successfully removed me from your life as wife and friend. What do your other friends think of your suicidal tendencies? Do not contact me when you are having suicidal tendencies in the future. Thank you.

Nearly as soon as she pushes send, Hunter calls. He is laughing. "I just want to clarify that I didn't call you as my last call."

"Oh." Hunter's laughter makes Cayleen feel silly.

"I was calling you as Logan's mom. Telling you where I'm at," Hunter says in a mocking tone.

"Oh, okay. Please don't contact me as anything other than Logan's mom from now on."

"I won't. And I didn't."

"Okay, well since we have that straight, goodbye," Cayleen says.

"Bye."

Cayleen continues in her prayer time. She teeters on whether Hunter is laughing at her to cover his suicidal tendencies or if he's trying to play with her emotions and get her sympathy. She realizes she has no choice. She has to treat it as a serious threat to Logan. "God, I'm not sure what else to do except treat it as Logan's mom. He contacted me as Logan's mom—I have to treat the situation with Logan's best interests in mind."

At school, after staying for prayer that morning, Cayleen asks to talk with all the teachers. Nap time runs between noon and two o'clock. After her prayer meeting at noon, she can stop by to talk with the teachers.

At one thirty, Cayleen prays while walking into the school. "Lord, give me the words to speak to Logan's teachers. Thank you for letting Hunter and I decide on a Christian school that allows your words to be spoken and prayers be made to you."

Standing in front of the three teachers Logan sees most, Cayleen says, "Logan's dad called me yesterday with suicidal tendencies." Cayleen's voice breaks, and tears fall down her cheeks. "Logan doesn't spend that much time with his dad, but he does have fifty-fifty parenting time."

The main teacher says, "Yeah, and without a court order, we can't do anything on our end."

"I completely understand that. I'm not asking you all to do anything. If you wouldn't mind calling me if his dad does show up to pick him up, that would be great. Maybe ask him to have a conference or something? I can be here in fifteen minutes and would drop everything to be here."

Another teacher says, "Do you think he's going to try to pick him up?"

Cayleen shakes her head. "I don't know. I don't know what he's thinking right now. I'm not sure if he was even serious or just trying to play me." Cayleen attempts a laugh through the tears. "I doubt it. Hunter hasn't worked a day since Logan started school, and he's only picked him up from school once."

The teachers nod.

Cayleen says, "I can tell you ya'll would be sick of me if I didn't have a job! I'd be here so much. I come for prayer, lunch, and show-and-tell—and that's with a job!" Cayleen smiles.

The teachers all smile at her.

Logan's main teacher reaches out to hug Cayleen. "I'm sorry, dear. Please let us know if we can do anything."

The second teacher also hugs Cayleen. "Logan's a great kid, Cayleen."

"I know. Thank you." Cayleen's voice is stronger, but tears stream down her cheeks. "I'm a little concerned about what his dad's telling him—things that a four-year-old maybe doesn't need to hear. If you all hear anything, please let me know."

As soon as Cayleen is back in the car, she texts Hunter again:

> The last time you were in this state, you did not have Logan for overnights nor did you see him alone for quite some time. Maybe if you'd like to see Logan, we can arrange for a visit with all three of us to meet somewhere? Thank you.

This time, it takes two hours for Hunter to call.

Hunter says, "Cayleen, I called the school. What did you tell them? If this is how you're going to be, I'm going to start exercising my fifty-fifty parenting time starting tonight!"

Cayleen breaks into tears at the thought of Hunter picking up

Logan to get back at Cayleen for her behavior. "Hunter, this is not about you and me! Can't you see that? This is about a little boy."

"I know that, Cayleen! A boy needs his father in his life."

Cayleen wishes Hunter would take that pride into his and Logan's daily life rather than just being able to puff his chest and proudly state that he's a father. Cayleen knows this anger all too well. She also knows that Hunter will hit the roof—hiring attorneys, going to the school, anything to protect his pride and image regardless of what it means for their son—if Cayleen further angers him. She must calm the anger and sidestep the ego and pride that have him raging mad in the first place. "Hunter, the last time you threatened suicide, you didn't see Logan for a month."

"That's not true. Your text said that, but that is not true! When did that happen?"

"You called me at the end of May, saying you were suicidal, Hunter." Cayleen pauses. "Then we had Logan's birthday, and you didn't have parenting time for a while." Cayleen had written all the overnights Hunter had taken over the summer. She thought better than to spill that fact on the phone—in case his attorney was going to be involved.

"All the more reason for us to get back to fifty-fifty parenting time now. A boy needs his father in his life."

Cayleen can sense the words coming directly from James through Hunter's mouth. Cayleen turns the mouthpiece toward her nose so Hunter can't hear and starts praying. Understanding floods through Cayleen, starting at her chest. *That's why it took an hour to call. Hunter called the school and James to see how to handle the conversation.*

"What?" Hunter stops his ranting. He'd heard her prayers.

"Oh, sorry. You called me with suicidal tendencies, Hunter. That's a really big deal."

"What do you mean? Eighty million people have suicidal tendencies. It's really common, Cayleen."

Cayleen wonders where he gets his statistics. She's not heard anyone in her life talking about suicide before even though at least three of their high school friends had committed suicide since graduation. "Okay," Cayleen says. "To me, suicide, suicidal thoughts, or suicidal tendencies are not common. I've never thought I'm going to get a gun and kill myself, or I'm going to take a bunch of pills and overdose so I never wake up."

"I've never thought those things either," Hunter says.

Cayleen says, "When you called me yesterday saying you had suicidal tendencies, what exactly are those thoughts to you?"

Hunter says, "Being down, not seeing a way out, not knowing how things are going to turn out, hopelessness."

"So that's not suicidal tendencies to me. Suicidal tendencies, to me, means you have thought of killing yourself—and you've thought of how to do it. Is that the case?"

Hunter says, "No."

"Okay, well, feelings of helplessness you've described seem to fit with where you are in your life based on what is going on in your circumstances. If you haven't thought of how to take your own life, I think we're in a much better place."

Hunter agrees to take Logan on Friday night—not reinforcing his fifty-fifty parenting time, even though Cayleen has already sent the email to cancel her work trip.

Cayleen hangs up and sets the phone on her desk. She clasps her hands and rests her head on her hands. "God, I've never prayed for you to remove Hunter from our lives. Lord, if it is your will, and best for Logan, take Hunter out of our lives. Put him back in when Logan is old enough to handle it, if you don't take him from our lives permanently. I just can't see how Hunter using his parenting time to get back at me is good for Logan. Logan is your son too, Lord. Jesus, protect Logan, and if in protecting Logan, you remove Hunter from our lives, so be it."

> The earnest prayer of a righteous person has great
> power and produces wonderful results.
> —James 5:16(b)

Cayleen pulls up to Hunter's driveway on Saturday morning. She has no regret for not taking her work trip even though everything was okay between Logan and Hunter the night before. She could not have risked being needed and not being able to be there for her son.

Cayleen walks to the door and rings the bell. She hears scurrying and Logan's excited voice behind the closed door. When Hunter opens the door, Logan is nowhere to be seen.

Hunter says, "He wants to hide and have you find him."

Cayleen's eyes widen. "Is that okay with you?" Cayleen has not set foot in Hunter's house—their family home—in quite some time.

"Yeah," Hunter says. "But there's something I'd like to talk about with you first."

Cayleen stops before she enters the home. If they will have a long discussion, she would prefer to be outside. "Okay. What's up?"

Hunter shoves a hand through his salt-and-pepper hair. He had gray hair from his time in the military overseas, but Cayleen finally realizes the past three years of divorce have not aged him well. "I've got to move to Washington."

Cayleen is stunned to silence. *Thank you, Jesus!* "Oh."

Hunter says, "With the layoff and not being able to find a job here in town ... and I can't find a place that will rent to me for a decent amount of money once I close on this house next week ... I'm going to have a go of it in Washington. A friend said he could help me out for a while until I get my feet under me."

Cayleen said a silent prayer, blessing whatever friend Hunter was referring to for helping him out. "Oh, okay."

"I'll be done with the closing Monday and drive to Washington. I've got an interview on Friday."

Hope surges within Cayleen. Hunter has a job to keep him there. *Hallelujah!* Covering her excitement as best she can, she says, "Okay. A job would be good."

"Yeah, the market here is not enough to make a living."

Cayleen's thoughts drift to the second interview she's had with the school in town. *Talk about not making a living!* She is moving from a private-sector, well-paying job to a pay cut in half, but if God's leading her in that direction, she will be obedient. She may not see the way, but with God, there is a way. With Hunter not working, it is just a matter of time before he tries to take her to court to pay him child support. Hunter leaving is showing Cayleen God's way is best.

"Well, let me know what you'd like to do regarding Logan. You're welcome to take him when you are in town." Cayleen knew Hunter wouldn't think of taking Logan to Washington. A long trip like that would be difficult for Hunter. The last time Hunter tried to take Logan out of town was only three hours in a car. Hunter ended up bringing Logan home a day early on a three-day trip.

"Yeah, I'm not sure when I'm going to make it back to town just yet. I'll have to see how it goes."

Calm sweeps through Cayleen. Peace like a wave washes her from head to toe in warmth and contentment. *I love you. I love Logan. I will make everything okay.*

Cayleen hides her smile from Hunter as she walks past him in search of her hiding son.

> The wicked die and disappear, but the
> family of the godly stands firm.
> —Proverbs 12:7

CHAPTER 32

When the bell rings, Cayleen stands nervously in the gym and waits for her middle school students to appear and meet her.

The school that hired Cayleen worked out better than she could have imagined for herself and Logan. The school is kindergarten through eighth grade—so Logan will be going to school with her next year. It is not a private school like the school Logan currently attends; it will also not be as expensive.

When Cayleen first applied for her certificate and then with the school district, she saw red in a vision. Thinking she would work for the high school in Spring Forks that had red colors, Cayleen took her petitions to God and asked for a modified schedule so she could take Logan to school, pick him up from school, have the same holidays, and afford to keep him in a good school. With one move, God answered all those prayers with a school Cayleen had never heard of.

Cayleen smiles as the students file in and sit by grade. She has six one-hour classes. The maximum class size is twenty-three students. *What a miracle!* When she was teaching before, her smallest class was twenty-four students—and most had more than thirty.

As the principal starts to introduce Cayleen, she smiles and remembers how far she has come in the past three months. The last bit of Cayleen's time with Liz and Jeannie was not pleasant, but Cayleen realized it was God making her move rather than blaming either of the two individuals.

Once Cayleen had her two interviews with the school—one

being substitute teaching the students to see if it was a good fit—the change happened quickly. Cayleen was only given three weeks' notice before the start of school. She had given notice to Liz before signing a formal offer with the school in order to give Liz two weeks' notice and give herself a week of downtime before starting teaching.

Liz's reaction to Cayleen's notice helped make the transition easier for Cayleen. Since Liz didn't come into the office on Fridays, Cayleen had tried to call. Cayleen knew Liz didn't answer Cayleen's phone calls, but she would listen to the messages. She left a voice mail stating she needed to give notice. Cayleen followed up with an email stating the same thing. Rather than call, Liz emailed stating how deeply sorry she was to see Cayleen go, and as soon as she was off of her conference call, she would come into the office to discuss it. The email read as though Liz has blind carbon-copied the higher ups in the company who may be concerned about Cayleen leaving. Cayleen is doubtful Liz feels sorry she is leaving.

Three hours later, Liz arrived in the office. She pulled her son, who also works for the company, into her office. Cayleen heard some laughs and small talk. He left half an hour later, and Liz pulled Cayleen into her office. "What's going on? Why are you leaving?"

"I've been hired as a teacher, and they need me to start at the beginning of January. I'm sorry for the short notice, but it's really all I have been given."

Liz looked away, typing something. "Oh, well. I was ready to negotiate to offer for you to stay, but if you're going to teaching, I can't compete with that." Topic closed.

Cayleen felt cut short, Liz hadn't even offered anything to try to get her to stay.

Liz said, "Two weeks is not enough time to get a replacement." Tears well in Liz's eyes. "Do you have any idea how much work this leaves me to do? You'll just have to teach me everything, and I'll have to do it."

Cayleen feels no regret for only giving two weeks' notice. With the introductions in the gym over, Cayleen walks to her new classroom with her class, feeling that she is where she should be. Over Christmas break, she had prepared the room, figured out the curriculum, and got her feet under her.

As she enters the classroom, the students are seated. She asks them to get up and form a circle at the front of the room. Cayleen brings a pad of paper and a pen to write with. Trust starts day one.

"Okay. So, for our warm-up today, I'd like you to tell me your name and one thing that would totally make your day or that you secretly hope for." Cayleen smiles, making eye contact with most students in the circle. "I'll start. I'm Ms. Jamison, and it would make me super happy to see a flash mob." A grin spreads across Cayleen's face.

"A flash mob?"

"Wha—?"

Cayleen giggles. "No being mean or questioning other people's ideas. We're sharing without judgment. I would love to see a flash mob. Everyone moving in choreographed movements? It would be so cool!" Cayleen turns to the girl on her right. "You're next."

"I think a three-foot-tall mochachino would be amazing right now," the girl says with her eyes halfway open.

"It sounds like eight o'clock is early for you to be waking up after having break, huh?" Cayleen asks. "Eight o'clock is early—break or no break. And can you tell me your name?" Cayleen still doesn't have computer access to get the rosters.

"Emi."

"Thank you, Emi." Cayleen makes eye contact with the next girl. "You ready?"

Yes, and the Lord will deliver me from every evil attack
and will bring me safely into his heavenly Kingdom.
All glory to God forever and ever! Amen.
—2 Timothy 4:18

CHAPTER 33

Over a year later, Cayleen is testing her eighth-grade class. She watches the students for wandering eyes, which seldom happens in such a great school, but Cayleen must maintain a rough exterior to prevent it all the same.

Over the intercom, the secretary says, "Please excuse this interruption. We have a message for Ms. Jamison."

Cayleen looks up, confused about why they didn't use her classroom phone.

All the students in her class are moving. The boys all move to the sides, and the girls move toward the front.

Tristin, one of her eighth-grade boys, says, "Please come with me, Ms. Jamison." He smiles.

The secretary's voice is counting down, "Three ... two ... one."

Bells signal the start of a Bruno Mars song over the loudspeaker. She is ushered to her chair at the front of the room and sits as the girls break into a careful dance. Between desks and chairs, the girls dance. The same dance. *Flash mob?* Cayleen smiles, and tears well up in her eyes.

As the girls dance toward the door, the boys move Cayleen toward the door, open it, and usher her out of her room.

In the hallway, Cayleen is shocked to see her sixth-grade students standing along the lockers and moving their arms to the music. As she passes, they point toward the gym. The eighth-grade girls dance in front of Cayleen, the eighth-grade boys usher alongside her, and the sixth-grade students join as she passes. Joyful tears spill from Cayleen's cheeks.

The song plays over the loud speaker: "I think I wanna marry you!"

In the gym, the entire school is seated in the bleachers. Cayleen follows the eighth-grade girls dancing and the eighth-grade boys at her sides. The seventh-grade girls are doing the same dance the eighth-grade girls were doing. The seventh-grade boys join in and flank the dancers.

As Cayleen approaches, the song is still playing through the loudspeaker. The dancers join in the center of the floor, and tears of joy flow down Cayleen's cheeks.

The music slows, and the dancers part. In the center, Justin is on one knee. Cayleen couldn't see him through the dancers, but there is no doubt in Cayleen's mind who would be behind all this. She and Justin had started dating the first semester she was teaching—intentionally dating to see if they were a good fit for each other rather than having a physical relationship to bind them together emotionally. Next to Justin, Logan is holding a bouquet of flowers. The girls part and welcome Cayleen to the center.

"Ms. Jamison, please come with me." Tristin walks through the opening in the sea of girls, and Cayleen follows closely behind. Cayleen's smile doesn't stop, and the tears of joy keep flowing. In the center, Tristin joins the circle of girls and stands to the side.

Justin puts an arm around Logan and whispers in his ear. The song ends, and the gym is oddly quiet for the number of students. Logan, smiling and shy in front of all the people, reaches out and hands Cayleen the flowers.

Cayleen accepts the flowers and kisses Logan on the forehead.

Logan exchanges a silly look with Justin. "My mom's crying, Justin! Sheesh! Just like you said she would."

Cayleen starts laughing.

Justin starts laughing, still on one knee, and reaches his hand toward Cayleen. "I think you know what this all means, but in case you don't, will you marry me?"

Between his thumb and first finger, he's holding a ring that shimmers under the fluorescent lights of the gym.

"Yes."

The gym erupts in giddy screams and applause.

CPSIA information can be obtained
at www.ICGtesting.com
Printed in the USA
LVOW11*2248110318
569415LV00002BA/9/P

9 781973 616085